DIARY

OF AN

EVIL

OVERLORD

LORNA REID

Dream big.
Or, at least, dream *better*.

Mischief, thou art afoot;
Take thou what course thou wilt.

Anthony, *Julius Caesar Act III, Sc. II*
William Shakespeare

MARL

25TH MARL

It is the first day of spring, and I'm forced to take stock (and perhaps, finally, put this terminally dull birthday diary to good use). I'm a thirty-something evil Overlord, living in his parents' home in Wretch, one of the most limp-wristed, nauseating kingdoms in the Eastern Reaches. And not even in the good neighbourhood either, thanks to my father losing our more palatial domain in a drunken poker game when I was just two years old.

Despite returning home after several years away, and promptly inheriting the castle after my parents' recent, untimely demise, I've yet to make my mark—largely thanks to stupid minions, wilfully obtuse staff, and a rancorous and frustratingly indestructible grandmother.

The west wing of the castle is falling down after being undermined by a band of dwarves, the kitchens are overrun with pike-rats, and the builders have walked off the restoration of the torture chamber for health and safety reasons.

Worse, I can't locate any substantial gold reserve or the key to the dungeons. Perhaps the key slipped out of my father's pocket when he fell out of a window in the north tower. I searched high and low as soon as his funeral was out of the way, but to no avail. Perhaps I should have asked him where it was before I pushed him.

26TH MARL

Today's torture: a tedious meeting with my ex-father's soon-to-be-ex legal advisor, Yanna Stropoffavich—fiery hair, smouldering green eyes, and a glare that could sever a pair of testicles at fifty paces. Swiftly dispensing with any pleasantries, she informed me that, along with coming into possession of this sorry excuse for a castle and its surrounds, I had a duty to see to its restoration and upkeep.

"*Whatever the cost,*" she said, smirking.

"Given its current state of neglect, that cost would appear to be *very* high," I said, eyeballing a teetering stack of bills that balanced on the edge of one of my father's numerous desks.

Her eyebrows twitched and her nostrils flared in what I suspected was a silent snort. I shoved the bills off the desk and into an already overflowing bin where they instead escaped over the floor.

"Who actually made that rule and what wizened baggage *actually* upholds it, because I have *zero intention* of spending any of the pittance of gold remaining in the main vault on anything but new décor for my chambers, and a few assassins to round out my forces."

In fact, I wanted them for prestige purposes, and to aid in the settlement of some childhood grudges, but I wasn't going to say that - something in her haughty demeanour suggested she wouldn't approve.

Yanna poked one of the bills with the pointy tip of a violent-red leather boot and her mouth hitched into a nasty smile. "It is not just a rule, but a law, enshrined in the magical fabric of the land since time began, and if you don't want a tenacious banshee to be sent from the nether-realms to plague your existence and shrivel *your* nether-realms, then I suggest you crack out the cash and start getting those… *pretty* hands dirty."

I scoffed at this, but she went on to detail the rather more realistic and worrying fact that I would receive a stiff fine from the Evil Domicile Inspectorate, among other things.

"This is outrageous." I kicked the bin across the room and hit a scamp that was chewing on the doorframe. It skittered off, shrieking and flapping its dangly ears. "I'm a *fucking* Overlord, feared throughout the lands." I chose to ignore her (this time, audible) snort. "I'll be damned if any little committee is going to dictate to me. I'll have them murdered in their beds."

Yanna inhaled, and my eyes travelled automatically to the top of her corset.

"You could, of course, opt for the violent route, but rules are rules, red tape is red tape, and you wouldn't be the first to try." She opened a shiny black dragon-scale briefcase and removed a pamphlet, which she handed to me. The pictures inside were disturbing.

"As you can see, the remains of others who have tried can be viewed by appointment at the Gallery of Skulls just off the main vestibule of the Evil Domain Inspectorate Headquarters." She whipped the pamphlet away and slid it back into the case. "Genitalia belonging to the skulls' owners is traditionally pickled and kept among other trinkets of amusement in the main waiting room. I've seen them in the flesh, so to speak."

With that, she looked me up and down and made some comment under her breath about small jars, before packing the rest of her paperwork into her briefcase and sweeping out of the room. How she actually swept in her impossibly high spike-heeled boots is beyond me.

I need to investigate her claims further, as if I don't have enough to do. I haven't even begun clearing out my parents' chambers so that I can move in; I need to give a pep talk to the staff who have been slacking off since the funeral and, rather irritatingly, I need to set about finding the source of the smell coming from the library—I've already had a number of written complaints from the librarian, despite only being Overlord for the better part of two days. Oh, and that sodding dungeon key—how can I give the staff a decent pep talk with no threat of the dungeon to hold over them, let alone keep the local heroes and rival

Overlords at bay without the hideous fire demon that my parents have housed there for years.

27TH MARL

I spent most of yesterday afternoon avoiding visiting my grandmother and searching for Reginald, my father's ancient manservant and Head of Staff, to order him to call a staff meeting since I refuse to go down to the staff quarters alone (or at all, come to think of it). Last time I ventured down there as a child, the troll-goblin hybrid that my stupidly progressive parents had hired as a cook tried to pickle me as part of the winter provisions.

Why am I doing the running around anyway? I'm in charge now, and they can fucking well come to me. I need to find Reginald. He needs to be more present—it's no good him sulking because I'm now the Overlord. That wig-burning accident was years ago. Besides, what's a good manservant without some sort of maiming or deformity anyway? He also has a key to every room and hidden passage in the castle (of which there are many), which would also solve the dungeon key issue.

LATER

After ringing the minion bell (minions may be separate from army or staff, but they are just as useless) for fifteen minutes two of the wastrels finally appeared, tugging their long brown ears and gambolling about in their irritatingly twitchy way. Of all the minions who could have responded, it had to be scamps. The very name imbues them with endearing qualities that they simply don't possess. I find them generally repugnant, but they have their uses. My father used to use them for 'smash, grab, and terrorise' raids on local villages and townships—if there is one thing scamps do well, it is breaking things. In fact, they spend most of their time destroying things - when they aren't eating, sleeping, and humping (one another, furniture, the dogs, etc.).

I showed them a picture of Reginald and ordered them to seek. They belched and ran off down the hall. However, after they had attacked their third suit of armour and simultaneously urinated on both a 500-year-old vase and a sleeping guard, I decided to dispense with their services and find someone with half a brain to help me.

MUCH LATER

Despair. I honestly expected this to be easier. I thought that the day after the funeral, I would be perched on the family's fabled black throne, sipping Blue Viper cocktails and snapping out orders as the gold and infamy rolled in. Instead, I had to round up some mutinous-looking staff and send out a search party for Reginald. The doddery, deaf old fool has probably got lost in the catacombs again.

My parents lost five manservants in there before installing a number of safety exits—the Health and Safety people weren't best pleased (they are the most feared and loathed bureaucratic arm of the EDI). I remember my own hair-raising experiences in there only too well. My parents were bitterly disappointed when I managed to find my way out, especially since the exits had been mysteriously blocked off.

28TH MARL

I ignored the sarcastic note delivered first thing by my grandmother's favourite servant, and decided to avoid her threatened visit by hiding out in the library and enquiring there about Reginald. I'd not visited it for a number of years, the last time being before I went on my extended break.

An unfamiliar librarian was busy moping over a number of rare volumes that had been partially eaten by scamps. Knowledge is usually enough of a repellent for most of the minions in this castle, but the base nature of scamps knows no bounds, and even the hallowed ground of the library is not sacrosanct. I spent many happy childhood days here, playing ~~with~~ by myself in the stacks and plotting the downfall of my family, so it is vexing, to say the least, that it has been violated.

The librarian didn't know where Reginald was and spent more time blowing her nose, scowling over damaged books, and fingering a large spot on her neck than paying attention to my questions. Her long, blonde hair and abundant (but appealing) form, clad in a voluminous blue dress with a white skull motif, were rather surprising—surely a librarian in an evil castle should be a hunchbacked old man who molests anything with a pulse and pins insects to cards for a hobby? People should be terrified to return a book late, not afraid of infectious skin diseases and a bad attitude.

"I don't mean to complain…"

Her complaint cut through my reverie.

"But the smell is absolutely unbearable now. And I *have* mentioned it already. Are you actually going to do anything about it? We *do* matter down here, you know."

"It's probably the result of the scamps' papery snacking. As soon as the damn staff buck their ideas up, I'll have it dealt with. And perhaps sort out some kind of scamp repellent."

She seemed sceptical, but it shut her up. She blew her nose on a large, red hanky. It took a while to make out that she was talking through the folds of twisting cloth that were being wedged and swirled up her nostrils.

"One of the more sober barbarians said they last saw Reginald a few days ago, setting off to investigate the flooding tunnels beneath the castle. You are aware that the waters are over and above the approved levels set out by the Evil Domicile Inspectorate Health and Safety people? They sent a letter—it ended up on my desk by mistake."

I could feel a vein start to pulse in my neck.

"Anyway." She shoved the hanky down the front of her dress. "No one has seen him since."

Perfect. Just *perfect*.

29ᵀᴴ MARL

The search team found Reginald this morning beneath the library. It appeared that he had fallen into a deep section of floodwater in the maze of passages and caverns beneath the castle that led to a large underground river.

The massive bunch of keys that he carried around on his belt had weighed him down, and he had been unable to drag his useless bones out. When the waters receded, his body was left festering beneath the sodding library. Now the whole place smells like a corpse and the more superstitious minions are talking about burning it down to ensure his spirit doesn't return.

I'm incandescent with rage. How *absolutely* typically fucking selfish of him. He has deserted me in my hour of need and ensured that it will take more than a large bowl of potpourri to sort out the smell, that's for damn sure.

At least I have the keys. I also have three more increasingly bitter and pissed-off notes from my grandmother.

30ᵀᴴ MARL

With my new keys, I was finally able to access my parents'

chambers and have a proper snoop. Instead of the plush, exotic interior, chock-full of hidden secrets, mystical wonders, and rare treasures, the reality was a trifle more disappointing. It's draughty. And damp. And the curtains are so full of mould that even the moths have abandoned them in disgust.

I quickly gave up my exploration of the many cupboards and wardrobes and, instead, concentrated on the areas where the good stuff is usually to be found — under the bed, the bedside drawers, and under the mattress.

LATER

I am still reeling. It wasn't so much that my fingers came into contact with what turned out to be a penis pump, hidden at the bottom of my father's chest, or even the pile of well-thumbed *Wicked Wench* and *Dirty Dwarf* magazines that were jammed down the back of his bedside table—I had expected such things, to be honest—it was the wig, the muscle enhancers, and the stacked heels.

All my life, I have looked up to my father—literally. I had admired him (albeit grudgingly) for his imposing height, bulging don't-fuck-with-me muscles and full head of luscious locks. Now I find that he was an average-sized balding man with bugger-all muscle definition.

Any hope that my mother would redeem the situation was soon dashed when close inspection of her underwear drawer revealed some squishy, scamp-gut breast enhancers. I wonder if my father knew. He fell in love with her because of her assets (and also the fact that she could kill five peasants with one well-aimed arrow).

Further mining through some very lacy and racy garments revealed what looked like a girdle and thigh-reducing leg-corsets.

My mother has been my template of womanhood, the one against whom all mistresses and potential wives were to be measured. Now it seems that those measurements are to be adjusted by several inches. No wonder, with all these trusses, that she couldn't run away from the boulder trap that I set in one of the lower corridors last week. Still, from the looks of things, she died thinner than she had ever dreamed.

EVEN LATER

My mother's smut collection is double that of my father's. The top end of her bed was shored up with copies of *Polish My Dirk!*, *Hung Heroes*, and *Shaven Elf.* I am speechless. My mother *loathed* elves. I have taken a few magazines away with me. The pile was overflowing, and I was loath to leave a mess on the floor.

31ST MARL

It would seem that my teething problems are not yet over. Despite locating the keys to the castle, it would appear that, as far as the dungeons go, only the key to the main vestibule and torture chamber is present (which I have not yet had the time to investigate thus far). Frustratingly, the lower-level key is missing, which means that I don't yet have much of a way of keeping staff and minions in line, especially as the torture chamber is still out of commission, thanks to the useless builders walking out.

I was hoping to be in possession of all keys so that staff mutiny would be averted, but no such fucking luck. I'm still having problems getting anyone to respond when I summon them. I strained my arm yanking on the damn staff bell for ten minutes this morning, and there is no way I can trust scamps to fetch me lunch or do laundry. I lost a fine pair of boots to that mistake already this week after a scamp ate them.

Half the minions are spending their time wallowing in the hot springs beneath the south side of the castle, while the others are either lounging in their lairs, eating one another, or steadily drinking their way through the contents of the more accessible wine cellars. A few more adventurous ones who don't seem to have an aversion to fresh air have been wandering around, trashing the surrounding countryside.

Yanna has presented me with three bills for missing livestock in the past few days. I told her I wasn't paying them. Fuck Overlord/peon relations; I'm sick to the back teeth of politics already—these people should be grateful they have lives, let alone livestock.

ANVIL

1ST ANVIL

Still no dungeon key. As such, the serving staff are being even more obtuse and wilfully insubordinate. My washing hasn't been done since before the funeral, and my food is sent up at least an hour late every day and is of suspicious origin. Yesterday's chops had fur on them, there was a claw in my lunch stew today, and there were several black flecks in the sticky pudding which, upon closer examination, appeared to have wings.

I decided to return to my parents' chamber to continue my investigation into their private lives and hopefully turn up something that could be of use to me, along with the damned key.

2ND ANVIL

Found the following in a chest at the bottom of my mother's walk-in wardrobe:

- A large, wooden puzzle-box
- Stack of old documents and papers
- Book, titled *Torture, Treachery, and Traps: How to Deal with Your Mother-In-Law* by Mercy Trench
- A pouch of gold
- An empty jewellery box
- A case of tiny phials (likely, poisons)
- A handwritten manuscript for a book on advanced strategy and tactics
- An extremely compromising photo of a man and a large, tentacled, water demon (will have to find out who this is and if he is worth blackmailing)
- A jar containing a pickled human head. The woman

inside looks familiar, but I can't place her

* Miscellaneous bits of torture equipment and strange items whose use I can't even fathom

I spent half an hour using various pieces of the torture equipment trying to prise the bloody puzzle box open and failing. There is clearly something inside because it rattles. In the end, I put it aside and decided to turn my attention to other matters, such as perhaps squeezing the surrounding towns for whatever wealth I can wring out of them until I turn up the real gold stash that I am certain my parents must have had—the main vault is running perilously low, and I will need more working capital. That said, I can barely get the staff to do anything, let alone attack anyone.

3RD ANVIL

I managed to find a guard who was only half-drunk and made him accompany me to the kitchens to confront some of the staff.
It didn't go well.

Things started off fine enough when I told them that I realised that this change in leadership had come as a massive blow. It was when I explained that if I was sent one more plate of cold, congealed shit for lunch they would be getting an even more massive blow that things started to teeter downhill.

As the greasy, stained peasants began to close in, I told them that their attitude was unacceptable and that I expected respect on pain of death.

It was at that point that the drunken mass in the corner that I had mistaken for a sack of rotting vegetables heaved itself to its feet and started to bellow about not having been paid for two months. I told the man/troll/thing that it had likely drunk more than a year's wages last night alone, and that it had better get back to work. I suggested that he started by scraping the black slime from the work surface and removing the dead pike-rat from the trap under the vast kitchen table. It was being eaten by another pike-rat at the time.

Several of the staff picked up rolling pins but ignored the rats. It was at this point that my guard seemed to sober up, as he made a hasty exit.

LATER

Still can't remove the fish-soup stains from my shirt. Having a vat of it hurled at you will pretty much ruin even the most resilient of decorative waistcoats.

Staff issues will be put on hold until I can sort out the dungeons and get the renovation of the torture chamber back on track. I'm starting to despise this place. Why did my father have to be such an incompetent card player? Why did he never try and reclaim our rightful lands?

4TH ANVIL

After switching tactics, my grandmother has decided to lay on a guilt trip by sending up a photo of me as a young boy, eating candy floss while sitting on her lap. Of course, what it didn't show was that two seconds afterwards, she ate it, right before she dropped and stampeded over me when she heard the chimes of the ice-cream wagon.

I remember consoling myself by planting a hornet's nest in her bed, thinking that would kill her (succeeding where my father had continually failed). It didn't work. Two servants were stung to death, however. She blamed my father for a crude attempt at killing her, leading my mother to consign him to the sofa for a fortnight. Highly hypocritical of her, I thought, since she got rid of *her* mother-in-law within two months of marrying my father.

I planned to ignore her, but a second note arrived, demanding that I "Get my useless backside along to her chambers now" before she has to move up into one of the empty suites along the hall to "keep tabs" on me. I made a hasty decision to visit her. Hopefully, she won't have realised that the pit-trap in the botanical garden where the funeral service was held was more than just subsidence— I don't need the earache.

LATER

The first thing she said wasn't, "how are you holding up at the loss of your parents?" or "welcome, my only grandchild", but to simply point out (loudly, and in front of several smirking members of staff) that I smelled of fish.

She then spent an hour shovelling white chocolate truffles into her face in between telling me what a failure I was, both as a grandson and an Overlord. I tuned her out after a while and studied the hair on her upper lip while planning my next attempt on her miserable, corpulent life. The last attempt saw ten members of staff and three minions lose their lives. One or two may well have lived, despite their injuries, but it was easier to have the pit filled in, rather than fish them out.

After cheering herself up by demeaning me, she fished a wad of tissue from her ample bustier and dissolved into tears over her "poor daughter" and how she had "thrown her life away on a good-for-nothing Overlord with a tiny castle."

I told her I refused to listen to her insult my father's modest erection—especially given the stressful circumstances in which he managed it—and bid her good day, but not before I had emptied a full phial of one of my mother's best poisons into her hot goats' milk.

5TH ANVIL

I called a meeting with Yanna this morning to see if she could do anything about the damned builders. I explained that I wanted the torture chamber finished as soon as possible. She said she would "have a word" with the foreman and get back to me.

Every time I come into the office, she is there, sifting through cupboards and stacks of papers, or on her hands and knees in some provocative pose, buried in old folders and parchments. I don't know if she is trying to seduce me or is an astonishingly hard worker.

LATER

I heard from the staff member who brought me my soup tonight that one of my grandmother's servants had taken a fit and died. *Sake.* Can't anything just go my way?

6TH ANVIL

Popped by the office late evening to find Yanna on a set of steps, fishing around on the top shelf of a cupboard. She nearly fell off the ladder with shock when I appeared. She shoved a set of papers back on the shelf and hurried down to rummage in her bag, then thrust some documents at me to sign. These were for something called Minion Underworld Group—some charity, presumably. I joked about the ladder, and she went red and blocked my view by leaning over me. Her black leather corset proved very distracting, and I quickly forgot to ask her to join me for dinner.

7TH ANVIL

Caught Yanna in the office again, waiting for me. She was on all fours, groping under the floorboards near my mother's desk. Her red face matched her underwear. She said some forms had slipped between the floorboards. She was looking stressed, so I decided not to risk pressing the issue about the foreman—she is one of the few staff who is actually doing their fucking job, so the last thing that I want is her walking out.

LATER

I have decided to try and spend the night in my parents' chambers now that I have changed the bedding and sorted the curtains out. It felt odd; I hadn't cleared away their things, and their portrait glared down from the opposite wall. I could feel their eyes burning into me, even when I retreated under the covers. Somehow, all desire to open *Shaven Elf* and busy myself shrivelled away.

8TH ANVIL

1.17 AM

Am still shaking as I write. Any sympathy I may have had for my wretched parents has deserted me faster than my bladder control. At 12:30 am, I put down my mother's manuscript and extinguished the bedside light, thinking I would be lulled to sleep with dreams of Yanna, only to wake up to an odd metallic creaking.

I rolled over in time to see the moonlight catch on something and barely made it out of the bed before a spiked platform hurtled down and crushed it. That bed was 200 years old, and now, thanks to the two-foot spikes pinning what's left of it to the floor, it is little more than ornate firewood.

I swear the portrait on the wall was smirking at me when I gathered my shredded nerves—and even more shredded bedding—and retreated back to my own chambers.

9TH ANVIL

Little comfort to be had from breakfast. The bastard kitchen staff think that they are being funny by sending up a steaming hot bowl of fish soup for every meal. I stayed in bed all day reading my mother's manuscript. It is actually a work of genius.

10TH ANVIL

Yanna arrived at my quarters to "check up on me" and caught me stuffing a copy of *Shaven Elf* back between the pages of my mother's manuscript. Thankfully she said nothing—she seemed more interested in my chambers and enquired about the accident in my parents' quarters. She even offered to go and investigate the mechanism and check for further traps while I rested, but I'm sick of the sight of these four walls and need to stretch my legs. It had nothing to do with the black leather skirt and goblin-boned red satin corset.

LATER

Yanna obviously knows nothing about checking for traps. Rather than being careful about each and every item that she examined, she was far too quick to pull open drawers and feel down the back of cupboards. That's a fine way to lose a hand. When I pointed this out, she looked irritated, but she soon stopped.

11TH ANVIL

Yanna was nowhere to be found today, and so I decided to stay in my chambers and page through the papers I found in my mother's chest. Among them were a few nasty letters from my grandmother, urging her to divorce my father and find someone with a big castle. She is so shallow. My father did the best with what he had.

Yes, this tiny domain may have been at the arse end of the lands, comprised mainly of swamps, impenetrable forests, and dwarves with bad attitudes (are there any other kind?), but the renovation of what had been a mouldering ruin was impressive, given the stressful circumstances. Shame that it has never risen above being a *newly-renovated*, mouldering ruin.

We've been the laughing stock of the surrounding domains for years—something I aim to remedy. However, if I can't even get my torture chamber back in working action, whipping my army and rag-tag band of assorted minions into shape will be a little tricky. Especially as our minions are overshadowed fifteen to one by every one of the surrounding domains' forces. It is a wonder that my father managed to keep order in this festering land… having a fire demon in the dungeon, with which to threaten the locals, always helps, though. It stemmed some of the more serious Hero invasions and kept rival Overlords at bay, since fire demons are extremely rare (read: expensive).

12TH ANVIL

Among the oldest bundles of papers were a number of items from my schooldays, which proved most fascinating. I wasn't aware my parents took all that much interest. They'd never been the most nostalgic types, either. The proposed bill of sale for my five-year-old self that I turned up today just proves it. The life I could have had as the adopted son of a silk merchant has haunted me all day. My father's rotten reputation must have rubbed off on me, to the point where they couldn't even give me away. That merchant will be laughing on the other side of his bejewelled palace before much longer.

Found this old school report in a small, scamp-skin folder:

BLOODSPIRE ACADEMY

TUTOR: MISS TINKLE | STUDENT: NATHANIEL EVERGRIM
DATE: 25TH MARL, 69AMR

SARCASM AND CRUEL WIT
Possesses the sort of cutting and cruel wit that only the bitter and underachieving can boast.

TORTURE
Only when he talks. Nasty ideas, but too lazy to see them through.

STRATEGIC PLANNING
Has a cunning streak, but needs to cultivate patience.

DOMAIN MANAGEMENT
Lacks authority and proper organisational skills. Couldn't organise a piss-up in a dead dwarf's helmet, let alone a brewery.

COMBAT SKILLS
Running towards the enemy would help. Otherwise, his sword skills are passable. Better with ranged weapons; they suit his nasty but cowardly temperament.

DIPLOMACY
Can talk endlessly, but a penchant for sarcasm and one-upmanship are ultimately unhelpful.

CREATIVE EVIL
Surprisingly inventive. Wickedly so. The school inspector lost three fingers last week, and we have received record numbers of complaints from parents of other students.

PSYCHOLOGICAL TERROR

Not a chance. Ever. Tight leather trousers with gold braiding don't help, either.

SACRILEGIOUS EDUCATION

Surprisingly adequate. Petty desecration of local religious shrines is second to none, displaying a spiteful, if childish, streak that could be of use, however minimal.

DARK COMBAT (POISONS, TRAPS, ETC.)

Excels at this subject. Innate cowardice and fear of confrontation are a big plus. His inventiveness in this area is nothing short of terrifying – staff are now afraid to use the school's water coolers.

SUMMARY

A tendency to blame others for his failings is a huge flaw, and he will never learn if he can't accept responsibility. The combination of Dark Combat and Creative Evil skills, not to mention his petty, spiteful streak and inability to get on with others is a dangerous combination, but not in the way you had undoubtedly hoped. May we suggest his immediate destruction for your own safety.

D. W. Treadwater

D. W. Treadwater | Headteacher

13TH ANVIL

Trying to figure out why my parents kept a letter of complaint from the school about some petty childhood incident. It was in regard to my tricking the school bully into knocking me unconscious and stealing a small treasure chest. A small treasure chest which ended up poisoning him and half the class when it was opened, leading him to get the blame (posthumously). They suggested that he would never have opened it if I hadn't manipulated him, and that it may well have been my intention from the start. They could prove nothing, however.

My father had scrawled a note in the margin, presumably to clarify his thoughts before writing a response:

> *There is only one thing more amusing than being stuck with something worthless, and that is making someone you hate move heavens and earth to possess it.*

The whole thing was clipped to my school report and a dog-eared map of the whole domain. As I was shoving the useless nonsense under the bed, I knocked that stupid puzzle box onto the floor. I spent a further hour prodding and stroking it, but to no avail. It must contain something important to be this difficult; I got my devious streak from my mother.

The only other thing of interest among the papers was a photograph of my beaming father, cradling a tiny kraken. I distinctly remember flushing it down the privy in a fit of rage in my teens when he refused to let me murder everyone at the school graduation for laughing at my crushed-velvet shirt. He had been heartbroken and didn't speak to me for nearly two years.

My mother replaced it with a sabre-toothed lion, but he never took to it. He used it in a failed attempt on my grandmother's life a few years later. The skin's still decorating her bedroom floor, so I'm told.

14TH ANVIL

Still can't open the puzzle box.

15TH ANVIL

No luck with the box. The rattle is starting to infuriate me.

16TH ANVIL

Had a dream last night that I was scratching at a wall, driving splinters underneath my nails in my desperation to get out. The walls started to close in on me, sliding and grating in violent hisses of polished wood. I realised that I was inside the puzzle box and then the rattling started, filling my head until I woke up screaming with the puzzle box bouncing around under my pillow as I turned and writhed. Am starting to loathe the sight of it.

18TH ANVIL

I was in the office today, shovelling most of my parents' useless papers (and countless bills) into the fire when the post arrived. The staff member who brought it said that he thought the scary woman would have been here, as she usually takes it all in.

Yanna arrived at that moment and the man scurried out, cringing under her withering glance. I wonder how she does it. I just look bewildered when I try, and my mirror has seen plenty of practice.

She helped herself to an envelope addressed to her and

retreated to the desk in the corner to read the contents while I made the most of a bag of hard toffees that I had found in one of my father's many desks. He had at least seven. Every time one would get laden with paper and junk, he would abandon it and get another. I keep expecting to turn up a dead minion beneath all the crap.

I was surprised to receive so many letters, but the reason soon became clear. I am 'eligible', apparently. They were all from young men and women, introducing themselves and stating their availability should I decide to take a mistress/master. There was so much scent on the letters that it started to give me a tight chest.

I was sifting through the more appealing applicants, contemplating whether I should risk poisoning by eating some sweets found in my mother's desk (I am that desperate, thanks to the kitchen staff) when a screech from Yanna made me jump.

She erupted across the room and flung a screwed-up piece of paper into the fireplace before storming out and slamming the door—no mean feat, considering that it has been wedged open with a dried troll liver for the last five years, to the point where the hinges have seized.

In her fury, she never noticed that her letter had bounced off the pile I had just added and fallen down the back of the grate. I fished it out. It was in code, so I pocketed it for later.

I considered burning the puzzle box, but suspect my mother had planned for that eventuality. I would have, so I refrained. She had also excelled in Dark Combat.

19TH ANVIL

4:15 AM

Finally cracked the code in Yanna's letter. If you can call it a letter anyway. It was just two lines long and read:

"My displeasure can take many forms—most bad. Do what you have to, regardless of your desires. S."

Sounds like a hokey proverb—the sort some of the more upmarket eateries in the larger towns have inscribed on the inside of mud-crab shells to amuse the tourists after dinner. Perhaps it is a note from an overbearing relative, in which case I can sympathise. Speaking of which, my mother's manuscript included a wonderful scheme that I will have to try out on my grandmother, although where I will find a suitable rock is beyond me.

20TH ANVIL

I set the application letters aside in favour of ridding myself of my grandmother, making it my morning's goal. I bribed a large barbarian with the promise of the key to the only remaining full wine cellar in return for him carrying a large rock from the garden up to my grandmother's quarters. We had just installed it, along with my mother's trap-spring mechanism, in the dumbwaiter that serves my grandmother's chambers (she was wallowing in the bath at the time) when a member of staff appeared and handed me a note.

Mr Evergrim, I would very much enjoy the pleasure of your company this evening in my humble quarters. Should the mood strike you for dinner, fine wine, and finer company, then I will be pleased to receive you at 7 pm.
    Yours, Yanna.

My jolt of astonishment nearly triggered the trap, and I had to take a firm grip of the suddenly sweaty wooden lever to finish the job. I then sent the barbarian packing with a fake version of the promised key and hurried off to spruce myself up for dinner. I know that it is eight hours away yet, but I need to calm my nerves. To be honest, I don't know whether I am more excited by the thought of an evening in Yanna's quarters or a decent meal that doesn't involve fish.

21ST ANVIL

Woke up feeling positive for the first time since I realised just what a pain inheriting this place would turn out to be. The evening was incredible. Despite a last-minute panic that Yanna would present me with fish soup for dinner, I arrived on time to be rewarded with the sight of her in a low-cut black silk dress and knee-length stiletto boots. It is a sign of my increasing starvation at the hands of the cursed staff here that the dinner, spread out over the table in the centre of her living quarters, was more appealing than she was.

There was a silver cloche in the centre, hiding some delicacy, and there were so many candles decorating the room that I am surprised there was any oxygen left.

Yanna's hair was cascading over her shoulders, brushing skin that looked almost as delicious as the vast pork roast and bowls of steaming vegetables. She planted a heavy kiss on my cheek, but all I could see was the chocolate pudding waiting on the side table. I think at that point that I started to openly salivate—until Yanna stepped in front of me, replacing my view of paradise with a rather different, if not equally appealing one.

She seemed irritated and leaned repeatedly to block my view when I tried to lean around her to eye up the dish of cheese-bread. I finally clicked and quickly explained my situation with the staff, omitting the soup incident.

Her eyebrows descended and the scowl vanished from her scarlet lips as she led me to the table. She told me that such things shouldn't worry me—a good mistress would be able to take care of them. I explained that I didn't have one, and she just smirked. She swept away the silver cloche from the centre of the table and told me to consider it her application.

The head of the foreman who led the walkout on the torture chamber restoration was sitting atop a bed of wilted greens, his half-lidded eyes staring morosely into the face of a baked trout studded with almond truffles.

I've found my mistress. I've also now developed a strong revulsion for wilted greens.

22ND ANVIL

Restoration of the torture chamber is back on track and progressing at a blisteringly swift pace. I helped myself to a large bunch of flowers from my grandmother's strictly off-limits area of the garden and presented them to Yanna over an early breakfast. The staff had excelled themselves, with three types of eggs, seven types of bread, a mound of fried potatoes, and so much bacon and sliced meat on the tray that I couldn't see the pattern. Yanna explained that, as of today, there would be no more trouble from the staff.

I was pleased to see that the foreman's head had vanished from her quarters—apparently, her first job as mistress had been to make it a permanent feature in the kitchen. The staff were suddenly very motivated, by all accounts.

I had to apologise for my lack of sexual energy the previous evening; I had eaten so much that the only thing I could raise was my head—over the sink as I brought half of it up. Thankfully, she didn't seem to mind at all.

I was going to suggest we consummate the mistress/Overlord relationship before breakfast started to repeat on me, but a cowering servant darted in and handed me a letter.

> *My quarters at your earliest convenience. That means NOW. Also, you can damn well replace the flowers you brutalised this morning. P.S. Do you know anything about the big boulder in my dumbwaiter? I lost two decent servants and a triple-layer chocolate sponge dessert.*
>
> *Your loving and eternally patient grandmother.*

Any ardour I had was promptly extinguished. I may as well have poured ice over my groin at the thought of going anywhere near my grandmother while she was breakfasting. Runny egg yolk sliding down a wrinkled, heaving bosom is enough to turn a barbarian's stomach—the thought certainly made me regret eating so heartily.

Yanna had to go and draw up some contract or other, so I excused myself and made the trek to my grandmother's chambers, cursing the servants who keep falling like flies in her stead. Still, it is another two pockets off the payroll, so that is a small saving grace. At this rate, the only people left in the damn castle will be her and me. Suddenly, the dank stone corridors began to close in on me, and I shivered.

LATER

I arrived at my grandmother's chambers to find a servant scrubbing bloodstains off the floor by the dumbwaiter. I tried not to stare while my grandmother poured herself a stein of tea and laced it with alcohol. I told her she couldn't keep summoning me like this, that I was the Overlord and had better things to do with my time.

"Like bumping bones with that fiery stick creature," was her reply. Her lip curled so much that her moustache almost vanished up her left nostril. Despite having had a daughter, she disapproves of sex. She claims it is undignified, messy, and leads to heartburn. The fact that her last husband's heart exploded while they were mid-passion may have something to do with her attitude. It must have been how those two servants felt as the boulder crushed the breath out of them.

I told her that my love life was none of her business, but she snorted so hard that her tea sprayed over the gilded dog centrepiece on her coffee table. "She's a strumpet. She's after our money."

Her money! I let it slide as I retorted: "What money? We don't *have* any fucking money."

"We will do," she snapped. I asked her what she meant, but she guzzled the rest of her tea and waved me away.

23ᴿᴰ ANVIL

No sign of Yanna for the rest of the day, yesterday. I spent my time pondering my grandmother's words and resolved to find out what she meant. I'll have to delve further into my parents' affairs.

I was unlocking their chambers when Yanna appeared. She handed me a contract and asked whether or not I needed her pen. I nodded and watched as she plucked one from inside her half-laced corset. My mouth went dry, and I could barely read the first few lines of the contract because of the distraction. She had to explain that it was a standard Overlord/mistress contract, but my mind had blacked out at a rather insistent thigh rubbing against my groin. Yanna flipped to the last page for me, 'to save time' while burying her tongue in my mouth—a good legal advisor should be able to multitask—and I scribbled what I could remember of my name as she shoved me backwards into the room and onto the remains of the bed.

24TH ANVIL

Woke up with my face buried in a shredded pillow. Yanna was splashing around in the bathroom. I hope she checked all the bottles of lotion with a poison-stick before using anything. One of my mother's maids made that mistake years ago and ended up with half her hand melted away by an acidic concoction of my mother's that had been left to deter theft.

After yesterday's activities, I appear to have recovered. In fact, I feel like I'm on top of the world. Even my parents' chambers seem less gloomy today. It took a moment to realise that the reason was because Yanna had removed the curtains and thrown open the windows. My parents' portrait was also nowhere to be seen. For a moment, it felt odd, but as I surveyed the wreckage of the bed, the feeling quickly passed. Anyway, looking into the faces of my parents over Yanna's shoulder as she bounced up and down was not exactly the most erotic experience I've ever had.

25TH ANVIL

Yanna has insisted that, as Overlord, I should take my parents' chambers as my own and completely renovate them. She said she would personally oversee this, along with clearing out all documents and rubbish. When I started to complain that it was a lot of hassle, she made the excellent point that it would help expunge their memory from the castle and so ensure better cooperation from all staff, who may well have lingering loyalties.

I acquiesced and set off for the library to see if I could get some help with the cursed puzzle box. I also sent a message to my grandmother that I would be visiting that afternoon. I am determined to extract more information on this money situation.

The library books on puzzle boxes were all useless—not from an informational viewpoint, but from the fact that someone had removed relevant pages and replaced them with pictures of naked elves. My mother has a sick sense of humour.

The librarian was also unimpressed at the damaged books and confiscated the pictures.

LATER

My grandmother knows more than she is letting on. She says that I will just "bungle things", especially if I'm distracted by "*that harpy*" and that my father's plan should "be allowed to run its course". I'm incandescent. No one seems to trust my abilities. Granted, I don't have many at this moment in time, but where in the job description of 'Overlord' does it say that I have to suffer such fucking outrages.

29TH ANVIL

I considered asking Yanna about the puzzle box, but she is currently obsessed with the renovation of my parents' chambers and has been working some of the staff and minions into the ground, helping her. I have never seen someone so diligent... she is even ripping out the built-in wardrobes and pulling the carpet up.

I suggested stopping for lunch after another hunt for something useful in the library, but when I poked my head in, she was busy haranguing three exhausted-looking staff members about not promptly clearing away the carcass of an orc who had fallen victim to a spike-wall trap behind one of the wardrobes.

As sexy as she looks while angry, I retreated and enjoyed a quiet but luxurious lunch of various smoked and sweet delicacies. The staff are still too terrified to mess me about, even more so when Yanna is around. The table legs threaten to give way with every meal.

30TH ANVIL

Before she set off to continue her renovations, I picked Yanna's brain about my grandmother and how to get her to open up to me. I didn't bore her with details—I'd rather she didn't know that I'm concerned about money. When I mentioned last night that perhaps she had better opt for the cheaper shrieker-skin rug, rather than the extortionately priced fellephant skin, her eyes turned to terrifying slits, and she slammed the bathroom door so hard that the doorjamb splintered.

Her suggestion was bribery and if that didn't work, take harsher measures. I replied that death was about the harshest measure one could take, but she just shook her head and smirked.

I opted to try her suggestion and sent for the pastry chef, with whom I spent the afternoon concocting a series of sugary delicacies. I was forced to endure the chef's complaints about scratching behind the kitchen walls. Has she forgotten where she works? I would be worried if there *wasn't* scratching.

MAJA

1ST MAJA

Mid-morning, when I could be sure that the expectation of the horrific vision of my grandmother in a nightdress would be minimal, I made my way to her chambers, leading a small procession of staff bearing silver platters of sweet treats, chocolates, and pastries. I don't think I have ever seen my grandmother smile so much, not since my father fell down a spiral staircase and broke his leg three years ago.

As she tucked into her second platter of champagne truffles, she began to warm to me, in that she actively engaged me in conversation that wasn't laden with contempt or criticism.

I lamented at the state of the castle and tried to convince her that the reason I was so inattentive was guilt at the fact that I couldn't provide a better life for her. She looked suspicious, so I diverted her all-too-sharp mind onto the white chocolate cupcakes. I told her that my ultimate aim was to own a domain in a land such as Copperwald, which is renowned for its culinary stars, and that any decent castle should have a proper pastry kitchen, rather than the converted bathroom that we utilise.

I could almost see the nasty little cogs turning in the grey depths behind her beady eyes and threw in a last, casual remark: "Of course, this little banquet is more than just a celebration for you, it is a fond farewell to the pastry chef and her assistant, as we can no longer afford to keep them in our employ."

As her many chins fell like a column of fleshy dominos, I added that she should pace herself as the treats before her were all that she'd likely see for some time.

She began to choke on a piece of candied fruit—what a dilemma. Here was my chance to watch the life ebb out of her, finally, and I had to throw it away for the greater good. A slap between her shoulder-blades sent the fruit pinwheeling into the beard of a lurking servant, and she grabbed my arm so tightly that the blood vanished.

For a long moment, she hung onto me, until I thought that the arm was lost, and then ordered me to sit down. She said that my father had been working on a plan to recover our fortunes and regain what had once been ours, but that the specifics had always been kept from her. However, not long after they had been sorting through some papers among my old school things, they came across *something* that had pointed to a valuable revenue source. Some sort of rare ore, by all accounts. Since then, for some reason, our gold reserves had been depleting at a rapid rate—she had no idea *where* they were spending it, or *why*.

Success! She also told me that she would be personally paying for the chef and her assistant so, sadly, that avenue of exploitation is now closed off to me.

2ND MAJA

Long after Yanna had exhausted herself of my body and fallen asleep, I remained awake, turning over the conversation with my grandmother. Rare ore? As far as I was aware, all we possessed were a few mines and some useless swampland. If it were true, and my father had found rare ore or minerals, then our land would skyrocket in value, drawing more wealth, business, and trade.

It would make up for my being unable to locate any hidden gold vaults and curtail any potential mutinies. However, the chance of attack from Heroes and other Overlords would increase—no wonder he kept it quiet. Why I haven't managed to find any pertinent documents, however, is of concern. There should be reports, surveys, maps, and more. The thought of ploughing through my father's office to find them leaves me cold. Surely he wouldn't have been stupid enough to leave them there anyway. I could ask Yanna if she found any—she was always in there at one point.

There is a possibility that they are locked away in the lower dungeons somewhere. When I reached to rummage in my bedside drawer for a notebook to set down my plans, my fingers grazed that infernal puzzle box of my mother's.

I lay back in the sliver of moonlight that was peeking from between the stupidly expensive curtains that Yanna had insisted on, and studied the polished wood, stroking the grain, trying to draw some clue from it. The rattle did nothing but torment. It suddenly occurred to me that the dungeon key I was looking for could well be in this box. I resolved to head back to the library and demand assistance in opening it.

3RD MAJA

I was forced to vacate my chambers early this morning, as Yanna was arranging fittings for new wardrobes and carpets. When I told her to tread carefully, as there wasn't the gold for anything in the Skeins catalogue (which, in itself, costs five pieces of gold), she threw a volcanic tantrum. She can clean up the smashed water jug and broken mirror herself, as far as I'm concerned.

Mopping my face off and picking shards of glass from my hair, I made my way down to the library, avoiding a troll and a shard beast squabbling over a dead, half-eaten scamp. They shouldn't even be in the half-decent part of the castle. This is what happens when you can't access the sodding dungeons. One look at the fire demon and there would be far fewer fights and no corpses left lying around the corridors. I stepped in the remains of a rotting scamp yesterday. In bare feet. It was like treading in half-melted sausage jam, but with more flies.

At least the torture chamber should be nearly finished by

now, which means that at least I now have that threat to hold over the wretched staff and minions. If we were ever invaded by heroes, we could also use it to turn them to our cause, but even the local Heroes' Guild now finds our castle to be a laughable waste of time.

According to last week's local paper, the guild president was quoted as saying that the only things to be carried away from the castle were fleas and a nasty cough.

Bastard.

If I had any blood assassins left, I'd have his guts decorating my new study before the week was out. As it was, all I could afford to do was send a few scamps round to smash the guild's windows two days ago. The corpses were sent back this morning, folded into a giant leather envelope with a bill inside for damages.

They can sodding well sue me. I left it on Yanna's desk to deal with earlier, which is another reason she is in a bad mood. The blood stained the wood, but I refused to allow the purchase of a replacement. Her lips pulled into a tight line and, in one incensed move, she managed to upend the desk onto a waiting servant. While she was looking around for things to throw, I had made my escape. I'm starting to regret not just declaring celibacy.

I got diverted from the library by a message from one of the low-level lackeys I employ, telling me that the torture chamber had been completed—finally, some good news. I hastened down to the dungeon vestibule to investigate, wondering which minions I should use to test it out. The kitchen staff are all high on my list, as are the howler wraiths nesting in the east tower. I barely slept last night for the wails of fornicating wraiths and rumbling stone.

LATER

Of all the stupid, incompetent, wretched bags of flesh to have ever existed. After spending twenty minutes shouting up at the east tower to get the attention of a howler wraith, and then sending them after the departed workmen, my efforts were all in vain. They have retreated to whatever slum of stupidity my father plucked them from. Only a solitary, abandoned tool bag remains, sitting under a cluster of stools near the torture chamber door, along with an overflowing helmet of cigarette ends, half a sandwich, an abandoned glove, and a cheap porn magazine.

In addition to not being able to access the lower dungeons, I now can't even access the former ruin of the torture chamber, thanks to the fucking spikes on the door handle. I can't look through the keyhole because there is a spike sticking out of it. The spikes on the door have spikes. The hinges have spikes, and the key to the door has spikes.

The wraiths wisely departed and sat cackling at me from the tower rafters while I went on the hunt for a scamp to kick. I found none. Not even dropping a chair out of a window onto a warlock who was reading quietly in the herb garden made me feel better.

I returned to my quarters to get Yanna to deal with it. I had to fight through a sea of milling people, some of whom appeared to be wearing a half-vomited-up rainbow. Yanna finally noticed me, bobbing and pushing at the back of the throng and swept up, flourishing a book of fabric swatches. Given her jovial mood, she had clearly spent more money. I'm beginning to see the downside of a high-maintenance mistress.

"Isn't it adorable; these fabrics are imported from the Red Mountains—exclusive designs." I barely saw them whizz past my face before she thrust the book at a hovering woman—dressed in a bright yellow fabric-cocoon of some kind, and clutching a large cushion—and snatched up a large board. "This is called a mood board."

"How apt." She ignored my acid tone.

"This is a visualisation of what the room will look like.

Burgundies... purple for the walls, and some velvet upholstery for the new furniture I've commissioned." I looked at the sea of swatches, pasted-on sketches of ornate furniture, feathers, and other jumbled nonsense.

"I'm supposed to make head or tail of this?"

"No, you're supposed to be grateful I've sorted out this place, and to shut up and pay for it." She thrust the board into the arms of a nearby lackey, dressed in what can only be described as a tie-dye tent, and planted her hands on her hips.

"Don't I fucking know it," I hissed.

"It's a mistress' privilege to decorate as she sees fit. Read your contract," she snapped. I felt my blood pressure rise.

"I'm dwelling here too, and I *refuse* to sleep in something resembling a giant bruise." I folded my arms. This would be the end of it.

All bustling stopped. One woman's tape measure zip-snapped back into its holster, sounding nastily loud in the sudden, deafening silence.

I had no idea mood boards could hurt so much.

With the slamming door cutting off the sniggering and laughter, I staggered away and spent five minutes hiding behind a suit of armour, trying to prise it from around my neck and back over my head, with fabric and glue-covered feathers tickling my nose.

Not for the first time did I regret killing my parents. In fact, dying was probably their last act of spite against me, knowing what I would be faced with.

I used the hideous board as a urinary target and then slunk downstairs to find someone to bully. I deserve respect. I have a castle, lands, a fire demon (albeit one that I can't yet access), and a potential super-haul in some mysterious ore. Yet I get no consideration.

I reached the library without seeing a single small minion to pick on and had to head inside, angry and dejected, so the woman who worked there would have to do.

I eventually located her on the upper gallery, boarding up a hole in one of the bookcases. "What do you want?" She spat nails out of her mouth and dropped her hammer into a mouldy-looking leather tool bag.

I was taken aback.

"Some fucking respect," I countered.

She snorted and gave her wilder-than-usual hair a flick back over her ears. It didn't dare move after that.

"Look in the fiction section, under 'R'." She turned her back, gave the board a kick with a scuffed hobnail boot that defied her colourful ensemble, before stalking away and shoving the tool bag under a desk that was overflowing with record cards and books that had seen better days.

I tried again. "You'd do well to remember your damn place. I won't be spoken to like this; I'm sick of it." She wasn't Yanna; I knew that, but she was far less volatile. Or so I thought.

She marched towards me, pulling a stray nail from her corset, and glared up into my face. I started to reconsider my assessment of her temperament. "What's my name?"

I blinked.

"What is my name?" she repeated, slower.

"I don't know."

She stepped back, giving a smile of bitter triumph.

"Exactly, and yet you talk about respect. If you manage to find any in this putrid castle, perhaps you'd be kind enough to send some *my* way."

"How dare—"

"Look." She ran a ripped sleeve over her forehead. "I've spent the best part of two days plugging up more scamp holes, I've had to scrape what was left of a warlock off the ceiling when he used the wrong incantation from one of the high-level spell books, half the culinary section has now been eaten by minions, there's a weird damp patch on the ceiling, I've not been paid in three months, and I got *three* papercuts this morning—*at the same time.*"

She gathered herself and took a breath. "So. What was it you really wanted?"

I shook my head, hardly remembering. "Erm. Have you heard any rumours about rare ore deposits? Minerals?"

"What kind?"

"I've no idea."

She pondered and shook her head. "No, but your father spent a lot of time looking up books on mining, ores, and things like that. He asked if I knew any specialists in the field."

Could this be it? "And did you?"

"Yes."

"Who? Where? I need to speak to them. This could be the key to everything."

"Like being paid?"

I waved her off. "Yes, yes. Twice bloody over, all right."

"Sharri Smith. Part-time lecturer at Cindertop University."

"And where can I find her?"

"Six foot under at Needleford Cemetery, last I heard." She sat down and started slamming books around the desk, looking for inspiration for how best to ignore me.

"She's dead? She fucking can't be?"

"She appears to be under that impression." She ruffled a stack of cards together and then yelped and dropped them to suck her finger.

I'd had enough. "This is your fault!" I screamed at her. She looked up from her latest papercut, startled. "Why couldn't you have been more helpful to my useless father, then you might actually know what his precious fucking plan to pull us out of this mess was. Then at least I could buy competent staff." I kicked the desk, my boot connecting hard with the ancient leg.

It gave. Suddenly, and with malice.

I remember the leathery cascade and then the dull ache at the back of my head as it complained about its rough meeting with the stone floor. Something was crushing my chest, forcing my ribs inwards with a steady, cruel weight. I smelled the sweet, decaying aroma of books.

"Fuck." The light dimmed a little as someone leaned over me. Wild tendrils of hair reached down towards me, framing a round, flushed face with smooth angelic skin.

"You still alive?"

"I wish I wasn't."

"I could always leave you," she said. Something resembling a smile may have flicked over her face. Or it could have been wind. I didn't care; I was fast starting to blackout. She shifted a few books and the pressure on my ribs began to lift.

"Yanna would love that. She could turn the whole damn castle into a fabric tribute to a fried blood clot." I tried to move, but my arms were pinned by several giant volumes. On giants, annoyingly enough.

"You have to help me."

"I should be able to shift them." She looked at the heap that was smothering my body. "If I were being paid…"

"No, I mean, *help* me." It all came spilling out. Perhaps the lack of blood in my extremities was making me light-headed, perhaps that smile—real or imagined—was the only true fragment of kindness I'd seen for a long time, and it broke me, but the foolish, weak words tumbled out.

"I've got a mistress who's spending what little gold we have left, a castle that's falling down around me, minions who won't do anything except eat one another (and everything else), a dungeon I can't open, a torture chamber I can't access, a grandmother who spites me by *refusing* to die, a bedchamber that resembles a haemorrhoid, a mystery revenue stream that could save us all, and a damn puzzle box that is driving me insane. INSANE."

As soon as I mentioned it, it began digging into my hip from my pocket—hateful, jagging wood.

"My name's Francis."

I blinked, momentarily thrown off. "What?"

"My name's Francis."

I swallowed and tried to take a breath, but my lungs were at crush point.

"Nathaniel. I… my name's Nathaniel."

Francis nodded.

"I will pay you. And I'll get you a helper to scare the scamps away." I hoped I didn't sound too desperate. I *was*, but I didn't want to *sound* like it.

She nodded again, thoughtful. She leaned down and started hauling books off me, each one easing the weight by a fraction until the blood began to seep back in, sending a riot of aggravating tingles through every twitching limb. The sight of her in her skull-motif corset above me was enough to make me wish she'd leave some of the books in place. Thankfully the blood had better places to be, and I was spared that additional insult.

"See if you can speak to anyone else in Needleford who may know more about this ore business. Given that Sharri Smith was run over by a wagon in suspicious circumstances, she was probably killed for what she knew."

"What were the circumstances?"

"She was tied down in the middle of the road."

"Oh."

She heaved a book off my legs and paused to wipe her forehead. "So was a colleague of hers who was a cartographer."

"Maps. Ore and maps." It got me wondering. Another few books and my arms were free. Bruised, tingling, but free. After a few minutes massaging my limbs, I was able to struggle up, with her help.

"I should get back. I need to get that damn torture chamber open, then perhaps I'll get some fucking respect around here and restore discipline. I'll need a decent army if I'm to keep any ore I do manage to find. As soon as we get anything decent, though, someone will want to march in and take it."

"Head of the Army's been... Busy," Francis said, avoiding my gaze.

"Whatever," I said, feeling a little better. "He can start doing his job. If Yanna has calmed down, she can go and deal with him—take this situation by the head."

"From what I hear, she's already doing that," she muttered, starting to stack a few books into a neat pile. I just nodded. If Yanna already had matters in hand, then I wouldn't interfere. It meant that, at least, despite blighting our bedchamber, that she was doing her job, which appeared to be a rare thing around this place.

As I straightened my waistcoat, the damn puzzle box fell out of my pocket and slid down a book to land at Francis' feet. She scooped it up and studied it, giving it a gentle shake.

"I couldn't find much help in this place on how to open them. So much for a decent library. I'm surprised my father didn't shut the whole thing down." I was feeling much better, and my aching body was fuelling a peevishness that clung to every word.

Francis glared at me and then, without a word, dropped the box over the railing to the floor below, where it clattered on the stone beside another overburdened desk. It appeared she operated in a similar way to my father.

"How childish," I sneered.

She gave me a withering look, hauled a vast book from the floor, staggered to the railing, and then dropped it. The book smacked the puzzle box, and there was a green snap of light to compliment the cracking noise. A puff of green acid erupted and, in seconds, dissolved the book.

"Problem solved," she said, dusting her hands. I stared at her for a moment and then tottered downstairs as fast as my bruised legs would carry me.

I batted away the thin, pungent haze and shoved the melted remains of the book away with my boot, hoping that all traces of the acid had gone. I should probably have considered that beforehand, to be honest. Anyhow. Lying on the floor where the box had once been, were two small keys—as I had suspected!

Francis leaned past me and poured a jug of water over everything, sending any remnants of acid swirling down a nearby grate in the floor. I picked up and stared at the fruits of my nemesis' death.

"All that fuss for a couple of keys."

"If one's the dungeon key, a great many creatures in this festering castle will soon be very sorry for their lazy, nasty little lives," I replied, briefly considering her face if I decided to consign her to a cell for a week. She narrowed her eyes, and I had a brief moment of panic that she was a mind reader.

She turned her back, however, and flumped down in a chair whose stuffing was escaping from a dozen or so rips and frays, and began colouring between the thick lines of a 'Strictly NO Scamps Allowed' sign with a bright red pen.

Given her help, I decided to be considerate and not remind her that she was simply making pretty-coloured food for them.

I studied the keys. One was solid and tastefully ornate, while the other was thick, chunky, and possessed of a satisfying heft. I remember my father making such a joke about himself during a drunken dinner party some years ago. My grandmother had been disgusted and had refused to speak to him for three months. He told me it was the happiest time of his life.

The decorative loops and bold skull at the top of the chunky key were unfamiliar, but it couldn't be anything but the desperately needed dungeon key. Buoyed up by my success, I hobbled away to help myself to a victory tipple from the wine cellar, only to be accosted outside the library door by one of my grandmother's lackeys.

"Sir, your grandmother requests your presence."

"Tell her I'm the pissing Overlord, and if she wants to speak to me, she can damn well come and find me."

"She said that if that was the case, I was to give you this." The shaking young man in an oversized uniform handed over a note and took two steps back.

It simply read:

> *Ores and whores. Both of which seem to be an issue for you. Bring me some rose pastries when you come, my dumbwaiter is still broken, and the servants don't move fast enough.*
>   *Your eternally patient grandmother.*

This was all I needed. I was about to take it out on her lackey, but he had fled back up a nearby staircase. I vowed to scour my mother's manuscript for more death ideas.

4TH MAJA

I spent the night in the bed in my old chambers, rather than return to face Yanna and whatever hideous furnishings she and her cadre of putrescently-dressed helpers had managed to spew over our quarters. The number of cushions appears to grow daily.

The visit to my grandmother had played on my mind half the night, meaning that my usual disposition was somewhat soured.

Between spoonfuls of a vile lavender pudding (I lied and told her that the pastries had been eaten by a rogue scamp because I couldn't be bothered going to the kitchen), she told me that she had heard 'disturbing rumblings.' This didn't surprise me, given the punishment she regularly meted out to her gastrointestinal system, but she started on about Yanna and how she was paying regular visits to the guard chambers.

I told her that Yanna was doing her job and keeping the damn army in line so that we actually had people to fight, should we suddenly become a worthwhile target. At that, her beady little eyes lit up, and she said she had heard that I was investigating the ore situation. She demanded to know why I hadn't made more progress and why I had been wasting time lurking around the library.

"Nothing good ever came out of one of those," she said with a sniff.

I tried to point out that they were repositories of great knowledge, but she just snorted into her tea. Her general loathing of books was compounded every birthday by my father's yearly gift of a thoughtful volume, such as *How Not to Be a Burden on Your Family*, *Knowing When to Quit*, and *Why Don't You Just Die?*.

I told her that I was going to be investigating reports by an ore specialist and she seemed placated. Perhaps the lavender had a calming effect, who knows.

Today, with the dungeon key in hand, I plan on ordering a posse of minions to track down those obtuse, useless workmen and throw them in the cells. And once they open the damn torture chamber, they will be its first guests.

LATER—STABLES BEHIND THE CASTLE

I was busy giving orders to a small group of soldiers whom I was sending out on the trail of the workmen when one of the staff responsible for the upkeep of the stables and other buildings actually questioned me.

"What are you going to do when you find 'em then? Can't exactly torture 'em, can you?" he pulled a long nail from behind his ear and started hammering a piece of wood over a hole in the stable door, drowning out my response and necessitating a louder volume, which somewhat watered down my sarcasm.

"I was of the understanding that that was what torture chambers were for."

"Yeah, but yours is busted."

"Would you like to find out?"

"Eh?"

Thump, hammer, bang.

"Would. You. Like. To. Find. Out?" I shouted between the thuds.

"I can take a look if you want, but I can't promise nuthin'." He took in a sharp breath and shook his head in a forlorn manner that I suspected was rehearsed.

"That's not what I—"

Crash. Bang.

"Eh?"

"I said... oh, forget it." He'd returned to his infernal hammering, and we were burning daylight. I'd rather be burning him, or the whole damn castle if my father had actually kept up the insurance payments (one of the first things I checked).

The tracking posse had just lit out when a servant came scurrying over, spluttering in the dust kicked up by half a dozen ageing horses ambling and limping away. I had a feeling the only thing the posse would be catching was a venereal disease in one of the town's licensed brothels.

"Sir?" It was the same lackey from yesterday. He was young and terrified—good. He should be. "Erm, there's some news."

"My grandmother's dead?"

"No, sir." He looked thoughtful. "Although, one of her servants got killed by a fireball that erupted from under a serving cloche."

Buggery fuck.

"What is it then?" My fine mood was starting to falter, and I didn't like it. Perhaps Yanna had discovered some hidden riches during her renovations.

"There's a man waiting in your office. He says he's..." He consulted a scrawl on his hand. "Mr Derrick Snide. Health and Safety Inspector."

The lights momentarily dimmed, and I felt the will to live begin to seep from my body. Why do these things keep happening to me? Isn't my life miserable enough?

"Tell him to come back next week."

"Erm... he says that your father had already put off the inspection twice before. He's here whether you like it or not. Erm. He says."

My foot put a fresh hole in the stable door beside the newly patched-up one, and I screamed at the assembled minions to temporarily disperse while I hobbled through the decaying castle to the office.

Each corridor and staircase made me cringe. They were bound to see problems everywhere. The fact that the handrails on many staircases had been melted down years prior and the metal sold was not a good start.

He was in my office when I arrived, perched on the edge of my chair as though the back was cursed, making notes. It made me nervous, and therefore in a bad mood. I made several attempts to slam the door and gave up, instead kicking over a bin to focus his attention on my entrance. The limp, admittedly, was a bit of a let-down.

Beady eyes peered through thick glasses beneath a neatly divided fringe of oiled black hair. "Mr Evergrim?"

"Yes."

"You are the Overlord of this domain?" His questioning tone appeared to teeter on the brink of incredulity.

"Why else would I be torturing myself by speaking to you, Mr Snide. And you appear to be in my chair."

"Indeed." He got up and shifted to a nearby chair, allowing me to take my seat and then wish I hadn't as one of the castors gave way and nearly pitched me into the man's lap. He made a tiny note on his clipboard.

"My name, as I trust you'll have already gathered, is Mr Derrick Snide. I'm here to carry out the much overdue annual inspection of your primary lair ahead of a greater, domain-wide inspection."

"Is this strictly necessary?" I demanded. I wished that we had a stack of gold left. How could I have nothing to bribe the man with? He adjusted his glasses and, with a sniff, tapped his pen against his clipboard.

"I'd say *perilously* overdue. And did I hear a scream just now?"

"It's an evil lair, what did you expect to hear?"

"Hmm. Certainly not woodworm and thunderticks in the walls." He gave me a sinister smile.

"The castle's just settling." Despite my abject hatred for every mouldering brick, I was starting to feel defensive.

"Settling or sinking? I understand you have some flooding issues…"

"Can we get this over with, I have better things to do," I snapped.

As he stood to leave, I wondered if I could foist him off on anyone else. Yanna perhaps. Or my grandmother.

"Let me explain how this works, Overlord Evergrim," he adjusted his glasses again and straightened his overly elaborate cravat.

I decided I hated him just for wearing it.

"You'll be accompanying me for the full course of my inspection. I shall raise any concerns or issues with what I find and, at the end, present you with a preliminary report as to my findings. A full report will be submitted to my office, and they will decide what action needs to be taken on your—or our—behalf."

"Sounds inconvenient," I said. He smirked, as only a person who adored his nasty little job could, and then headed into the corridor. He waved his pen as he walked, asking all manner of inane questions while I desperately wondered where I could ditch him… or, rather, *pieces* of him.

"The records state that you have two hundred and eighty-seven minions currently domiciled here, forty-five members of staff, and a small army of around seven hundred and fifty. Is that currently correct."

"Probably not. Many of them have either died, deserted, or eaten one another. I have no idea."

"That is a serious offence. What happens if there is a fire?"

He stopped his inspection of a hole in the wall that looked out over the herb garden and stared at me.

"Then the place will be warm for the first time in fucking years."

"You need to take an immediate roll-call," he said, scribbling furiously on his clipboard. "Disgraceful. As for the consumption of minions by other minions, that is frowned upon. Don't you have separate domiciles for hostiles?"

"What?"

"Hostile minions—those who don't get along with any or specific minions. They need separate housing with their own facilities. This all should have been in the handbook, Overlord Evergrim."

"What handbook? I inherited this shitty place from my father."

"Yes, I heard he took a tumble." The man peered through the hole in the wall. I lamented the fact that he wouldn't fit. Giving him a shove would have done little but get him jammed, sadly.

"Are you aware that there is a decomposing warlock down there, pinned to a bed of parsley by a chair?"

My shrug seemed to irritate him, at least, that's what his twitching eyebrows seemed to suggest.

"Experimental organic compost," I said.

"You should get yourself a copy of the handbook. These things are all clearly stated. On the subject of minions, I shall need to inspect the domiciles first-hand. And as for fire safety, what precautions do you have?"

Our wandering was taking us closer than I would have liked to my grandmother's quarters. That was all I needed, her sitting him down and telling him everything I had ever done wrong.

"We have a large pond. And a river flows under the castle and out down the Shard River towards that halfwit Sergi Grimhaven's domain."

I got that look again.

"Fire alarms, water buckets, automatic dousing spells, gathering points, safety notices?"

I shook my head.

"Do your minions know what they should do in the event of fire?"

"Run?"

"Overlord Evergrim, this *really* is not good enough. You have a responsibility to every minion currently domiciled under your roof."

"We've only got half of a roof. Does that mean I get half off?"

The nib of his pen bent as he jerked, spurting ink over his notes.

"No, it does NOT." He rammed his glasses so far up his face that he nearly squashed his eyeballs. "These issues are level-one priority and need to be addressed *immediately*."

He scribbled something in tiny writing on a piece of paper and then pulled a vented box from his shoulder bag. Inside was a small, leathery creature with dark wings and a small tube attached to a scaly leg—a homing macrex. Part of the scamp family and more intelligent than all of their brethren put together. This wasn't good.

Ignoring my protests, he stuffed the message into the tube and released it from the nearest window. As he closed the window, it fell off its hinges, and the glass smashed over the floor. I could feel his glare burning into me, so I studied the ceiling until he had moved on, hoping he wouldn't look up and notice the hole where an acid imp had exploded last year—one of my father's attempts on my grandmother's life. I was hoping to emulate it, but with more success. Hopefully, by tonight, I will be one problem less, at least.

5ᵀᴴ MAJA

I rarely have cause to thank my grandmother, let alone be glad of her repeated attempts to defy death but, yesterday, I did. After writing a damning report on the lack of handrails on the staircases and the Hero damage to one of the towers, which now teetered in high winds, Mr Snide decided to talk to the staff about their living conditions. I directed him to my grandmother's quarters and lurked in the corner while she interrogated him and verbally abused me for letting a strange man into her quarters.

While her staff quailed under her gaze and answered that they were very happy in their jobs and had never seen, or been a party to, a breach in regulations *at any time*, my eyes moved to the dumbwaiter. I groaned quietly at the sacrifice required.

I suggested that my grandmother had a snack sent up from the kitchen, which naturally set her off on a rant about how the dumbwaiter hadn't been fixed since the boulder incident.

Mr Snide went to inspect it, and I hurried behind a marble statue of a semi-naked barbarian (my grandmother hung her dressing gown over the 'unmentionable bits') and waited.

Along with Mr Snide, two servants were killed in the blast. To my eternal chagrin, my grandmother had been protected by her vast stein of tea and one of her larger servants (now not so large).

With the toe of my boot, I nudged the pair of glasses and dissolving pen, sitting in the sad, fizzing green puddle by the dumbwaiter. Though my grandmother was now shrieking about the loss of staff and the destruction of her dumbwaiter, and how useless I was that I couldn't control my minions, it was worth it— even if the stench of burning flesh and hair was making me gag.

I decided that, to avoid further trouble from H&S, I would have to install the damn fire safety things. To spite my grandmother for not dying in the blast, I removed and sold her barbarian statue while she was paying a visit to the kitchens to verbally abuse the staff. It will pay nicely for the plush wank I'm expected to decorate this castle with.

6TH MAJA

Woke up to find Yanna draped over my nether regions. Not unpleasant. She said that we should take a break from the castle, as the decaying corridors and halls were a drain on our relationship. I agreed, wondering if we could seize a nice holiday place in one of the less shitty towns on the outskirts of the domain. She suggested Needleford. She *is* after my damn money. Probably to buy a boatload more cushions. I walked into what was formerly my parents' quarters this morning and thought there had been some sort of odd fabric-breeding program going on. I actually summoned the head warlock to get him to explain but was told that he was missing. Typical.

When I explained to Yanna that Needleford was unpleasant this time of year and that, besides, no ore had actually yet been located, her eyes narrowed. I told her that I had sent a letter to a number of persons and societies in the town, but had yet to hear anything positive.

She said she had forgotten a meeting and then hurried off. I decided to send several of my more competent staff members on an excursion to Needleford to see what they could discover about the ore and my father's own investigations. In the meantime, I would have to continue my search for any information that I could. As if I didn't have enough to do.

As I poured myself into the same breeches that I'd been wearing the day before, I found the keys that Francis had finally freed from the puzzle box. If one was the dungeon key (I had yet to try it, what with all the distractions) it struck me that the important paperwork might be housed in whatever chest, container, or cupboard the other of them fit. I just had to find it.

A passing duo of scamps was shown the smaller, ornate key, and I sent them on their way to try and locate something that matched. In the meantime, I went down to the staff level and lurked outside the quarters until I had caught enough of the slackers, including the short builder from the stable, to form a second posse to go in search of the posse that had not yet returned.

They were not happy, but given that I intend to get the torture chamber opened up in the next few days, and made several mentions of it, they made a hasty trail to the stables.

As I was returning to my office to sift through paperwork, the scamps I had retained earlier came trotting down the corridor, holding a door. The pattern around the lock was similar, but not identical to the ornate key, and it didn't fit. Not that it would have done me much good as the wretched door was now in my possession, but its erstwhile location was not. Trying to explain this in anything less than a scream proved useless, and they slunk off.

7TH MAJA

No luck in my office and no luck with the fancy key. I have searched every chest, cupboard and door in the family's chambers, but to no avail. There are no floor safes, no wall safes, no hidden chests—nothing that I could find.

LATER

Several letters back from Needleford today. It would seem that my father had a small team of mineralogists and geologists working secretly in the area, but then the team were all either killed or vanished. Apparently, the useless locals now won't go near the swamps as they believe them to be cursed, which means I'm not likely to be able to hire anyone to explore further.

What did my father find? What was worth killing the team over and who did it? Our family's primary rival, Sergi Grimhaven, is the most likely suspect, other than my father himself, of course. Sergi and my family have always hated one another—I went to school with him. Since becoming Overlord of his parents' domain, he's become far too inflated with self-importance and has repeatedly threatened an invasion. I hope I survive long enough to actually mine some damn profit out of this miserable domain and rub it in his square face.

I had to know what was there but lacked the ability to pull strings and get the job done, so consulted with Yanna, against my better judgement—it isn't as though she can make off with a whole mine—and she sprang into action, making immediate arrangements to get a team out there to see what was what. Finally, our fortunes could be turning around.

10TH MAJA

I was busy inspecting the servants' access to the shaft of my grandmother's dumbwaiter to see whether it was possible to flood the thing with toxic gas when there was a nervous cough. It was the terrified servant again. His hair was an unusual shade of green, for some reason.

"Erm, Sir… there's an official to see you. Again."

"What do you mean *again*?" I slammed the half-melted dumbwaiter door shut and dusted off my hands. Murder would have to wait, sadly. He glanced at his hand and then cleared his throat.

"Miss Emilia Davenshire-Derby, Health and Safety Executive."

My insides wanted to melt out from between my buttocks. Why me?

"Tell her to bugger off."

"She's here to check our fire-safety compliance." His eyes were like saucers. Perhaps he had seen, as I had, that the few fire buckets we had had been used as scamp toilets for years. Anyone hurling that at a naked flame would likely be caught in a raging shit inferno.

"—and to carry on where my predecessor left off." The clipped voice belonged to a tall, stick of a woman with dark skin, short curled hair, flame-red clothes, and a terrifying-looking troll-skin clipboard.

"How do you know he… passed away." I couldn't not ask. I had thought it wasn't quite prudent to tell them that their man had been melted. They might look upon us unfavourably.

"His tracking signal was abruptly terminated," she said, her eyes boring into mine. I cleared my throat. The young man stared at the ground. He had been one of the unlucky ones tasked with mopping up the acidy mess.

"Yes, it was a sad accident—no fault of our own."

"Indeed. I'll be investigating, of course, but…" she looked around the kitchen and wrinkled her nose in disdain. "I think, given where we are, we'd best start here."

Oh no. No, no, no. I was fully aware that there was a dead rat in the coffee jar and that the foreman's head was still mounted on the wall above the refrigerating cupboard.

"I noted on my way in that there is a bathtub outside, full of cut chips in water."

"Yes, we consume a great many." I suspected that that was about to change.

"You are aware that the tub is housed beneath the pigeon coop? Not only that, but there appears to be a decomposing scamp floating in it."

I barely flinched, but the young servant twitched. Given how he clutched his stomach, I guessed what he had eaten for dinner the previous evening.

"I'll have a word with the cook." The stupid bastard.

She sniffed and made a few notes in red on her clipboard. While she was inspecting the pantries, I had the servant—whose name, I was told in a shaky voice, was Gawain—remove the dead rat from the coffee jar while I filled an old bucket with water and placed it near the door beneath a hastily drawn fire-safety notice.

"There's a dead goblin among the potato sacks; the flour weevils appear to have become magically engorged and have taken over three shelves, conducting war with some equally large spiders; and your supply of milk expired two years ago." She emerged, brushing dust from her sharp shoulders.

"If you are planning on classifying it as a new life form, you have to submit the relevant forms in triplicate to this address." She ripped off a piece of paper and handed it to me.

"This magical leakage, wherever it has come from, needs to be dealt with. Flour weevils can be a serious threat to other minions and a kitchen pollutant if they get bigger."

I assured her that the moronic minions who had been practising magic in the kitchens would be hunted down and fed to the spiders.

Gawain appeared to pale at this notion and made his excuses and left, probably to warn the rest of the absent kitchen staff. Frankly, I'm amazed they can count to ten, let alone cast spells.

I got bored of her tutting and scribbling and watched an ancient horse kicking and gnawing the stable door that had been recently repaired. It reminded me... I'd need that builder bloke if this pain in the arse wanted to go anywhere near the torture chamber. I certainly couldn't rely upon the wastrels who had buggered off.

Just as the official pain was launching into a lecture about a severed head being hung above a food storage area, with subsequent drippage of fluids onto cream and cooked products being a hazard, I noticed my second search posse returning and slipped out to greet them. Or, rather, demand to know where the rest of the bastards were and where the workmen were that I tasked them with finding.

It appeared that the original posse had indeed caught up with the builders at a tavern in Red Oak, a town half a day from here. After a few pints of ale, they had been convinced to give up their lowly paid jobs here and join the sodding building crew.

"They said a troll would be a great addition," one of them explained, raising their voice to be heard over the sound of me kicking another hole in the stable door. "They said they wouldn't need a ladder to do the fiddly bits then." He shuffled his feet, blinking repeatedly.

"You're telling me that my search posse has deserted to join those useless slacker bastards? Why didn't you drag them back here? And where is the rest of your group?" I demanded.

The pathetic misfits standing before me shared sheepish glances. Of the twelve or so people and creatures I had sent out, only three remained. Two humans and one shuffling magpie demon—human-looking but scrawny, with black and white streaked hair and green-black eyes.

"They joined the others," replied the sulky looking magpie demon, fingering a lucky-leaf necklace around his neck.

"And you didn't out of a crushing sense of duty and loyalty?" I sneered. They fidgeted, the woman with shoulder-length purple hair glaring at me in defiance.

"I couldn't spit far enough," the magpie demon muttered, staring at the ground and balling veiny fists.

"I hate milky tea," confessed the purple-haired woman.

"I worked too quickly; they said I had no idea about pacing

myself," said the builder, looking surprisingly dejected as he scratched his sandy-haired head.

"Staff who know the meaning of the word work?" I snorted, aware of Gawain sidling up, trying to get my attention.

"For your information, the only reason you still have walls still standing is because of people like us," snapped the woman.

I blinked and stared at her for her sheer audacity. How did she think that she could speak to me like that and live?

"Trudy!" the magpie demon hissed, flinching when I looked at him.

I stared at Trudy, imagining seeing her writhing in a pit of flesh-eating flour-weevils. Then I lifted my gaze until they followed it to the wall beyond the stables. It was leaning outward like the half-peeled paper case of an ancient cupcake. Globs of plaster clung hopefully to its walls while cables and ropes tethered it to the ground to apparently prevent it from escaping into the river beyond.

"It appears you missed your calling," I said, distracted from considering what grisly fate was to befall them by Gawain frantically pointing behind me. The inspector was picking her way across the yard. Joy. Of. Joys.

Gawain and the motley group in front of me formed an impromptu wall to block her view of the precarious wall behind them. For a moment, I felt a stab of surprised gratitude.

"I think I've seen enough here, Overlord Evergrim. Now I'd very much like to inspect your dungeon."

There was a snort from Trudy. I gave her a look.

"I'll need to check over your equipment—" Another snort cut the inspector short.

"Would you like to come inside?"

Trudy laughed so hard that she nearly had a fit, and it had clearly spread to the others who were also snickering. I shot one last withering glare at them and led the Health and Safety woman away, gesturing to Dave to follow. He trotted along behind, totting his tool bag and stuffing what looked like a candied eyeball into his mouth with a weathered, meaty hand.

Word had clearly got around about the inspection because servants fell away before us, leaving corridors strangely empty of corpses, scamp faeces, and broken weaponry. If this place were to be shut down, they would have nowhere else to linger and sponge off.

We reached the entrance to the dungeon without incident and paused at the top of the gloomy staircase.

"Hmm." H&S woman peered down the steps, worn smooth by centuries of use—none recent, sadly. "The slime on the steps, is it of the non-slip variety?"

"No, it bloody isn't!"

"In that case, there needs to be hazard signage for staff."

I couldn't bring myself to speak.

"Oh, nothing *elaborate*," she said, seeing my face. "Something like: 'Caution: Slippery Surfaces' or something similar."

"It's a dungeon. A fucking *dungeon*. I don't *want* people to mind their step; I want them to die horribly. Unless it's me." I rubbed my head, trying to stave off the fast-advancing headache.

"I could knock something up. Wouldn't take long," piped up Dave, crunching on another eyeball. He nudged me. He *actually* nudged me. With his body.

"Well, see that you do before the follow-up." She reached for the handrail, only for it to crunch out of its ancient moorings and clang onto the stairs—another red note. I looked at Dave, and he gave me a 'don't worry about it' look, which petrified me.

After she had picked her way down a set of perfectly acceptable steps—things weren't helped by Dave slipping down the last few—we arrived in the grand vestibule.

"The torture chamber?" She looked at the spike-blighted door.

"Yes."

"Elaborate, but impressive." She nodded, and I felt my body relax, finally. "The spikes are all sterile?"

Headache riding nearer.

"They... *what?*" my voice was fading faster than my patience, and I wished that I could just open the damn door long enough to slam it in her face.

"They's brand new!" chimed in Dave.

For the first time since making his acquaintance, I didn't want to drown him. "How about you get the door open. *Safely.*" I growled, pinching his elbow until he squeaked and almost choked on one of his wretched eyeballs. "And I'll go over the other details with Miss Derby."

He scuttled to the door and pulled open his battered red tool bag. "Right," Miss Derby continued, trying not to listen to the words of a filthy folksong about a halfling's bucket as Dave set to work.

"Once I've inspected the torture chamber, we'll move on to the dungeon. We'll be covering the basics once we're down there. Rusty chains are fine, but we do recommend that all prisoners are inoculated prior to incarceration. It isn't law, but we like to recommend it."

I rolled my eyes. This had to be a joke. Perhaps it was a hazing? That had to be it. A terrible, pain-inducing hazing. A joke; a Hate-O-Gram.

"Got it open," said Dave, tossing his hammer back into his bag, whistling happily to himself.

"About damn time." I could finally see the newly-renovated chamber for myself, although I was dreading it, given the quality of the workmen. It turned out, however, that it was actually pretty well done—racks, chains, benches, whips, spikes, all clean, pristine, and correct. For once, we got what looked like a red tick.

"It looks… surprisingly *good*, Mr Evergrim." Miss Derby nodded and moved about, touching spikes and testing equipment. "You *are* missing some necessary signage, however."

"Colour me fucking surprised." Headache now at a gallop. No amount of nose pinching and rubbing was going to stop it.

"The chart on hygiene, including what to do if you or part of you is vomited or bled on… It should hang above the wash-hand basin, which appears to be absent."

"It's outside; the plumber is on holiday, we're working on it." I lied, planting an elbow in Dave's ribs as he made to quiz me.

"Hmm. Well, of course, your torturer will be using sterilised gloves and an eye-shield? Again, not law, but recommended."

"Rather kills the intimidating torturer look, somewhat." All sarcasm was lost upon her. I suspected that they trained it out of them in whatever bastard school they recruited these people from.

"Oh, where is your first aid kit?" She looked around, pen poised.

"Are you *fucking dicking* with me?" That was it; I couldn't take any more. I had to get out. The light bouncing off all the spikes was making my eyes swim and exacerbating my headache, which had finally arrived with a vengeance.

"Well, perhaps we can move on?"

"Fine." Anything to end this misery. We headed for the door to the rest of the dungeon and fished the dungeon key from my pocket. It didn't work. I twisted and wrenched it, but nothing happened. Feeling her eyes boring into me, and smelling the sweet candied eyeballs that Dave was shunting around his mouth, I started to feel sick.

I pulled out the other key and jammed it into the lock, knowing it wouldn't work, but hoping against all hope…

nothing. I tried the thick skull-topped key again. And again. And then I took a much closer look. The embossed grinning skull had some details that I had previously overlooked. It was wearing a hat. A jester's hat. My stomach reacted as if I'd been punched with a brick. A jester. A joker. A joke. My mother's joke. The key was fake.

"Is there a problem?" the inspector quizzed, hoisting one eyebrow aloft.

I suddenly knew that my day was about to get infinitely worse.

11TH MAJA

Yanna had vanished early—something about helping the Head of the Army with some tactical manoeuvres—leaving me to the whole delicious width of our vast new bed. My delight was to be short-lived, however, as there was a tentative knock at the door. It was the librarian, Francis.

"Sorry to disturb you, but..." she stopped, and her gaze lingered. I realised that I had put on Yanna's dressing gown by mistake and that it didn't meet at the front to prevent anything from escaping.

I ducked behind the door, pulled on my own robe and invited her in. "Erm... I know that you have a lot on, what with the inspections," she said, stroking the spine of a tatty book in her hand. I moved to a small table and picked up the wine carafe.

"Not anymore," I replied, pouring myself a drink and smiling at the memories from the previous day.

"Oh yes, I heard the inspector was crushed to death by a spiked door falling off its hinges. Will it cause us any trouble?"

"Your job's safe," I sniped, knowing damn well that was all any of them cared about. She flushed but said nothing.

"Not that it did me any good, since she had already sent out an immediate report that I did not have access to my own fucking dungeons."

I threw my glass against the wall, and it smashed over one of Yanna's precious goblin-boned corsets, which were displayed on mannequins in the corner. I admit I screamed just a little.

"Why? Why do the Gods hate me?"

"You want a list, or…"

"Shut up, unless you can figure out this key thing or get wine stains out of corsets." I examined the article and shuddered. I'd seen her throw a servant down the stairs a few days prior for dribbling candle wax on one of her boots. I don't bounce well.

"She's got worse out of it, I imagine," she muttered, examining her hands.

"Meaning what?" I gave up and stuffed it down the back of the love seat, covering it with one of the many cushions that adorned every piece of soft furniture.

As I went to haul myself up, something jagged me from inside one of the cushions. I poked around at the seam and found a sliver of paper.

"What's that?"

I shook my head and tugged it free.

"*Can you confirm existence of rare ore seams or not? S.*" I read.

I looked at Francis. She looked at the other cushions. With a nod from me, she joined me, and we pulled open each one. There were two more notes secreted among them, one from S and one in Yanna's writing, placating S.

"S… Well, Overlord Sergi's is the closest domain." Francis' voice was cautious.

"Yes. The pathetic *worm*."

She played with the book in her hands, turning it over and over while my mind spun and whirred. I looked up at the large portrait of Yanna on the wall.

What to do? Oddly, the betrayal was no real hardship. I'd have been surprised if she hadn't stabbed me in the back at some point, I just hadn't expected it so soon. I had been looking forward to an acerbic back and forth, a challenge. How vexing.

"What will you do?"

Could I just kill her? Would it prompt Sergi to invade if he assumed that she had been killed to defend our secrets?

"You could use her to plant false information?" Francis said, eyeing the cushions.

"Now I know what all those mood boards and boudoir decorators were doing… smuggling." At least *they* would be easier to deal with. I sat, lost in thought.

Francis said nothing for a while before eventually clearing her throat. "Erm, you promised me a helper to scare away the scamps. I haven't yet had one."

"This is what you are bothering me with?!" I shrieked, waving the notes and useless dungeon key in her face. "My mistress is consorting with the enemy, and I have to figure out how best to deal with it, without bringing chaos down on us all. Speaking of which, do you know what will happen when Health and Safety get that report? We can't access the dungeon. I was told repeatedly, with much sighing, that it was a serious offence."

"So, you'll get a fine," Francis said.

"That we can't pay. But, besides that, as soon as the news leaks, we'll be a target for every pea-brained Hero in the fucking domain. Do you think that the scrappy remains of this army will deter anyone? I can't even keep any prisoners."

"That means you don't have to *feed* any prisoners, so it's not all bad."

I opened my mouth to be sarcastic but realised she had a point. As I hauled myself up and got dressed behind a screen, I listened to her whine on about the decrepit library, the scamp problem, the arrogant warlocks, and everything else that I didn't give a toss about.

To shut her up, I promised I would have a helper for her before the day was out, but she had to help track down the door that fit the ornate mystery key. It *had* to be something important—it certainly wasn't for the dungeon, anyway. It was my last hope.

I should have known that fate would not be that kind to me, that nothing would be that fucking simple. At least if we found something useful, I'd be making progress.

Francis took a pencil rubbing of the pattern and set off rather keenly. I imagined it would do her good to get out of the library. The smell of so much decaying paper can't be good for a person. The librarian in our previous castle became addicted. It took years for him to be weaned off books before he fell off the wagon and was eventually arrested in the grand library in Shatterhalt, rolling naked in their restricted section and rubbing ancient documents over his genitals.

I had a servant locate Yanna and suggested that, given her powers of deduction, she should perhaps go to Needleford and investigate the ore claims herself—there was no one better to terrify information out of the townsfolk. While she was away, I would have the chance to deal with her 'advisors' and manage the flow of information to my rival

Yanna sent a message back suggesting that she would need an armed escort to prevent kidnap attempts and I told her to take whomever she deemed necessary. I vacated the quarters before she arrived to pack.

I located Gawain in the kitchen where he was reading a magic-stained book and had him take a sack-load of cushions (empty), three pairs of Yanna's riding boots from the stables (to spite her), and some old statues to the market to get enough gold to pay for the new bloody fire signage and some provisions. He told me he wasn't qualified to drive a wagon, so I had him locate the misfit builder-reject crew from the previous day and get them to take him. I also tasked him with arranging meeting points for the fire safety nonsense. He seemed flattered at the responsibility, and it was a load off my shoulders.

LATER

I decided to tackle the dungeon once and for all. It didn't go well. I couldn't force the door, so I gathered several grumbling minions and had them use a rock troll as a battering ram. He didn't protest much, on account of being drunk, and things seemed to be going well until his head fell off and shattered.

To say that it dampened morale somewhat would be an understatement. There were distinctly mutinous mutterings as I had them carry its body up several flights of stairs and install it in my grandmother's quarters in lieu of the missing statue that she has been sending me nasty notes about.

Thankfully, she was wallowing in the bath at the time, but the look from her servants said that there would be trouble ahead. I made myself scarce and left the rest of the minions to slink back to their quarters.

I returned to stare at the dungeon door. This place hates me, I swear. It's like every brick has been conjured by my parents to torment me. To be bested by a simple door? It's the only damn thing in any sort of decent shape in the whole rotten place. When this place has long since crumbled into the river, that pissing door will still be standing, mark my words.

Since one was a joke key, and the ornate one from the puzzle box wasn't for the dungeon door, then what? We haven't yet found anything worth opening. I could seriously use some hidden gold. Or a weapons stash. Or a cupboard full of ice demons. Or some anti-Health-and-Safety repellent.

14TH MAJA

No word from Yanna, no word from Francis. Gawain came back with a reasonable sum of gold from the market, which was something. My grandmother, however, has been far from silent. Seven nasty notes demanding that I remove that 'obscene eyesore' from her chambers at once. I ignored her. It's time I got far tougher around here. I just need a dungeon to help back it up. At least the torture chamber is in working order, although the absence of a torturer is now a problem. I hadn't considered that before. I could do it, but can barely operate any of the equipment—my training schedule has seriously lapsed—I also managed to cut myself on a sharp edge that wasn't actually supposed to be there. Good thing the Health and Safety woman is now shoring up the castle's compost heap.

15TH MAJA

I received word from Yanna today that she conducted several interrogations of locals and that, despite several of them dying, she managed to discover that eighteen months ago, rumours started to circulate about a rich ore seam beneath the Needleford swamps.

They don't know where it started, but several experts were brought in to advise and evaluate. It was all 'hush-hush'. And then, suddenly, a few months ago, most of them turned up dead. Anyone who saw anything was also killed. Yanna suspects that they were bumped off because my parents want to keep the ore secret lest someone else gets there first or decides to simply invade.

I'm inclined to agree.

The only thing to be taken from the swamps was firewood, apparently. There was little else of use there for anyone but loggers.

I told her we are in a precarious position, especially as the Health and Safety report had gone in. We are vulnerable to Hero and Overlord attack. She told me to get the damn minions back on track and that she would personally arrange a torturer when she returned.

On the subject of torture, it reminded me that I needed to deal with her 'advisors', who are due to arrive back at some point this afternoon, according to Yanna.

LATER

I thought it best to rehearse my lines just now, to try and make sure that I can actually stop laughing when it comes time to explain to Yanna what happened to her people.

- ☠ It was a senseless tragedy.

- ☠ Who knows how the acid got up there in the first place?

- ☠ Spontaneous acidic combustion is not unheard of—Tangian Spices are best avoided this time of year. Perhaps it was indigestion?

- ☠ I suspect a bungled murder plot against us, utilising your cushions as explosive acid devices—I suggest the immediate destruction of the remaining ones for our safety.

- ☠ No, there is no truth to the rumour that I was seen in the gallery above the entrance vestibule, holding any ropes.

☠ I was not dancing down the corridor after the tragedy; I was running in panic to fetch help.

☠ I don't know what happened to the cushions that they were bringing back with them. They were also probably melted—a true shame.

☠ Look on the bright side, the green puddle of their remains would make a lovely organic mood board.

☠ No, I am not smiling; I am grimacing.

16TH MAJA

Had a nightmare that I was being suffocated by sentient silk cushions and woke to find that a heap of them had slid over my face. I'm starting to have a panic attack every time I walk into the chambers now.

After pulling myself together, I took a slug of my father's best whiskey and summoned Gawain. I demanded an update on the signage. He said that he had posted fire notices around the minion and staff quarters and in all the major work areas (a laughable concept, since most of them think that work is only something that happens to other people).

The fire meeting point was in the grand courtyard at the front of the castle. He suggested that for mine and Yanna's safety that we should have one of the posters in our quarters. I told him that fire would be too afraid to burn Yanna and he seemed disappointed.

He said, rather sullenly, I thought, that it had taken him ages to draw the posters. I told him that my grandmother could use one, and it terrified the rebellion right out of him. I've never seen someone move so slowly in all my life. Rather him than me. I could paper my office with the notes she has sent over the last few days.

LATER

I was forced to have dinner later than usual thanks to the absence of kitchen staff. It appeared that they were sulking in their lairs again over lack of pay and poor working conditions. I sent a member of staff down to rouse the cook, but only his right foot returned, hurled up the staircase.

I eventually located Gawain in the main pantry, muttering over the same stained book he'd had days before. He looked terrified—always a good sign—and rushed out, asking if he could do anything for me. After catching sight of the book cover, I told him that there *bloody well was.*

Magic? In the kitchen? He went pale. He pleaded with me not to tell the warlocks, as they were snobby and cliquey. They selfishly believed that only warlocks, those born into warlock families, and those with either a cleft chin or high-end suede shoes had the right to practise magic.

He said he'd been studying it for six months now—he aspired to be more than just a servant. I told him to get rid of the flour weevils who now appeared to be waging war on the resident rat population, and we would discuss it.

First, however, I told him to get me my damn dinner, which he did. In his eagerness to please, he gossiped a great deal about the other staff and was most forthcoming. The humans and hybrids are on the verge of a walkout, and they know that I can't do a damn thing about it. They know I can't pay them.

"I give them a roof over their miserable heads," I reminded him.

He looked at the ground as he stirred a pot of rice.

"Not much of one, so they say. Some of them are complaining that the damp is making them ill. They are talking about making their own report to the next Health and Safety person."

That's all I needed, mutinous bastards. Talk about a low blow.

"And the minions. They don't care so much, they'll sleep anywhere, but they want pay and food, and proper entertainment. They are scared of Yanna, but you…"

He looked away again. "Erm. Anyway, now some of the vampires have taken up residence in the wine cellar and are threatening all the barbarians who go near there. So that's massively annoying them, as they don't detox well. They need alcohol to function—it makes them impervious to pain."

They'd know about bloody pain if I could find a decent torturer.

"The dark fairies are waging war with the brick gnomes over access to the weird psychedelic mushrooms in the cellars, the last remaining toxic tentacle was cooked yesterday after it had a heart attack cos of a near-miss with a flour weevil, and the sinister hounds dug so far down in their lair that they managed to undermine one of the walls. It crushed five bloats and two night terrors when it collapsed."

He saw my face and fell silent.

I fell into a depression.

17TH MAJA

When my half-eaten morning newspapers finally turned up at lunch, I felt like crawling into a grave beside my parents.

Heroes' Guild Confident for Prosperous Quarter

Armourzon Report Sales of Swords and Mining Equipment up 175%

Local Castle Reportedly Condemned: Overlord Seen Crying

Am disgusted. I'm sending a strongly worded letter to the editor, delivered into his stomach clenched in the fist of a troll. I was crying because I opened a cupboard door and was almost drowned in silky cushions and velvet comforters. Long-range seeing eye spells are illegal for everyone but Overlords.

Via a seer spell, I complained to Yanna. She said to burn down their presses, rather than write a letter. I sent some harpies over to do just that and felt better.

18TH MAJA

The harpies returned but had been unsuccessful. Apparently, the local press office was made fireproof six months ago, after they ran a story on a local brimstone construction firm and were on the receiving end of some nasty reprisals. Perhaps I should hire the firm.

LATER

Just realised why I haven't heard from that wretched librarian woman about the ornate key. I had Gawain lure a riverlurk up from the lairs and then promised it all the goop that it wanted to follow me to the library.

"*What* is that?"

It wasn't the sort of gratitude I had been expecting from the wretched woman, that was for certain.

"Your new helper. You're welcome. Now, your progress on the key, please?"

She watched the lurk prod and poke the piles of volumes that had been recently mended and cleaned. "You thought it prudent to send an aquatic creature to help in a library?"

"You take what you can get," I snapped, fed up with her repeated flinching anytime it went near one of the books.

"This wasn't the bargain," she hissed at me. "How is it going to scare away scamps?"

"It's big, isn't it?"

"You're six foot, and you don't scare anyone." Her arms folded and I wished I had a torturer to give them a good stretching on the rack.

Anyway, what a fucking outrage, I'm at least six foot three in stacked heels.

"Take it, leave it, or fucking quit." I was done with insolence, stupidity, destruction, and rebellion from everyone under what was left of my roof.

"It's a fucking *vegetarian* creature. It won't scare scamps."

As we spoke, the scaly grey lurk pulled up one of the grates in the floor and ran a nail around the edges of the stone lip in the floor, and then sucked a substantial quantity of green gunk off the tip. I felt my stomach start to rebel against its frugal breakfast.

"Would you like a fire demon instead? That would go down well in here."

"I heard you don't even know if it's still alive because you can't open a *door*."

Ouch.

"Shouldn't you be milling around the tower with the rest of the harpies?"

"Shouldn't you be fluffing cushions in your quarters and hoping your mistress gets home in time to scare off the local meathead Heroes when they decide to invade?"

"That won't happen."

I was dreading it happening.

"Well, I heard from one of your grandmother's spies, who heard it from a local delivery man, who heard it from his best friend's brother's girlfriend's sister that they're planning an attack."

I felt suddenly very cold. A headache began to sidle around my lowered defences.

"I need to inspire my troops."

"Pay them, you mean," she snorted, watching the lurk scraping lichen off the bars of the grate with its rounded teeth.

"I need to find that ore; I need to find that door—it *must* be the secret behind all this. There must be documents with details, or maps, something."

"I haven't been able to find it. Maybe your mother hid it in your grandmother's quarters," Francis joked.

My blood turned to ice. She clearly saw the will to live slip away from me and hastened to dismiss the idea. "It's okay, she wasn't *that* cruel. She was more a prankster."

"If I'd been hiding it, that's what I'd have done." My voice was a bare whisper.

There was a cough from behind me. It was Gawain, now sporting bright orange hair that smelled of magic. Our conversation had clearly not involved enough pain.

"Uhmmm. Excuse me, sir."

"What fresh torment awaits?"

"You want to hear it all?"

I braced myself and nodded. Francis leaned closer.

"The harpies have abandoned the tower and left, three of the barbarians have absconded to take up work in the local brothel—they say they don't get nearly so badly screwed there…"

I stored Francis' snort for a rainy-day piece of torture. "The gnomes have killed two dark fairies, and in reprisal, the other fairies are bricking up the cellar doors with mud and… other moist substances to 'starve and stench them to death'."

Fuck *sake*. Gods, I *hated* fairies.

"The kitchen staff have now voted on an official strike since that woman made you take the head down from the kitchen, and the ah, the flour weevils have taken over one of the first-floor landings above the kitchen. The cook tried to go up there and lost his arms this morning. He had to vote for the strike with his foot."

There was a long silence as I tried to wake myself up, but, alas, it was not a horrible dream.

"Have you heard anything more from Yanna's team about the ore?" Francis enquired, touching my arm and stirring me from my trance.

"No. Nothing."

"Oh, and here's the post, sir. There's something in here from over that way." Gawain thrust a handful of charred letters into my hand.

I found one with a Needleford postmark and ripped it open.

"Well?" Francis asked after several long minutes. I thrust the report at her and slumped down into a chair which groaned and let out a puff of stuffing that smelled too much like dried urine. I was beyond caring.

"Ah. They didn't find anything. How is that possible?"

"Maybe the first lot of reports were wrong?" suggested Gawain, playing with a lock of his magically damaged hair.

"Then why were so many people killed to cover it up?" I mumbled. "I need to find it."

"You need to find a great many things," said Francis. "Money, manners, and patience being among them." She marched away to supervise the lurk, who was now scratching mould from the spine of a large book.

"And some bloody respect. Try calling me 'sir'."

"Sorry, can't hear you over the sound of my indifference," she shouted back.

"You need to be more useful. I need either that ore, or the dungeon key to hunt for any remaining treasure vaults to bloody pay anyone," I shouted after her.

"Then the key is still missing? Tut *tut*."

My head turned so fast that my neck clicked. An officious man in a pinstripe suit was shaking his head and making notes on a large, red clipboard. Is there some sort of demonic factory that produces these things?

He had red hair and a monocle, and his combover could only be described as ambitious.

"Gods alive." I slithered down into a chair and wished for the fibres to strangle me. "Don't you people *ever* make a noise?"

"Only at the annual H and S conference," he replied.

"Sounds riveting."

"Indeed. Making notes on the state of the cutlery and the safety of the catering wagons can get rather raucous." He cleared his throat, twirled his moustache, and looked me over. "My name is Cecil Hawthorne-DeWinter. I am a level *three* executive and a veteran of some thirty years in service. I will not fall down stairs, become impaled on spikes, or get melted by traps, nor fall foul of aggrieved minions or other *accidents*." He gave me a severe look. So severe, one of his eyebrows temporarily masqueraded as a cowlick.

"Let's get this over with. I don't suppose I can bribe you with a pet flour weevil and some silk cushions?"

"I have turned down bribes of gold, precious gems, and rose-smothered cottages full of country lads and lasses who would make your hair curl with their erotic talents. I will, sadly, have to forgo your kind offer of cushions."

Bastard.

"The cushions are dead nice. All silky. The kind that you can catch your dry skin on." It was a brave attempt by Gawain, but, sadly, it was to no avail.

"Given the nature of my predecessors' visits, I feel that it is better I roam unaccompanied. I don't want to be helped into any accidents. Nor do I plan on being steered away from areas in need."

Bastard.

"Enjoy yourself." I gave him a wave and wished I hadn't used up every scrap of acid on Yanna's damn people.

He sniffed, made a few notes, and then marched out. If I didn't know that most of the weapons in the armoury had been melted down or sold off, I'd have taken a broadsword and whipped off his square head.

"Now what?" Gawain ventured.

"Now you go and spy on him; keep me informed. I'm going to go and speak to the warlocks to see if they can use their magic on the damn dungeon door before that pain in the arse gets down there."

"And this?" Francis had returned and pointed to the lurk, who was leaning against a bookcase, swishing its thick, curved tail and picking out its teeth with a quill.

"All yours. Now, find that door."

"Find me a decent scamp deterrent." Folded arms.

"My grandmother is several floors up. Take her."

At that moment, a scamp rattled out of a hole beneath a bookcase and paused to urinate on a heap of mouldering tomes. The lurk looked down, and in a movement so fast that I barely registered it, it scooped up the scamp, moulded it into a ball and hurled it through the window. As the last tinkle of broken glass faded, I turned to Francis, said precisely nothing that my smirk couldn't convey, and left.

LATER

I arrived at the warlocks' plush lair to find them squabbling over whether or not to desert. Apparently, that decision could only be made by the head warlock, who had been absent for some days.

During the heated debate, I pulled aside one young initiate and had him fire up one of the expensive magic mirrors that my father forked out for several years ago, and called Yanna. The warlocks would clearly be at this for some time, especially as a third of them kept falling asleep. So much for getting them to open the dungeon door.

Yanna seemed flushed and irritated at having been disturbed, so I decided to wait to give her the sad news about her advisors. I told her that if she wanted a fucking castle to come back to, then she had better beg, borrow, or berate another crew into exploring the swamplands more thoroughly in search of ore deposits. Then get her arse home and take care of the mutinies, sue the local paper for libel, and then write a cease-and-desist letter to the local Heroes' Guild over their invasion preparations.

I didn't wait for an answer and went to cheer myself up by planning another attempt on my grandmother's life. It has become a challenging hobby now. Perhaps I could put a flour weevil in her bed?

19ᵀᴴ MAJA

Against all the odds, it seemed as though the hardy Health and Safety man survived the night and has combed at least a fifth of the castle, according to my young spy. He has examined the lairs, the kitchen, the back yard, several sections of the castle, and the graveyard, among other places. I wonder if a visit to my darling grandmother could be his undoing?

My breakfast was non-existent, and according to Gawain, the rest of the cook was seen entering the pantry but never returned. Perfect. I grabbed the first person I could find in the kitchen and made a battlefield promotion to head cook and then helped myself to a gammon sandwich with thrice-deep-fried pickles (a local speciality, considered so harmful to health that it is in the process as being reclassified as a weapon by the EDI).

I retreated with it to my office to read the papers.

The morning's headlines:

Local Overlord to Marry a Whelk

Giant Weevil-esque Creature Seen in Local Woodland—Investigation On-going

My Night of Passion With a Haunted Scabbard

H&S Rumoured to Be Condemning Local Castle

I was just binning the rags, wondering if the scabbard had been bejewelled, when Gawain peered round my office door and then nodded to someone behind him. Two staff members shuffled in, carrying the body of the Health and Safety veteran. His clipboard had been placed neatly on his chest.

"What now?"

"He's dead."

"Really?" My acidity appeared lost upon him. Things were indeed looking up!

Feeling far happier than I had done in days, I was about to order him be dropped into the river or fed to some of the less discerning minions when I caught sight of the man's face.

I brushed away his errant combover and stared. In the centre of his forehead was a large, red indentation. It was a keyhole, surrounded by ornate detailing. My heart jolted.

"Where did you find him? What happened?"

"He tripped over a loose rug and fell headfirst into a door. Broke his neck," said Gawain.

"So much for invincible. What door?"

"Cleaning cupboard, two floors up."

"Cleaning cupboard? No wonder no one ever fucking found it." My fortunes could well be turning. I could feel the gears of the universe slowly start to move back in my favour.

"Get Francis to meet me up there, now."

"What about—"

"Dispose of him." I swept out in my usual masterful way, almost snagging one of my frilled shirt cuffs on a door splinter, and marched along until out of sight, before running like buggery.

TOO MUCH LATER

"Where have you been?" I snapped, as Francis dawdled into sight.

"Scraping dead scamp off the library ceiling with a pole." She looked smug.

"Key."

She handed it over, and I jammed it in the lock, barely able to turn it for excitement. Instead of returning to the library, she lingered behind me, craning to see.

At the last moment, I realised what I was doing and pulled back. I told her to turn the key. It could be my mother's last trap. She refused. In a rage at the delay, I found a member of my grandmother's staff on the next floor and had him do it. A hidden blade nipped off one finger, and I sent him on his way, snivelling, while I pushed open the door.

I hate my mother.

I hate her so *very* much.

20TH MAJA

Francis and Gawain found me the following morning, still sitting staring into the room beyond the door. Francis pushed a mug of cocoa into my hands.

"Um… how are things?" Her voice was quiet, tentative. I think she thought I may have had a breakdown. I was contemplating how to resurrect my mother in order that I could condemn her to a life of misery and damnation.

"Have you, uhhmm, tried any of them yet, sir?" Gawain asked, peeping inside.

"No. I have not." The steam warmed my face, and the drink scalded my raw throat. The previous day's screaming had not been good for it.

The cupboard was large, and in the centre of the back wall was a small door, halfway up the wall. It was locked. Every other surface—walls, floor, and even ceiling, were smothered in keys. Big keys, small keys, shiny ones, rusty ones, ornate, plain, broken. Keys. Fucking keys. Keys hung on hooks or lay on the floor, mocking me. KEYS EVERYWHERE.

"If you just went about it in an organised manner, you'd be in before you knew it. Do one at a time and then discard them so you don't get mixed up," said Francis, rolling her eyes.

"And then what? Find a small cubby full of keys, with a small door at the back, and the same thing in that one?"

"That would be *seriously* funny—" Gawain stuttered to a halt as I glared murder at him. "Uhmm, I mean, not at all, really. Terrible, even." He started playing with his fringe and shuffling. Francis took pity on him and motioned him away.

21ST MAJA

I was summoned to my grandmother's quarters today and actually decided to go along, if only to eat something. Only her staff are brave enough to enter the kitchens now, thanks to the weevils. In a toss-up between a pastry-deprived woman and a horde of mutated flour weevils, the nasty, demanding old woman wins every time.

After gorging a fully cooked breakfast, I had to endure her snide remarks about Yanna and my failures as an Overlord. I was too busy fighting off acid reflux to care much, however, but it relaxes her to berate someone, so I started picking my teeth out with one of her lethal hairpins and let her have at it.

"…and of *course,* she's turning this mission into her own private holiday, you know. I'd love to go to Needleford; I'd *jump* at the chance."

"I'll happily arrange a trip to the swamp for you," I replied, wondering how long she would take to sink.

"Of course," she said, ignoring me but changing tack, "I

haven't been on holiday in years."

Lies. She goes on regular tea-room binges and booze-ups with a posse of her elderly friends. Many of the tea rooms across several of the domains keep in special monogrammed tea sets for them as they are such good customers. She thinks nothing of fraternising with the enemy—Sergi's grandmother is one of her oldest cohorts.

"No one thinks of *me*. No one asks if *I'd* like to go anywhere. No, send the young strumpet off, *gallivanting*." One dramatic gesture saw half a cup of tea slopped over the feet of a lingering servant.

"I'm thinking of going to Needleford myself and personally supervising, to be honest. I'm sick of the incompetence with which I seem to be surrounded."

"Hmmph. Well, you'll be lucky if you have a castle to come back to, from what I hear."

"What do you hear? *How* do you hear?"

"I get told things. You never tell me, no; I'm left here, *all on my own*." She was off, blowing her nose and making dark comments about my abilities as an Overlord. My eyes rolled more than a tumbleweed in a hurricane.

"I'll wait for Yanna to return, she can keep an eye on things. Besides, she has jobs to get on with, including staving off the local Heroes' Guild."

"Hmmphh. Drunkards and fantasists. Couldn't find the business end of a sword if it was lodged in their backsides."

That, we did agree on.

"Well, even they can figure out to simply push the castle door and it will fall in, thanks to the rot." I helped myself to a strawberry pastry and took my leave before I had to listen to any more abuse.

I hadn't been jesting—I wanted to find out what the hell my father had discovered, once and for all, and capitalise on it. Before someone else did. I needed Yanna to get her arse back to the castle first, however. I also needed some sort of transport for my escort party. I was not travelling alone, and the carriage Yanna had taken was not large enough. I had a sinking feeling who I would need to speak to.

LATER

"I SAID, it needs to be ready as soon as possible." My throat was killing me.

"When?" *Thump. Bang. Crash.*

"AS SOON AS POSSIBLE." Dave stopped hammering the wall of the stable and removed several nails from between his lips. There was a nasty, low inrush of air.

"I dunno about that. Have you seen the few wagons we got left?"

"Yes, but…" *Thump. Bang.*

"I mean." He paused his assault for a moment. "Your lady took the best one, and she ain't come back yet." *Crash. Pause.* "There *is* one what might do. Needs a bit of work, mind."

"See to it. As soon as Yanna gets back, I'll be taking hers, and I will also need an escort and some guards." There was a snicker, and I looked around to find the failed search posse sitting on a broken flatbed wagon, eating sandwiches.

"You find that amusing?"

The magpie demon looked away and started scratching at an old nail with his finger.

"Half the army are on strike, you know?" said Trudy. "You won't get the rest of the slackers anywhere, especially with the Head of the Army away. They've been mostly stripping off fixtures from the lower levels of the castle and selling them for gambling money."

"Is this why most doors are now hanging off their hinges or don't have handles?"

"Yeah." The magpie demon sniffed and took a huge bite of sandwich. It took me a moment to realise that I had lost the thread of conversation and was watching him, salivating.

"Where did you get that? I thought no one could access the kitchens now."

"We snuck in while those things were asleep. They'd just eaten someone," said Trudy. "Had to rescue that young wannabe warlock, too. The one with orange hair. He was hiding on top of the fridge cupboard."

"You should have left him, since he's the one responsible for that particular fucking mess." I snatched away the sandwich, downed it in three bites, and then promptly vomited it back up. I could feel their eyes on the back of my neck as I finished retching behind the stables.

"Yeah. scamp meat is an acquired taste, Overlord." Her smirking tone ate into me until I turned around.

"You can make yourselves useful. Help Dave sort out a working wagon and find some weapons. You'll be accompanying me to Needleford. I'd suggest something arrow-proof."

Their glares followed me back to the castle, but I relished the small victory. It was short-lived, however, when the scamp sandwich repeated on me again, this time in a more alarming way. I barely made the staff thunderchute—their charming, common name for the privy—the small hole that runs down the inside of the castle, with various, unpleasant access points. The door came off in my hands, narrowly missing crushing me, and the light fixtures had been liberated.

It wasn't until a few moments later, however, that I discovered the seat had also been sold. I considered screaming for help, but suffering the indignity of having some useless member

DIARY OF AN EVIL OVERLORD

of my staff prise me out from where I was wedged would have been too much. I would have had to have killed them before they spread gossip and I can't afford to lose anyone else.

I was left to extricate myself from the choking tunnel of stench. I tried to grab for the paper roll holder, but found that it too was missing. Someone will pay for this. *Anyone.*

It was with moments to spare that I hauled my backside free. My grandmother's voice could be heard somewhere above me. I fled. It's bad enough being present when the food is going in.

22ND MAJA

I arrived at the kitchens, near starving to death to find jostling staff and minions lurking outside. They quietened down when I approached and Gawain pushed through the crowd.

"We sent in a rock troll to distract them. He's stamped on a few for us and chased the others away. One of the kitchen staff went in just now to see what they could grab."

He was cut off by a bloodcurdling scream. Hats were removed from heads, and there was a background of low muttering.

"For crying out loud. Get in there, all of you." No one moved. "Or would you prefer more easy jobs, such as working for my grandmother?"

"Her staff don't do so well either," muttered someone from the back of the pack.

"Yeah. That pastry chef girl of hers has been trapped in the pastry kitchen for two days now."

"Weevils?" I asked.

"Yeah. No one can get to her. If she's still alive, that is."

I shot Gawain a look. Pastry was one of the few things to placate my grandmother. If she were to rampage, then on his soon-to-be-removed head be it.

"We have an army…"

"They have *bulk*," muttered another dissenter.

"Why *can't* the army deal with this, though?" complained someone.

"They said that they didn't sign up to deal with magical vermin, and anyway, they weren't paid enough," said the first pain.

"Maybe Dave can knock up some traps or something?" someone else suggested.

"They'd only eat 'em."

"I have an idea," I cut in. "I'll select one lucky person to brave the weevils and see if the wretched girl is still alive." I waved my finger about in front of the wincing crowd before pointing at Gawain.

"You." Before he could burst into tears, there was another bloodcurdling sound—my grandmother's voice. Several of the staff ran, while others who were penned-in near the door looked as though they would have palpitations. Someone muttered a brief incantation to the gods. I suspect, however, that they long have since given up on this place. I steeled myself.

"What are you rats doing lurking here? Why can't my servants get me my food? Where are my pastries, and *where* is my pastry chef?"

"Morning grandmother, you're looking radiant." Her fluffy blue dressing gown was wrapped around her, while silk slippers boldly strained to contain her feet and the acre of dry skin that enwreathed them. She was followed by a trail of servants, who looked relieved that someone else was about to get it in the neck for once.

"I'm hungry. And I want to know what you are doing about this *insufferable* staff problem, Nathaniel."

"I'm attending to the other important things that we discussed," I murmured. She was beyond reason, however.

"Why are you all out here? *Why* is no one in the kitchen?"

"Uhhmm. Weevils, ma'am," said Gawain. "They've turned a bit iffy." If there were awards being given out for understatements, then he'd be on the receiving end of one.

"*Nonsense.*" She marched past them into the kitchen and, for a moment, I thought one of my problems would be solved. Tentatively, the pack followed her in. As Overlord, I preserved myself by lurking at the back.

She stood alone in the kitchen. Everyone looked around, suddenly rather sheepish. On the floor were three squashed giant weevils. For some reason, they were a familiar shade of orange. Gawain ducked out of my sight behind my grandmother, who had planted her fists on her hips and was looking around in disgust.

"Well? I don't see any problem here." Several people caught sight of and backed away from the bloody scratch marks on the floor leading to one of the pantries. I also moved closer to the exit, shoving several cowering staff members out of the way.

"Where's my pastry chef?"

"Erm… no one's seen her or her assistant for days, ma'am," someone ventured. The path to the door of what we laughingly call the pastry kitchen was suspiciously unobstructed, but for a single human arm.

Everyone crept closer, taking courage in sheer numbers, before my grandmother strode forwards, scattering staff and rattled the door handle. It was locked. She hammered on the door. Nothing. A swift kick from her sent wood splintering, and the door gave way.

Everyone shuffled forwards, past a broken barricade of furniture, expecting the worst. The converted bathroom that had become the pastry kitchen was beset by shadows cast by the dying lamps, flickering in their fittings around the decaying plaster walls. All moveable furniture had been used to both barricade the door and a pantry in the far corner, in front of which were a heap of dead weevils. The strata of colours indicated that there were several magical generations present. There was green blood spattered over the corner, the windows, and the walls.

One weevil was pinned by the head to the wall by a carving knife, while two more appeared to have been crammed into the oven and crisped. It would explain the fatty smell. Still more lay around an odd heap in the centre of the room. I realised that it was a cupboard which had been dragged there—an obelisk among the chaos.

Someone squeaked in fear and pointed. Everyone followed their wavering finger and looked up. Atop the cupboard was some sort of harpy. Its straggly, curled hair hung down past its dark face, while clawed hands clutched something metallic. Its clothes were spattered in blood, red and green.

"That's her," Gawain whispered. "The pastry girl."

"Can't be, she's not that tall," someone said.

"She's perched on top of a cupboard, you fucking moron," came another voice.

"Well, I couldn't see properly from back 'ere."

"How can she be made of pastry?" asked another idiot.

"Girl. Get *down* from there now and explain yourself," thundered my grandmother.

Even I, with my limited patience, could see that was not a winning tactic, and the girl failed to move.

"Uhm." Gawain sidled forwards and craned up to the top of the cupboard. The girl's hand tightened on what looked like a kitchen knife that had been lashed to a thick ladle handle. "Miss… They're gone. It's safe."

She raised her head, surveyed us all, looked hard into the corner, and then down at Gawain. "They mostly come at night. *Mostly*." Everyone looked around at the failing lamps and began backing out of the room—everyone except my single-minded grandmother.

"My pastry chef?"

"Gone." The young woman nodded in the direction of the pile of bodies. For the first time, I noticed several uniformed body parts. The rescue parties, it would seem.

"Well, you just got a battlefield promotion. Stop dripping around up there and get down here."

The girl stared at me with the eyes of someone who has looked beyond the gates of the underworld to paths that even demons won't tread, and then saw my grandmother waiting for her. She tucked her weapon into her belt, which was already stuffed with improvised weaponry, including a nasty-looking whisk, and slithered down onto a ledge created by a splintered serving trolley.

She stopped, reached up, and passed a tray down to Gawain. The crowd fell silent as she pushed her hair back, straightened her back, and adjusted her filthy dress and bloodstained apron. She was missing one shoe, and her foot was wrapped in a bloody bandage.

She wiped blood from her face, smearing it over her dark skin, stuck out her chin and took the tray. With a deep breath, she presented it to my grandmother. Two dozen tiny cream and pastry delicacies glistened. I felt the crowd lean closer—I could practically hear the saliva bubbling in anxious, hungry mouths.

My grandmother took the tray.

Two sharp sniffs and, with a sneer, she thrust it back at the girl. "Cream's off."

I watched the girl inhale. Then exhale. There was a flutter of movement, and then the ladle/blade was underneath my grandmother's primary chin.

This would save me so much trouble.

"Eat them."

"You *what?*"

"I said, *eat them.*" Those pits of eyes burned into my grandmother's. "*Now.*"

The collective holding of breath was like the tide at Sinistrata Beach suddenly receding before a vast doom-laden wave.

"Do you *know* who I am?" my grandmother boomed.

The girl said nothing. Her eyes told me that the thread holding her reason over a perilous abyss had suddenly snapped.

"I've seen off hundreds of Hero invasions, survived wars, plagues, and a husband with a contagious skin disease. No assistant pastry chef is going to threaten *me.*"

"Assistant *to the* Pastry Chef. And you *will* eat them."

"Uhmm, how about we all go outside and get some fresh air?" Gawain chipped in. Several members of staff moved in and tried to prise the girl's arm down. It was like forcing down a lever that had been rusted in place for five generations. I suspect that it was more for the girl's benefit than my grandmother's. I've seen her hammer an orc into the ground with two blows of her fist. It was a small orc, mind, but it was still impressive.

"That would likely be best," I sighed, seeing the sudden chance to have my dirty work done for me evaporate.

"No. I want her head for her insolence."

"You'll be making your own pastries then?" I asked her. My grandmother digested the problem.

"Fine. Have her lashed."

"Haven't hired a torturer yet," I admitted. Seeing her face, I hastened to shift blame. "Yanna is supposed to be taking care of it."

"You can take it up with my predecessor if you like. What's

left of her is through there," the girl whispered. "Incidentally, she was carrying your handwritten recipe for gilded frost tarts when she… failed to return." The girl pointed at the door beyond the weevil pile, having offloaded the tray into the more than willing arms of several staff members, who didn't give a damn about off cream.

One troll had fished the crisped weevils out of the oven and was crunching on the heads.

My grandmother's lips pursed. Several servants backed away.

She marched to the corner and began kicking bodies and pieces of wood aside, while many of the staff began to sidle towards the kitchen door. I had a bad feeling and was about to follow their cue when there was a rumble from the back of the room near the sinks.

The cupboards burst open, and a swarm of huge orange weevils burst out. Everyone scattered. One darted ahead and got in front of us, forcing an abrupt halt. The pastry-chef girl barged me aside and hurled her knife/ladle, impaling the creature's head to the doorframe. I picked myself up and hurtled out of the door behind Gawain, who was towing the girl with him, refusing to let her stay and use the lethal-looking whisk she'd pulled from her belt.

The door slammed. Two things slammed against it. I let the staff drag furniture over to barricade it shut and then, despite my thumping heart, made a glorious discovery—my grandmother was still on the other side of the door. I allowed myself a little jig.

There was a loud banging from beyond and some high-pitched squealing. Then nothing. Several of the braver members of staff put their ears to the door.

"Nuthin'," one of them said. "She's 'ad it."

"They're already tapping on the bloody door," said someone else. She was right. *Tap, tap, tap-tap.*

"It's a pattern," said one of the more intelligent-looking

servants. One of my late grandmother's staff frowned. The look she gave her fellow staff filled my veins with fizzing shards of ice.

"Code. Sir, your grandmother used that code when she got trapped in the privy last year."

"I don't care," I said, "Leave her. That's an order." One of them, who had placed his ear to the door, cleared his throat and straightened up.

"Sir. She says, have you by chance lost a bunch of keys… one of them has spikes on?"

"What are you…" My heart plummeted, and I scrabbled in my waistcoat pocket.

My scream drove half the staff from the kitchen. Those who stayed, mainly my grandmother's staff, gave me sympathetic looks. I slumped down on a broken bench and let my head slip into my hands.

"Open. The. Door."

23RD MAJA

I was at the stables early. The castle has become insufferable. Despite there being holes in nearly every wall, ceiling, and floor, it has never felt so suffocating. The morning air was only marginally better than the smell of the castle, thanks to several minions frying a brace of dead pike-rats over a small fire. They were lucky to have found any. The weevils appear to have put paid to them.

"Well, you're all set. She's nice, ain't she?" Dave gave me a disgustingly cheerful grin, planted an inappropriate elbow in my ribs, and popped a candied eyeball into his mouth. I looked at the wagon. I recognised woodwork from various parts of the castle, and several shields which had been fashioned into shiny hubcaps for the wheels.

"Barely tolerable." I had just ordered Trudy to put my bags into the carriage when a procession of servants approached.

"The final mutiny?" I muttered. They'd regret it. They parted before me and my grandmother swept up, covered from head to foot in tweed. There was even a miniature tweed hat perched on her complex knotted hair. I struggled to take in what I was seeing.

"Since you can't be trusted to do anything yourself, I'm coming with you."

It was then that my eyes fell to the trail of bags in the arms of her servants.

"No. Absolutely not. Never."

Trudy snickered somewhere behind me.

"Put them in my carriage; the boy should have brought it around by now." She turned her back and began waving her servants towards an approaching carriage. It was fashioned from dark, stained wood, highly polished, and with gilded wheels and solid gold steps. I looked from it to mine. One of my shield hubcaps creaked and fell off. I looked at Dave, who pulled a face and shook his head. "Don't worry about it. Have it fixed in a jiff. Anyway, your lady'll be back soon with the other one, eh?"

"Grandmother, I insist you stay. I thought you were supervising the construction of a new pastry kitchen."

"I was, but my new pastry chef can deal with that. Besides, her behaviour is distinctly odd. Whoever heard of a chef sleeping on top of a cupboard and screaming to herself in the night?"

I'd also scream nightly if I worked with her.

"Sir, will you be riding with your grandmother, or will you be riding alone in your erm…" Gawain struggled to describe what Dave had cobbled together. I watched three servants help my grandmother into her carriage and begin to pass several large travelling bags inside.

"I…"

A clatter of hooves broke my terrible dilemma, and Yanna's party came clattering into the yard, her carriage—my carriage—

among them. Now in a foul mood, I marched over and ripped open the door to find her giggling with the Head of the Army.

"About fucking time. And what the hell are *you* doing in here?" I demanded, eyeing the man. Their smiles vanished, and he looked panicked.

"Ah… There was a… bandit attack just outside Slake. I agreed to personally accompany Miss Yanna in the event of another, sir. She was very distressed."

"Yes. She's a distressing kind of lady," I snapped.

He jumped down and took his place with his troops. I extended a hand and helped Yanna down. She was flushed, but as cool as ever. I was looking forward to her finding out about her advisors. And then I would need to consider how best to deal with her.

As the door slammed shut, one wheel snapped off and the whole carriage thunked into the ground on one side. One door groaned open and then fell off into the mud. Fucking perfect. Was this placed cursed or something?

"You need to have that fixed; we barely made it home."

"Stop buying cushions, and perhaps we could afford it."

A glare. "Someone has to make this mouldering heap vaguely habitable. So… you're going somewhere?"

"I was, yes. We have apparently been delayed. I intended to see what my own efforts can uncover since yours have failed." I was feeling peevish, and her eyes instantly narrowed.

"Really? Well, I suppose taking a detour on the way here and burning down the local paper as a surprise gift for you was a waste of time. That's the thanks I get?"

"I had no idea."

"You never do," she snapped. "It's why the carriage is so damaged—our escape was not uneventful. But fine. Bugger off and scour that damn swamp yourself then. In the meantime, I'll try and stop our home from being invaded by the local morons. At least with their obsession for tunnelling in, rather than actually using the front door, it will buy us some time."

She flicked her hair back and almost took my eye out.

"Stop wasting time with that strumpet; I want to be in Needleford as soon as possible." My grandmother leaned out of the carriage window and bellowed over the heads of her servants.

"Myrtle, how *delightful* to see you. You haven't choked to death yet then?" Yanna gave a beaming smile and waved daintily. My grandmother snorted and slammed her window shut.

"You're taking *her*? At least you won't have to worry about a grave—the swamp should about do it," Yanna muttered.

"My thinking exactly." I cleared my throat. "It would appear our trip has been delayed until the wagon can be repaired, Grandmother."

There was a volcanic eruption of protests and dark mutterings, which I shut my ears to.

"I wish I *was* going. Besides, the staff need time to fit her new pastry kitchen. Ours is now officially out of commission."

"Wonderful. So, apart from a lack of gold, a mutinous staff, a crumbling castle, health and safety issues, and, in all likelihood, a Hero attack that I will do my best to fend off legally… anything else I should be aware of?"

"Yes, that you signed on to be my mistress, knowing full well what a shithole this place is." I enjoyed her fury.

She glowered at me.

"Sort out the damn staff. Organise a raid on some of the wealthier outlying regions—no one local who could be persuaded to join a Hero attack, though, and use the money to pay the most important staff and get in more provisions. I have a dungeon to sort out, and it won't be long before Health and Safety are on our backs again."

She nodded and cracked her knuckles.

"Also…" I cast a glance at my grandmother's carriage, where she was dumping her bags back out of the window into the waiting arms of sweating servants.

"She can maintain her staff and that carriage, among other things. She *must* have her own gold supply. We need to find it. It will take her time to get up there if you can make it before she does. Uses anything and anyone to get in and out."

Yanna gave a wide, evil smile and strode off, staff falling in her wake like terrified petals. I watched the soldiers disperse, and then, with a heavy heart, ordered my escort party to help Dave sort out the damaged carriage.

I was now annoyed and would derive no enjoyment from telling Yanna about the liquidation of her vile advisors. Even that had been spoiled.

24TH MAJA

I decided to sulk in the library and talk to the only person who has really listened to me. Francis did her best to ignore me, using her new helper, Dagg, to shelve books while she sorted through the newly repaired pile.

"I just want money. Is that too much to ask?"

"My feelings exactly," Francis muttered, riffling through a stained volume on minion hygiene before giving up on it and tossing it in the bin.

"I've been trying to follow in my father's footsteps…"

"Perhaps that's your problem."

"What?"

"Try following in your mother's," she said, looking at me for the first time that morning.

"What's that supposed to mean."

"It means stop fantasising about chasing all over the countryside in search of some elusive ore and focus your efforts closer to home. First things first."

I didn't care for her tone and told her so. She shrugged and went back to the pile of books. Her words bothered me, so I lowered myself enough to speak to her again.

"What do you mean closer to home?"

"How did you *actually* become Overlord? Actually, don't answer that." She held up a hand. "Look, they had a reserve of gold; they *must* have. Something not in the main vaults. Use that first, then sort out these grand plans and this ore business. Have you looked in the dungeons yet?"

"I'm afraid to. And, anyway, I haven't found the key, remember, it was a fake. And the other one just led to that infernal cupboard. I'm not sorting through all those keys."

"Do it. Your mother did this for a reason. It wouldn't have all been for an elaborate prank. Go through the keys in that cupboard and find the one that opens that little door. Maybe you'll get some answers."

"In the meantime, the heroes…"

"Yanna held them off by having a Heroic Services Inspection Team check them out. Their armoury wasn't up to scratch, and there was a decomposing body in their main beer keg. It's bought you some time from that problem, at least."

At least we weren't the only ones with problems. Still, it didn't buoy me up much.

"Time for more creatures to desert, you mean."

"Then find the dungeon key – it is probably what is hidden in that key-cupboard – and check on that fire demon. Send some of the more violent creatures out to smash some stuff up—they'll enjoy that. Earn some cash. Finding the fire demon will also help ward off an attack from the other domains while you figure out the rest."

LORNA REID

"If that fails?"

"Then do what everyone else does," said Francis.

"Which is what?"

"Bugger off and nick it all from someone else. A castle, gold, whatever makes you happy."

"Nick a castle? You've seen what's left of the army?"

"Maybe everyone else is as bad off, but they all hide it too," she said.

I snorted. "Not likely. Vlansen Hammerdark is supposed to have an army of undead."

"He also has a rolling fine from the Health and Safety people for the poor hygiene in his castle, due to the fact that the bits falling off his undead are hazardous to public health."

It was news to me and cheered me up, somewhat. "Dare I ask how you know?" I had a sudden moment of panic that she might be a spy.

"I'm a spy."

Was she a seer?

She gave a colossal sigh. "His librarian got drunk at the annual Librarian's Picnic last year and blabbed it out."

Thank goodness for that.

She was right, as much as I hated to admit it. I had no clue what my father was playing at, but I could find out what my mother was up to. Even if it only led to a cache of gold.

25TH MAJA

Tried 77 keys.

26TH MAJA

Tried 84 keys

27TH MAJA

Nursed blisters.

28TH MAJA

Tried 132 keys.

29TH MAJA

Tried to melt door. Failed.

30TH MAJA

Francis eventually found the right key underneath a stone in the corner of the cupboard. I could feel her breath on my shoulder as she tiptoed to see past me as I opened the door.

The small door creaked back in a satisfying manner, and I waved away the dust that swirled around us.

Inside were several shelves. In the centre of one, on a silver dish, was a large, ornate key. It was the dungeon key, finally! I knew because someone had thoughtfully labelled it with a large tag that read 'Dungeon Key, don't lose or else'.

There was a small bag of gold, and a framed photograph of Sergi and me on a school trip, trying to drown someone in a water trough. On the top shelf was a row of jars. Inside each one was a crab, floating upside down in the murky water. Each jar contained a slightly larger crab and shell.

"Hermit crabs." Francis read the labels and wrinkled her nose. "Please don't tell me they are some sort of family delicacy."

"Fuck knows."

Why keep those? Was it another weird fetish of my parents'?

I poked at what looked like two empty snow globes and ran my hands through the dust to the far reaches of the cubby. There was nothing else there. This was it?

"Well… at least you got some gold and the key."

It was a start.

31ST MAJA

After strenuously denying noticing any missing cushions (now somewhere in the depths of the local market), I made my escape from Yanna and headed for the dungeons. I had my fearless posse of misfits with me: Gawain, Trudy, Chakk the magpie demon, and Dave. I didn't fool myself that they had agreed to come for any reason other than to harvest gossip for the rest of the staff.

Francis refused to come because she was busy colouring in a 'No Magic Allowed' sign for the restricted section. Apparently, two warlocks messed up a high-level incantation and sent a bookcase to one of the nastier demon dimensions. When they finally managed to retrieve it, under duress from Francis, they discovered that someone had gone through every book, deliberately pencilling in punctuation errors and bad grammar.

With a deep breath, I turned the key and yanked open the dungeon door. It failed to creak. Dave noted that we'd get marked down for that in an inspection by the EDI people. I immediately wished that I had taken an even deeper breath and then held it.

The smell was beyond vile. As a child, I made the mistake of accepting a dare by one of my school friends to smell my grandmother's slippers. I was bedridden for two days. When I recovered, I retaliated by pushing him down the school privy. We were no longer friends after that. Sergi always did have a nasty attitude.

Using Trudy and Gawain as a shield, I advanced down the steps. Sadly, halfway down, I was too busy masking my face with my cravat to notice the slime and skidded the rest of the way, cannoning into Trudy and ending up in an ungainly heap.

"Could have got me flowers first," she sniggered, removing my hand from her chest. I brushed myself down, ignored the childish snickering, and activated the magical lighting that my father had installed several years previously after being told that the dingy corridor was *too dingy*, and someone was likely to have an accident. I weep for the future.

"Peeorrr, smells like dinner, don't it?" Dave muttered.

"The cook's improving," said Chakk.

"Not now he's dead," said Trudy.

"Ah, yeah. Shouldn't talk ill of the dead, it's unlucky."

"Silence, all of you," I cautioned. I didn't want them upsetting the fire demon. We headed along to the large chamber at the west end of the dungeons, and I peered through the eyehole in the giant iron door.

Dave jostled with the others for a look, so I let them to it, breathing a sigh of relief. It was still there.

"Ohhh, ee's big," Dave said, getting shoved aside by Trudy, who screwed her eye to the hole.

"Why's he just standing there, why isn't he melting stuff?"

"We don't want him 'melting stuff' until we are ready," I informed her.

"What does it eat?" said Chakk, taking his turn to gawp.

"Brimstone. Of which we actually have plenty. And annoying staff, which we also have in abundance." I cracked my knuckles and clicked my neck to a more comfortable position. I felt better than I had in weeks.

"Where does it go to the toilet?" said Chakk.

"Right, we're done here." I had no intention of carrying on

this train of thought. "Spread out and check every room. I'm looking for hard, shiny stuff. We call it gold."

"What if we find gems, should we not mention them?" asked Chakk.

Dave nodded, having evidently been pondering this himself.

Trudy rolled her eyes and started picking threads out of her purple bodice that was the same shade as her hair.

"Yes. That would be nice, yes."

"Ore?" said Chakk.

"Yes."

"Diamonds?" said Dave.

"Those are gems. Yes."

"What about dead bodies?"

"What bodies?"

I turned to see Dave on tiptoes, peering into a cell along the corridor.

"There's bodies in 'ere! Corrr, that's what the smell is. Should 'ave found that key sooner.

Bugger.

"Hope it was no one important," sniggered Trudy, peering inside. I took great pleasure in seeing her retch and run to the nook under the stairs to vomit. I secretly hoped that she was right.

I ordered Dave to check the other cells for any surviving prisoners and dispatched Gawain to get them some food. Scamp meat or the food Yanna had plundered from several local farmsteads should do the trick.

The pair made off as fast they could, Dave's tools jiggling in his belt. I secretly envied them. The smell was seeping into my lungs. Is suspected it would take more than one shower to rid myself of it.

"You." I motioned to Chakk. "Go and get some trolls, they've got bugger all sense of smell. Get them down here with some fire sprites if there are any left. I want that cell purged." He nodded and took off at a run, but not before giving Trudy the finger. She grudgingly returned to helping me search every room and storage area.

"Here." I wandered into a room at the east end of the passageway. At the far end, half-buried in the shadows, was a stone door, its contours blending admirably in with the walls it clung to.

"It's locked." Trudy rattled the handle.

"Of course, it couldn't just be fucking easy." I gave it a kick.

It groaned and fell inward, crashing down and sending a puff of dust into the air. In the small room beyond, in the middle of the room, was a pathetic heap of gold. It wouldn't pay even a fifth of the minion or soldier salaries.

Silently, I circled the pile. Pinned to the wall behind it was an envelope, addressed to me, in my mother's handwriting. I tore it open and read the following:

Dear Son,

If it helps, then visualise me laughing uncontrollably as you read this. By now, you will have likely reached the end of your tether as far as money goes. Since I imagine one of the first things you did was to take your father's legal advisor to bed, what gold you see here will likely not last long. When she isn't sending illicit letters to her paymaster and your father's most hated rival, she's spending.

You won't find easy riches. Being Overlord is not what it appears. It's a game. Everyone is in the same boat, only with slightly different pieces or advantages. Play it better than they do; that's all you can do.

This is all that is left. The rest was spent on the one last gamble. *If you haven't figured out the truth about the ore, then*

I suggest you do so, before someone else, namely Sergi, decides to take what little this domain can offer before you are ready. It's time you actually used that brilliant brain of yours and worked for a living.

Also, please don't waste resources trying to kill your grandmother. You may need her. In a pinch, there is a secret exit to the castle starting from beneath the nymph trio statue in her parlour. She also keeps some gold there.

Your mother.

No wonder Yanna never found grandmother's gold. That statue is used to hang up worn stockings.

I sat down on a broken chair and re-read the letter while Trudy and Chakk, who had returned, shuffled and kicked at the edges of the coins, both no doubt silently fantasising about what they would do with it, were it theirs. So was I, to be honest.

To think it would have to go on minions or defences, or anything that wasn't for my immediate pleasure, was crushing. So... there *was* a grand plan. As for the rest, it made little sense. She spoke like Sergi's invasion was to be expected. Even planned. And just what did they spend the money on? What truth about the ore? Were there hidden riches in the damn swamp or not?

JUNN

1ST JUNN

I decided to check in and see how things were faring in the library and found myself once again pouring out my troubles to Francis, who was in the middle of cataloguing the remaining wildlife volumes. Anything with a picture of an animal on tended to get eaten, she had told me.

"So, you found gold and are still moping and moaning. Wish I had that problem." She slammed down a book and glared at me. "One of your famous flour weevils got in here this morning. It took three giant books, dropped from the balcony, to crush it. They're becoming a hazard."

"They aren't MY anything. Blame your ridiculous friend—the little excuse for a warlock." She harrumphed and went back to trying to ignore me.

"You'll be pleased to know that, for your services, I will be including you on the priority pay list." I paused for some sign of gratitude. There was none.

"About time." She felt the silence and looked up. "What?"

"There's something else."

"What?"

"What, *Overlord*. The ore. I need to research the swamp."

"Do it yourself, *Overlord*," she said quickly. "I've far too much to do. Get one of your hapless escort group to do it."

"I'm ordering YOU to do it. I have staff to pay, missing gold to locate—or at least whatever my parents spent it on, and, somehow, Yanna to deal with."

"Found out about the affair, did you? Took you long enough." She stood up, saw my face and then made an 'O' shape with her lips. I tried to process what she had said.

"Erm, ore? That sounds fine; I'll get on it." With a wide-eyed look, she snatched up a notebook from the desk and ran, leaving me standing there, staring blankly ahead. What did I do to deserve this? Aside from the obvious.

2ND JUNN

After a night spent deep in thought, I decided to hold off mentioning the cushions, the contact with Sergi, or the alleged dalliance, as I needed Yanna's assistance. I had her comb my parents' records for any large payments made in the year leading up to their demise. I want to know where the money went—it will bring me closer to discovering this 'one last gamble' before, as my mother suggested, it was too late.

"Here." She slapped a small, ripped piece of paper down on my desk. "There were payments out, but all records of them are gone. This was a scrap I found down the side of a desk. Whoever destroyed or removed all the relevant records must have missed it."

I studied the faded red type. "It's a receipt for the manufacture of an anchor." I frowned. "What did they want an anchor for?"

"Your father never had a naval fleet," said Yanna, looking equally as puzzled. "They were paid cash by the look of it. Can't really make out the name."

"Well," I said, suspecting there may well be someone who could help. "Never mind."

"That's it? What's the plan now?"

I shrugged, which seemed to enrage her, but I didn't care. I was bored of the nonsense.

"Ask Sergi. I have things to attend to." Without stopping to savour the flash of shock and anger on her face, I swept out of the room and made my way to the library.

LATER

"So?"

"This is a clue!" I waved the paper under Francis' nose.

"But you don't know to what," she said, fixing a spine back onto a book with some thick yellow paste. "Look, did you actually go out to that damn swamp?"

"Yanna did. There was nothing there. No mining, no works. Just swamp."

"There must be something there."

"There bloody wasn't. She said that there literally wasn't. Not even trees. Nothing."

She looked up. "What do you mean *not even trees?*"

"No trees. Just swamp. Gunge. Mud. Slime."

"No trees. At all?"

"Someone had cut them all down. Probably the locals. It was a bad winter. It's been a haven for loggers for a few years." I groaned and slumped against a bookcase. "Why can't this all just be easy?"

Francis shook her head. "Are you just going to sit there then? That won't help, you know."

"It helps my headache," I snapped.

"Sake. Well, you don't help mine. There are no trees and no ore. So, you have no money. Which means we'll be invaded for bloody nothing."

"Not now we have a fire demon."

"If it's not half dead by now. Has anyone fed it?"

I opened my eyes. Urgh.

3ᴿᴰ JUNN

"This sucks minotaur dick. I mean, why me?" Trudy demanded.

This had been going on for half an hour.

"You drew the short straw," I snapped, watching Dave finish strapping the tattered remains of a dragon-scale breastplate to her. It was two sizes too big and looked precarious in all its patchy, filthy glory. Much like everything else in this palace of ruin.

The complaining continued. "Look, what about all them— get one of those bastards to feed the fucking thing." She waved a thickly gloved hand at the crowd who had gathered behind us in the small lobby, corridors, and even the staircases. After all, it wasn't every day that you saw someone feeding a plate of brimstone crystals to a fire demon.

"Look at those barbarians," she raged. "*Look* at them— they've got more armour than I have and are nearly twice as tall as me."

Heads turned and several barbarians squatted in a futile attempt to look smaller.

"And look, there's a fucking cave troll."

The cave troll vanished from sight behind a screen of fluttering dark fairies.

"Cave troll, cave troll!" they chanted in their trilling little voices.

"Piss off, you," Trudy sniped.

"Dead girl, dead girl!" they trilled back.

She gave them a vigorous finger gesture.

"Too late, you've got all the kit on," said Dave. Many large minions and soldiers nodded vigorously, and the barbarians suddenly regained their former height.

"Anyway, if you want paid… eventually… you'll get on with it," I snapped. My feet were aching, and a nasty smell was drifting around. I was also suddenly conscious of contagious skin diseases. "Remember, if this thing dies, the moronic local heroes are going to toast what's left of this place. And then Sergi will have the rest."

Her furious response was cut off by Dave jamming what looked like a bucked wrapped in a wet carpet over her head. A small slit had been gouged out for her to see through.

"Right, get in there and feed it before we get stenched to death," I ordered. I motioned to the door, and Chakk and Gawain looked at one another and then, as one, turned the key and shoved the door open.

I felt the fetid, ragtag crowd behind me press closer, and a rumble of excitement rolled around the lobby. Above my shoulder, a red, glowing, disembodied eye hovered. One of the warlocks was using it to broadcast the show to the jostling mass at the back who were stretched up the stairs and down the surrounding passageways.

"Move." The voice, then the body cut through the crowd at my back. People, trolls, and worse fell back like matchsticks in a tidal wave.

"Yanna." I barely turned to acknowledge her but made sure to shift several inches to partially obscure her view. I nodded to a soldier who shoved the mutinous Trudy through the door.

"Bastards!" came the muffled yell.

Everyone crowded closer. Even Yanna got jostled a few times.

Trudy took a few steps towards the towering shape lurking in the shadows. Its eyes burned red holes in the darkness, and a red glow hung over the rocky floor around it.

Trudy suddenly thought better of what she was doing and turned back to the door, but stopped. With the mass of bodies filling the doorway and lobby, she'd never be able to retreat, even if she wanted to. And she clearly wanted to.

"Just chuck it and run," hissed Dave, poking his head around the doorframe.

"Yeah, just slide the tray over and fucking leg it; it's on a chain, ain't it?" shouted a soldier from somewhere behind us.

"It could melt that, though," said someone else.

"Couldn't," chimed another voice. "That's clearly dwarven blue steel."

"You'll find it's actually Endoran ice steel."

A heated argument ensued, while everyone else focussed on the thing in the darkness.

"C'mon!"

"You can do it."

"Kick its arse, then feed it!"

"Feed its arse?"

The hubbub of voices rose in support, with only a few jeers. I think perhaps they just wanted to see her being eaten. I know I was fifty-fifty. It would certainly save entertaining the morons for weeks.

Under the outsized breastplate, her shoulders tensed, and she took a step forward. And then another.

The fire demon didn't move, but its eyes smouldered. No one made a sound—only Trudy's boots scuffling on the floor.

"CHUCK IT!" shouted someone, making Trudy and half the crowd jump violently.

The tray slid in her hands, and she flailed, trying to keep it straight as the crystals slid and bunched against the lip, on the brink of escaping.

The idiot was furiously shushed, and the grim spectacle continued. After calming herself, she moved again.

"If she's got any sense, she'll put it down, slide it, and run like buggery."

I hadn't even noticed that Francis was beside me. I nodded.

"It would be a shame to lose one of the few competent staff members that we have," I said.

"Then you should have sent the sodding cave troll, or one of the dark fairies—at least they can fly out of harm's way."

"The fairies are on strike, and the cave troll has a hernia. I got a badly-written letter purporting to be from his doctor."

Francis' eyes widened, I imagine from trying to envisage what this fake hernia would look like, were it real. At least it shut her up. I was starting to regret wasting a decent staff member, and the internal admission was making me peevish.

"Can she just throw it?" said Gawain in a stage whisper.

Dave gave his patented 'suck in air and shake head' move.

Trudy took another step.

There was a low hissing growl that rumbled in my chest cavity before trailing off, and the eyes seemed to grow brighter. Minions tried to back away, but we were all penned in by the press of the crowd. If the situation turned nasty, we'd all be immolated before we could turn around. I suddenly wished we had better fire-safety measures.

Trudy's whole body trembled so much that her breastplate slid off one shoulder and the brimstone crystals shimmied on the tray. Slowly, she crouched down and put the tray on the floor. A piece of brimstone rattled off onto the ground, and everyone winced. I wondered if this was the day I was to die.

Nothing.

Before Trudy could stand up, a rat leapt out of a nearby crack in the floor and skittered past her towards the lurking terror. One of the warlocks grabbed at a holy symbol around his neck, Chakk squealed, and Dave's hand stopped, his hipflask halfway to his mouth.

The rat scuttled between its legs, barely visible in the dull glow, and leapt out of sight. There was an odd scrabbling sound.

A loud, protracted creak cut the atmosphere.

Trudy took another step and then pulled off her helmet. She then moved closer, mouth agape as she stared into the gloom.

Around me, there was an inrush of horror.

Her helmet thunked to the ground.

"Son of a—"

With a despicable groan, the demon teetered and fell forward. Screams rent the air around me, and Trudy dived out of the way as it smashed down on to the floor in a cloud of mould spores and dust.

She picked herself up, and I just stared at the thing. My parents' special terror. The scourge of our lands that had kept us safe for decades.

I felt the will to live leave me momentarily, and my body acted on autopilot as my mind began to shut down at the horror in front of me.

Laying in the dust was the pitiful wooden frame that had been propping up a flat cut-out of a fire demon. A wooden fire demon whose painted façade was now face-down on the filthy floor. One remaining eye flickered, and the spell powering the fierce glow finally popped out of existence.

The rats, whose nest had been constructed amidst the rotting timber supports, scattered, knocking a thin metal cone, which rattled to a halt against my boots. The small box that was attached to it hissed and growled, eventually turning to a farting noise before it, too, perished.

"Well." Francis' voice carried through the door behind me. "That's us fucked."

As the dancing spores and pirouetting dust motes began to stir me into a raging headache, I heard Yanna's boots clicking away amidst a growing rumble of anger from the crowd. Francis, as much as I loathed to think it, was right.

LATER

"What do you fucking *mean* they sold it?"

After fighting my way through an angry, jeering crowd, I had stormed as fast as I could up to my grandmother's quarters. Somehow, several of her servants had beaten me to it and were hovering nervously around the chamber doorway, whispering amongst themselves when I burst in. Her revelation at my angry news did not go down well with me.

The infernal woman just shrugged and slurped her tea.

"When? Where? Bloody *how*? You won't get one of those in a fucking mailing box."

"They sold it years ago. Nasty thing, anyway. It was old and flea-bitten."

"Flea-bitten?! How is that even *possible*? And how could they be so *stupid* as to sell our greatest deterrent and defence?"

"Don't speak ill of the dead," she snapped.

"It never stopped you," I snapped back.

She harrumphed and returned to her tea. Something about her demeanour, however, spoke ill. She looked worried. She was never worried.

"Anyway," she said, "they got a local carpenter to knock that one up, and the head warlock put some high-level magic on it to make it more realistic and stop anyone getting close enough to see what it was."

"Why didn't they tell me? Why didn't *you* tell me?"

"Why should I?" She shifted in her seat and looked away, a flash of something... something in her eyes... surely not regret. The woman wasn't capable. "It's *your* damn job to know everything."

"What I do know is that when word of this spreads—and I guarantee it's already beyond the castle—we won't be able to stop the moronic, entitled pricks at the Heroes' Guild from waltzing in here. And that's the happy option, because when Sergi or one of the others hears about it, we're worse than dead."

"No one will be stupid enough to spread a rumour that will

lose them the roof over their heads," she said.

"Gossip is currency, and in their damn cups, they'll certainly spill it. Besides, Yanna saw *everything*. I know who her damn paymaster is and he *will* attack. It's just a case of when."

"I told you not to get involved with her, just like your damn father. All libido and no brain."

"It wouldn't have made a fucking difference." I gave up arguing and left, slamming the door as hard as I could. Not for the first time did I consider resurrecting my parents and then buggering off and leaving them to the whole sorry mess. They'd done it to me after all. They'd acquiesced to their own murders to spite me, I just knew it.

4TH JUNN

I retreated to what was fast becoming a sanctuary of sorts. Few minions would set foot in the library, so I was safe from angry demands and reprisals. Francis, however, was not to be avoided.

"So… let's summarise." Her voice seemed to come from far away, against the backdrop of her helper scraping mould from various fixtures. The floor was cold at my back and was, I found, the best way to hold my headache at bay in an attempt to focus my mind.

"You only have a handful of gold."

"Yes."

"And a grand plan of which you know practically nothing."

"It involves swamps and ore, or something…" I protested.

"And Health and Safety are breathing down your neck—I'm amazed no one else has come out yet."

I gritted my teeth. "Yessss," I hissed, wishing she would shut up.

"Half the castle is falling down, and at least a fifth of the good part has now been taken over by magical weevils."

"Eugh." I covered my face with my hands and groaned.

"And your fire demon—Hero and rival-Overlord deterrent—is, in fact, a mouldy sheet of wood."

Someone started sobbing. It may have been me.

"And your erm... I mean, Miss Yanna... she's just run away with the Head of the Army... erm... sir," came Gawain's voice.

There was a sharp inrush of air from Francis, and I sat bolt upright.

"She WHAT?" I leapt up and grabbed him by the lapels of his plush blue uniform jacket.

"She... she... went off just now with him and the rest of them."

I dropped him, and he squeaked as he crashed to the floor.

"Rest of who?" Francis said, helping Gawain off the floor and shooting me a filthy look.

I was truly beyond caring at this point. I found myself longing for the days when it was just the collapsing west wing and a missing manservant plaguing me.

"Erm..." Gawain swallowed a few times and adjusted his collar. "Half the army went with them."

"Ohhh... you've gone dead pale..." said Francis. A blurry hand adorned with chunky skull rings waved in front of my eyes before they closed ahead of the loudest scream I had ever uttered. Two scamps and a bat fell out of the rafters in shock, and there was a startled yell along with a plume of blue magic from the high-magic section, followed by a demonic roar.

LATER

I marched straight to the barracks, with Francis and Gawain scuttling behind me like the world's most pathetic comet. The door had been locked and would not yield to repeated kicks, so I had to send Gawain to fetch Dave. Sadly, he arrived with the rest of the misfits.

"You need a hand with a job?" he asked, waving a bag of disgusting sweets under my nose.

Trudy sniggered.

"Open that door."

In two minutes, he had undone the hinges, and Trudy forced the door open.

I looked around the shambles of what had once been magnificent barracks. Tattered banners clung tenaciously to walls amid posters for the local brewery and several of the more risqué elf dance troupes.

"What is that *smell*?" said Francis.

"Don't ask," muttered Trudy.

I privately agreed. I also vowed not to touch anything. I valued my health too much.

The floor was a jumble of discarded, patchy armour, old bedding, mouldy mugs full of cigarette ends, and a dead scamp who appeared to have choked to death on the remains of a deflated football.

The place smelled of stale sweat, beer, piss, and armour polish, among other rank things. In defence against the olfactory assault, a bowl of potpourri lay on the chipped coffee table beside the cold fireplace in the common area—a forlorn attempt at cheer. It stood no chance.

There was no bickering, fighting, or complaints about drafts or pay—no clanking or swishing of weapons on rasps. It was as though time had stopped. Only it hadn't. It had marched inexorably on, and so had the bastards that had once been domiciled here.

"Messy buggers, ain't they?" Dave popped a candied eyeball into his mouth and clucked to himself. He shoved the paper bag at Trudy, who wrinkled her nose and went to poke through some of the footlockers at the end of the tattered bunks in the next room.

"Don't s'pose there's any food in there? Or shiny stuff?" asked Chakk, looking hopeful.

"No," she called back. "Only dirty mags, empty wine bottles, a boot brush that looks like the bristles have been eaten, and a small dagger."

"Where's the rest, then?" Dave asked, making a disgusting sucking noise over his confections.

"What? Dirty mags?" said Chakk, giving a bedframe a lick and then pulling a face.

This was a disgrace. The bastards hadn't left anything of use. Not that there had ever been anything much of use in here for a long time.

"The army," said Dave. "He said only half 'ad gone." He pointed a stubby finger at Gawain, who was tutting over a rip in one of his precious fire-safety notices.

"That's a point," said Francis, kicking at a rusted helmet.

"They're probably down the sodding pub," said Trudy. "I saw them leaving earlier. It's half price shots on 'show-your-scars day'."

I rolled my eyes.

"There's no way of catching up to Yanna? Any remaining wagons?" I asked Dave. He sucked in a breath and shook his head in what I took to be a definitive no.

"Only one we got is the knackered one that I'm repairing."

"And do what, exactly?" scoffed Francis. She turned to face me. "Even if you could catch up to her, you'd waste what few precious resources you have left trying to stop her playing pied piper to your band of rats. You could even end up dead."

She was right, and I hated it. Not as much as I despised

Yanna. I started fantasising about setting fire to all her cushions.

"She 'ad the right idea, though… buggering off before someone arrives to duff us all up," said Dave.

Francis' shoulders tensed in a way I had come to dread. "So. Now what? Because you know that as soon as the other lazy bastards get back tonight, pissed or not, they'll set off out of here too. As soon as they find out about that sodding fire demon."

Would she ever shut up? "Yes. I know!"

"If they ever come back," said Chakk, shrieking to avoid a black cat that skulked out from underneath a chair and bolted out of the door.

That was a nasty thought.

My mind raced over every possibility, of ways in which I could convince them to stay. I thanked my own good sense that I had hidden our paltry gold supply from the dungeon under my grandmother's sofa. At least Yanna couldn't take that. It was a minuscule saving grace.

"There's not even enough gold to pay them to stay," I muttered. There wasn't much left to sell, either. Unless we went into weevil farming.

"Sometimes it ain't what you got, but what you do wiv it."

I stared at Dave, and something clicked.

"So, I use it to get them to stay by doing…?"

"Eugh, just make an effort to raise sodding morale until you figure out what the fuck your parents had planned. Or we all get eaten by flour weevils," said Francis, giving an abandoned sword a test swing, only for the blade to shoot out of the hilt and just miss impaling Gawain.

"You ruined my poster! I took ages over that," he whined.

Francis looked guilty and hurried to pry the blade free from the wall/poster. "I'm so sorry," she said. To my disgust, tears welled up in his eyes. Dave made a valiant stab at fixing the situation while Trudy just muttered under her breath and wandered off to rummage through the cupboards—the ones that still had doors, anyway.

"I like the curly bits." Dave offered the whiner an eyeball while I looked about and wondered how I would fix this mess, and who I could blame if I couldn't. How did my parents deal with everyday petty nonsense? Is that what a manservant is for? Not that I had any gold with which to hire one, anyway. Perhaps I should have interred Reginald in the graveyard with a view to resurrecting him later, rather than posting his corpse in a large birthday card to Sergi for a practical joke.

"I used to do the curly bits on the posters back home for the town fayres and sports days," Gawain sniffed. I wondered what village had lost its idiot the day he became employed here. Perhaps that village had been consumed by giant flour weevils too.

I flicked at the ripped poster and eyed the overly elaborate swirls and loops. Something occurred to me. "Wait... how about we do our own day."

Brilliant.

"Rubbish," snorted Francis. "You think these cretins will go to a country fayre?"

I gave her my best glare. Always a complaint, never a solution.

"The nearest most of them get to a vegetable judging contest is when they look in a mirror to check how brown their teeth are."

Did she ever shut up?

"Shut up," I ordered. "I don't mean a country fayre... well..." In truth, I wasn't quite sure *what* I had meant. My brain was clicking and whirring in panic mode.

"You gotta have beer, then. The beer bit's always good," piped up Dave.

"Beer," I nodded. It was a start. "A sort of morale-day event. With beer." I wasn't the best when coming up with non-sadistic things. Traps, yes. Assassination ideas, absolutely. Nice games and fun things, nope. Luckily, I was surrounded by drippy idiots who, I suspected, would do most of the work for me.

"We need prizes," said Chakk, suddenly interested. "Shiny ones."

"Cheap ones," I corrected. "But shiny-ish."

He looked pleased.

"Competitions will certainly distract everyone and help them let off some steam," admitted Francis. "Especially violent competitions."

Gawain was already scribbling in a notebook.

As the ideas began to fly, I leaned over Gawain's shoulder and began to dictate.

The fact that it was only a day or so's worth of bandage over a festering wound weighed heavily on me, but if I could keep what was left of the troops and minions happy (ish) and alive until I sorted our mess out, then it could only be a good thing. I hoped I was right.

8TH JUNN

☠ MINION MORALE DAY ☠

WEST SIDE OF THE CASTLE—WASTE GROUND.

In the grounds to the west side, on a vast piece of scrappy, overgrown wasteland covered in rubble, weeds, and stony hillocks, it began. The sun had just grudgingly climbed into the sky, and the work that had frantically been going on for the last 72 plus hours was now culminating in this… folly? Genius? I heaved in a sigh and drew my cloak against my neck at the biting morning air.

Banners made from the fabric of eye-wateringly expensive cushions and bed linen fluttered on ropes strung between spears. I watched the growing crowd milling about and shuffled. The makeshift stage groaned ominously beneath my feet and, once again, I realised that my life was in the hands of a man who ate candied eyeballs and slept in a giant's wheelbarrow that had been brought back from Poppletop as a souvenir by my father, a decade ago.

"Are you going to do your speech or what?" demanded Francis, appearing in front of me like a curvy avenging angel, albeit one dressed in black and burgundy with silver skulls on her bodice beading. Her hair was slicked back into an ornate cluster of twists and knots that suited her, and she was clutching a familiar-looking clipboard.

Clearly, she was in a crabby mood about being press-ganged into the head role in the newly founded 'Committee to Plan Parties'. Tough. I had to stand on a fucking stage constructed out of the remains of my sodding fire demon.

"Nice clipboard," I said as conversationally as possible in order to annoy her. "Let's hope you don't end up on the same compost heap as its former owner."

Her eyes flickered. "No sense in it rotting with the Health and Safety woman, was there? That's real Hydra skin, that is. It's probably worth more than your castle." She hugged it defensively.

"Then maybe we should sell it," I snapped, rising to her bait.

"Over my dead body."

"It would certainly help make my day," I hissed, trying to avoid attracting any more attention than we already had. Fists clenched, I snatched the megaphone Dave had battered together from a metal bin lid and began my speech.

"Friends, minions, and countrymen… the most esteemed and faithful army in the East Lands," I shouted, my voice amplified as much as a wraith's fart.

Everyone looked around expectantly, wondering to whom I could possibly be referring. I'm sure I heard Trudy's familiar snort from somewhere.

I continued. "This is our—*your*—special day of fun, relaxation, and friendly competition. We have racing, high jumping, pie eating, scamp dunking and more. There will, of course, be prizes for our noble winners." I tried not to choke too much over the words. It didn't help that Francis' incredulous faces and Trudy's now very audible snickering and rude remarks were giving me an angry tic in my left eye.

"So, on that note, if our referees and organisers would like to get into position, let the games begin! Over to our *loyal* staff."

Francis shot me a foul look and stamped off. "Right. Fine. This way. Running race this way. Move. *Now.*"

"Where's the beer?" someone shouted and the crowd began to separate and flock towards the various flagged staging areas and events. In the distance, Francis and a trail of minions and soldiers arrived at the race track that had been roughly mown and flattened, thanks to some stolen sheep and a few begrudged spells from the warlocks.

I saw Francis wave a pen and nearly put out the eye of a small warlock holding one end of a starting tape, while a row of minions lined up behind it. I say tape. It was, in fact, a ribbon liberated from a wedding carriage that had passed through the town the previous day. Dave had been particularly proud of his acquisition, despite having come back with a shoe print from the best man on his backside.

Gawain shuffled up to the line and puffed out his chest. It looked like his uniform had been brushed to within an inch of its life, and there had been an attempt to shine his boots. His hair was still orange but now had blue tips. I had a nasty feeling that there would be another iteration of flour weevils to look forward to.

A whistle hung around his neck on a golden cord. It looked far too luxurious for this place, and I suddenly recognised it as one of Yanna's curtain ties. It gave me a stab of pleasure, as he blew the whistle for the first race, especially knowing how much she would have hated all this.

The first race went off without much of a hitch, bar one runner getting turned into a coat-stand by an elderly warlock and a fistfight at the finish line after some casual tripping. Still, the sudden violence set the tone for the rest of the day rather nicely. With the cheap medals awarded, people settled down and the day ground onwards.

As I moved around what we laughingly called our playing fields, observing and directing other people to break up some of the deadlier fights, I couldn't help but notice that people were enjoying themselves. It wasn't a common sight around here, not since the viewing gallery had been removed from the torture chamber. Before he quit, our torturer had complained that the vuvuzelas and rustling sweet wrappers put him off, and so my father made the decision to do away with it.

Even my grandmother's staff had been allowed out to watch, and I wondered where she was this day and whom she was plaguing. A few of the braver souls among her staff were even taking part—gods know they needed some ray of joy. Seeing one enter the three-legged race convinced me that some of them were here on a suicide mission, though. Especially given that there seemed to be some confusion as to what the name of the event actually meant. Two barbarians had pinned down a companion and attempted to saw off one of his legs before they were stopped by Francis, aided by Dagg.

Trudy and the other misfits had been assigned medical-aid

duties. They were, naturally, now working overtime. Fair play was just something that happened to other people, as far as my collection of idiots was concerned. Not that cheating is a bad philosophy; it's just when it gets costly in terms of property or manpower that I object.

I had just approached the pit to watch the weevil wrestling—a cave wraith was taking on a large orange weevil who had been dubbed Hammond—when Gawain came barrelling up.

Since the breathless little rat only appears when some disaster has happened, I am considering tattooing a skull on his forehead.

"Erm… sir…" He was wringing his hands as though his husband had just been shipped off to war.

"What disaster has befallen us this time?" I said over cheers and shouts from the pit crowd.

"Your grandmother…"

"She's dead?" The sun burst from behind the clouds, and suddenly butterflies began to dance over the weeds and piles of scamp excrement.

"No, sir."

Darkness.

"She's competing, sir. She insisted."

"She what?! Where? Gods tell me that she's not doing the high jump."

"Um, beer drinking, sir."

"Who the *fuck* let her do that? Do you know what she's like in her cups?"

Fear creased his face, and he looked as though he was going to be sick. He only nodded.

"*Who?*"

"F-Francis. She was angry because the warlocks were using magic to cheat at the high jump, and because you said earlier this morning that books didn't make worthy prizes."

"Only because most of these idiots would either eat them or just can't read!"

What was she playing at? Was she trying to evoke a heart attack to finish me off?

From the edge of the pit came a barrage of cheers, followed by a chorus of 'ohhhhhh's and 'ahhh's, and then a gurgling scream that was swiftly cut off. More cheers broke out, and coins, buttons, playing cards, and pages of saucy magazines changed hands. A troll fished a ripped cloak from the pit with a long boathook, and several warlocks and soldiers removed their hats for a moment of respect.

Hammond, it seemed, remained undefeated.

I left as another contender was 'helped' into the pit to a new chorus of cheers and a fresh flurry of bets.

I pushed my way through a knot of soldiers arguing about whether using a ladder for the high jump was actually cheating and found Francis breaking up a fight between two guards over a bronze (plated) medal and a bumper bag of candied eyeballs. Nearby, a troll was pummelling a drunk barbarian into the ground with his fist while clutching a tin trumpet to his chest.

"Enough!" Francis yelled at the guards. "Do you want another timeout?"

The two soldiers shook their heads and glared down at her from beneath dented helmets. "How about one of you gets the medal and one gets the candies, or you *share* the candies and take turns wearing the medal?"

They looked at one another, then down at Francis, whose hands were welded to her hips in fury, and gave sullen nods. They divided up the sweets and wandered off to a small platform (wardrobe doors) where two soldiers and an orc were attempting to eat large pies before the timer ticked down.

For a moment, my stomach growled, but then I saw what

looked like a scale slip out of one slice in a blob of congealed gravy and my appetite vanished.

"Brickwort… you got your prize back, stop crying and leave that barbarian alone. *Now.*" The troll stopped hammering on the man's head. "Get on to your next event. Try the scamp tossing."

The troll wiped his eyes and with a final poke to the man's head, left the barbarian and headed off to the scamp-tossing field, passing the high-jump crowd as he did.

Over the heads of the raucous cluster of bodies, I watched a warlock pinwheel through the air in a puff of blue magic, clearing the floating pole (curtain pole) by a ridiculous amount. It would have been more impressive had he not been so overambitious. The crunch as he hit the castle wall made even the rock trolls in the crowd wince.

Francis exhaled in a way that suggested aeons of hardship and turned finally to bring her full attitude to bear on me.

"What?"

"My grandmother. Why?"

She smirked.

I became decidedly more irked.

"Couldn't leave her out, even I wanted to. It was that or the scamp tossing, and I wasn't about to tell her she couldn't take part."

"Well, I can't afford to lose too many more scamps… the scamp wells got clogged up two years ago."

"You know everyone's cheating, don't you?" Francis scowled, waving her clipboard and nearly taking off Gawain's ear.

"You expected anything else?" I scoffed. How long had she been working here?

There was a distant scream from the castle. Heads around us turned. Francis sighed and scribbled something on her clipboard. What was it about clipboards that always brought out a pissy, officious, world-weary attitude in people?

"That'll be another hide and eater gone. You're going to have to seriously consider stopping that event because that rabid snapper has got five so far."

"Wait... what?!"

"The event." She waved her clipboard at me again. "Hide and go eat."

My mouth dropped. Actually dropped. I struggled to regain my composure.

"SEEK. Seek! It's bloody hide and go SEEK!" I was half-aware that spit was frothing at the corners of my mouth. "What the *fuck* is wrong with you?!"

Francis went scarlet and hurried away towards the castle, grabbing Dagg on the way.

I'd be lucky to see the day out with anyone left. I turned slowly, surveying the chaos, voices, laughs, screams, and the occasional flash-bang of magic settling over me like a mantle of gloom.

There were crowds everywhere, especially around the weevil pit, the beer-drinking contest, and the pie-eating stage. Over the heads of some more diminutive minions, I could see my grandmother wiping her mouth and slamming her empty stein down on a table that was creaking with empties and wizened bar snacks.

Her last upright opponent slithered down in his chair, and his glass thunked onto the stage. Two hellhounds bounded up to start lapping up the dregs while the crowd broke into a raucous cheer. She looked even happier than she had the time my father nearly choked to death on a swan bone.

I decided to leave her to it and edged away before I could be summoned, bothered, or berated.

Many enterprising villagers had got wind of the event and

had set up stalls. Unfortunately, as gold was thin on the ground, most of the merchandise was either stolen or bartered for dirty magazines and fixtures liberated from the castle or from other vendors.

One man left his stall for two minutes to relieve himself behind a bush, only to return and find it not only stripped bare of meat rolls and various pastries, but half the wood had also been taken. All that remained was a few scraps of canopy material fluttering against a bare wooden frame. Even most of the nails had gone.

Still, the villagers and some braver (stupider) heroes made good fodder for some of the events and, from the screams, Hammond was having a field day. The crowd around the weevil pit were now sporting an array of spoils, from hats and aprons to things like stall-bunting capes and bloodstained boots.

I allowed the thought to creep in that, perhaps, the day would end up a success of sorts. Finally, *something* was going to plan. It was a stupid thing to do because, *of course,* the Gods punished me. Immediately and with a vengeance.

Through the magical haze drifting over the field, he came.

Lo, a pale goat, and the man that sat on him was tall and lean, wearing a dark pinstriped suit and bowler hat. Briefcase and offensive clipboard in hand, he came and, I suspected, the demon realms followed with him. The sun went in, and my gut twisted.

In a panic, I turned to make sure that the crowds were obscuring the compost heap where his predecessors had been deposited. When I turned back, thankful for small mercies, I realised he had spotted me and had abandoned his mount. He strode towards me, confident, with a smirking smile.

Fuuuuuck.

He swept off his hat to reveal short, neat black hair. "James Pincher—Executive First-level Health and Safety. I'm here to perform a mandatory deep-level domain inspection." He shook my hand with a surprisingly firm grip and I felt calluses on his palms and fingers. Something in his eyes told me he wouldn't die easily.

"I will need clean, quiet, safe quarters and your full co-operation for the duration. The long duration. Or there will be... *penalties*." His mouth hitched in a tiny smirk, and I decided I hated him with a passion.

"You may have my new old quarters, Mr Cincher. I hope you like cushions."

"Pincher. And yes, I'm rather partial. I warn you; I plan to be thorough, and—"

I followed his gaze to the distant compost heap where a high-heeled shoe was poking out.

"—and I will pull no punches. Make no mistake, Mr Evergreen, this is deadly serious."

"Evergrim."

"It certainly is. I will shut you down and see you imprisoned—or worse."

I looked past the round glasses into green eyes that danced with devilish pleasure and knew he'd try his damnedest.

Somewhere behind him, Trudy was casting glances in our direction and blocking Chakk, who appeared to be pasting a fire-hazard warning on the back of a fire eater, who had been hired as a roaming entertainer. I resolved to up her non-existent pay.

"Could all this wait twenty-four hours or so? We're rather busy today."

"So I see. And no."

"Fine. If you'd like to go to your quarters, then, I'll have someone escort you."

"No." He looked around, scanning the crowds, drinking in the vomiting, the fights, the drunken fairies who were setting a sleeping warlock's cloak on fire. At that moment, a goblin toppled off the roof of the stall that he was capering on and fell onto a spear being brandished by one of the pit crowd.

"Something tells me that I'll find *much* more amusement here."

He was temporarily drowned out by cheers from the weevil crowd as the wriggling goblin was thrown, spear and all, into the pit. "And besides, I'd hate to miss anything." A flicker of a grin. "*Anything* at all."

His attention wandered to a fight that had just broken out at the staging area for the throwing contest. A large goblin had taken umbrage at having come third and had thrown the victor into a crevice at the base of the castle wall. The second-place winner was now locked in combat with him, right up until a chunk of masonry fell out of the side of the castle and squashed the pair of them.

Standing to one side, in a ripped blue cloak and tunic dress with a beaded bodice was my grandmother's pastry chef. Her black hair had been swept up into a complicated knot, and her boots looked more buckled, spiked, and terrifying than our torture chamber. She still held the ladle weapon that she had fashioned. A referee's badge clung to her cloak, the faint metallic shimmer in contrast against her dark skin and clothes.

She was motionless, emotionless, while others around her burst into raucous laughter and kicked at the green hands poking out from the stone, before divesting them of rings and bracelets. She blew the whistle and, wordlessly, handed a rosette to a small goblin who had been watching the chaos unfold. Two others bustled up to her, shrieking complaints. One accidentally poked her.

In a move I barely saw happen, she swung the ladle up and knocked the pair of them out in two deft swings. Her hand moved into the pouch at her side, and she dropped two rosettes onto the twitching bodies and then wiped her nose on her sleeve before wandering away, looking through people.

I was aware of Pincher's pen scratching away behind me on his infernal clipboard. I moved away to try and escape him, but he followed me around the field. Trudy and co. ran ahead to fix notices to various things and, in the distance, I could see Dave hammering a fire-rallying-point signpost into the ground.

Over by the old stables, a group was gathering to organise swampy bulldog. I decided to avoid them. Many of the gargoyles were loose in that section, and the last thing I needed was Pincher scratching away about that.

Our path eventually took us past the beer-drinking stage once more. A dead hellhound was being carved up and barbequed on a nearby meat vendor's cart—the smell of beer, singed fur, and roasting meat was oddly sweet, yet nauseating. I looked back to see some red notes being made.

Francis popped up in front of me and I uttered an embarrassing shriek. "What the fuck? What do you want, don't you have work to do?"

"Don't you have minions to pay?" she snapped back.

"Sir."

"*Sir.*"

"Pincher." The man pushed past me and extended his hand towards her. "James Pincher…"

"Let me guess. Health and Safety," she said, shaking it.

"Erm, yes." He tapped his glasses back up his nose and nodded. "Let me guess… that accent… Silverton?"

"Erm. Yes. How did you know?" She gave a curious smile.

"Well… I… get around, and very much enjoy the shires and towns out that way." He smiled. He *actually* smiled.

It was just as well because his goat was now turning slowly on a spit at one of the meat stalls and its hooves were being whittled into what looked like ashtrays.

I tuned out while they made small pleasantries and considered every way in which he was about to make my life a misery, and how hard I'd worked (or made everyone else work) to make the day a success. I still needed to sort out whether there was any truth to the ore rumours that could turn around our fortunes, and had the Heroes' Guild to worry about. And all Francis could do was make small talk about the local fauna and the listed architecture in the old quarter of Silverton. Rage overtook me when talk turned to book preservation.

"As I'm sure you are aware, Mr Pincher is here to make all of our lives more difficult. Perhaps you have somewhere else to be."

Their conversation stopped. Her smile vanished. It was momentarily terrifying.

"Well, it will certainly give *you* a brief respite from making our lives a misery," she said. "*Sir.*"

A smile flashed over Pincher's face and was as quickly concealed.

"Given the ineptitude I have to deal with, it's poor payback," I sniped.

Something seemed to snap behind her eyes, and I braced myself. She ripped off her whistle and tossed it, along with her clipboard, into a nearby vat of boiling fat in which several unidentified strips of meat were being fried.

"If you were half the Overlord that your father was and your mother *should* have been, then you wouldn't need people like me to run your poxy castle for you."

A red mist descended and my palms itched. I am twice the Overlord that my father was, and I didn't need to justify myself to a librarian or a smirking Health and Safety executive.

"Guards," I screamed. My voice rose and cracked, but my

rage carried me bullishly past embarrassment. Francis folded her arms and stared me in the eye as two soldiers plucked her by the elbows, giving one another looks from beneath their ill-fitting helmets. "Escort her to the dungeons, *now*."

I watched them vanish into the throng and felt Pincher's amusement. I had a troll fish out her clipboard and whistle and rinse them off in a puddle before I snatched them back and thrust them at Trudy who had been eavesdropping nearby.

"What the fuck?" she said.

"Battlefield promotion." It worked for my grandmother.

"This thing's got gobs of fat all over it," she protested. Ingrate.

I walked away with my Health and Safety shadow and spectated a number of events, trying to regain my calm.

A nervous cough drew my attention. It was the guards, returned.

"You put her in the dungeon?"

"Yessir."

"Very good. The key, please." Their shared look was not encouraging.

"Erm… what key?"

"To her cell, morons."

"Erm… well, when you said to escort her to the dungeons, sir, you never told us to PUT her in a cell, like. Just *in* the dungeons."

Pincher chuckled. Irritation ran its fiery nails down my body. Right before my voice broke.

"You mean that you left her freely roaming around down there? *Get back down there NOW.*"

They fled, barging into minions and pinballing off stalls and vanished back inside the castle.

I pinched the bridge of my nose and pretended that I couldn't hear a pencil scuffling over a sheaf of paper. "Having a good time?" I hissed.

"Oh, yes."

Smug satisfaction, thy name is Health and Safety. I sat down on a drunken orc that was being used as a bench by patrons of a fried-potato establishment and wondered if I could flee back to the mountains and jungles in which I had spent some of my gap years. Or perhaps open up a nice tea room somewhere. I could take up window-box gardening. I could become one of those weirdo Overlords who grow and manage miniature kingdoms in bell-jars and enter them in shows once a year.

I was in the middle of a long, elaborate fantasy about my own bell-jar kingdom and being able to crush Pincher and co with one swift stamp of my boot when the guards returned and sidled over to me. One shoved the other forward. He swallowed and pushed his helmet back.

Pincher's pencil was poised over his clipboard.

"Erm... Mr Overlord, sir. Erm... she's locked herself in, like."

"She *what?*"

"Erm, she's locked herself in a cell, with the key on the inside, like, with her. So no one can effing bother her, she says."

Pincher laughed.

My fists clenched into white-hot knots.

"What? Go and get her out, *now.*"

"Erm... yessir. But even if we *could* do that, then what do we do? Do we lock her right back in again?"

"Yes. No. Just..." I looked skyward for inspiration, or perhaps for a large comet to end it all. "Just... just... take her back to the fucking library. You're a liability, all of you."

"Erm... do you have a spare key, sir?"

"No, I DON'T."

Furious scratching from Pincher. I swore that his paper began to smoulder. It wasn't long before he chipped in, in his soft, low voice. "That's a serious offence, Mr Evergrim. Duplicates should be kept with the dungeon keeper at all times."

"We don't have one of those either."

"Indeed. This gets better and better."

"Piss off you two; I'll deal with her later, myself."

"Excuse me," Trudy said, looking loath to interrupt such undoubted good entertainment, but momentarily distracted by the speed of Pincher's pencil. "We've got teams gathered and waiting for swampy bulldog to start."

"Joy. Of. Joys. *Fine*." I followed her through the crowds heading for the area that had been staked out.

Two teams of craggy-looking minions had gathered and were facing off in the drizzle. A pathetic coloured flag on a stick jutted from a mound that had been piled up behind each team.

"Capture the flag—that's your objective," shouted Trudy over the noise. "No eating anyone, no serious biting, no name-calling, no immolations, and NO incantations." There were several groans of complaint. "When I blow the whistle, each team will retreat and regroup. Any unconscious team members will be removed and I'll signal for the next round. Clear?"

There was a dull murmur of assent. Many, no doubt, pondering the meaning of words like 'unconscious', 'retreat', and 'clear'. With a nod from me, Trudy blew the whistle. No sound emerged. She blew again, going red in the face and then, suddenly, a chunk of fat popped out of the hole and a shrill assaulted the air.

It was like watching two slow-moving landslides on a collision course. Shouts, growls, and screams rent the air as they met and the crowd cheered.

Helmets flew. Limbs flew higher. A small goblin flung himself into a puddle to extinguish a magical fire, and a cloud of dust and magical fog gradually half-obscured the scrum, while everyone strained for a better view, hardly able to see what and who they were cheering for.

Trudy batted smoke away and blew the whistle, and the kerfuffle eventually stopped. The blue team retreated back to their spot by the castle wall, adjusting armour and comparing dents.

Lying in a heap in the middle were most of the opposing team—bar one. The pastry chef, ladle in hand, stood alone among the fallen. Groaning trolls, whining soldiers, and sobbing goblins lay around her. She stooped down and scooped up a helmet which she then pulled onto her head, the tarnished silvery metal slipping neatly over her cornrows.

There was a collective guffaw from the blue team, many nudging one another and pointing. Coins, buttons, porn mags, and promissory notes were furiously exchanged among the watching crowd.

Dave had taken up position on top of a nearby stall, along with Gawain, and the place was so silent that I could hear him cracking his foul eyeballs.

"Hurr hurr hurr. Give up, girlie, you don't wanna get hurt, do you?" chuckled a hulking barbarian from the blue team.

"Yeah, hurt!" piped a smaller barbarian, peering round his companion.

"Just giz yer flag and no hard feelin's."

"Yeah, feelin's," came his echo again.

She stooped down, plucked up a severed goblin finger, and drew a bloody slash across each cheek. She let the finger fall back onto its erstwhile owner and then picked up a chunk of rock.

There was amusement among the crowd, and the opposing team laughed uproariously, slapping one another on the backs. Her stillness, however, was unsettling and, after a long moment, the laughter died and they began to shuffle in awkwardness and then annoyance. The crowd sensed... *something* and also quietened. It was eerie.

"Fine... go on then, girlie, I'll give you a free shot. Can't say I ain't a gentleman." He grinned round at the blue team, who, feeling temporarily buoyed up, guffawed obediently.

"Yeah, gentleman."

"Shaddup." He elbowed the smaller barbarian and then took a step forward. "Go on then. Right 'ere." He stuck out his chin and jabbed a thick finger into it.

Eyes moved to the pastry chef (assistant, to the). Her chest heaved in and out with several deep breaths, and then she hurled the rock. It sailed over the barbarian's head, and the blue team bellowed with laughter.

The rock tinked off the scrotum of a gargoyle atop the wall. With a rattle, it began to rock. And then it fell. The barbarian never knew what hit him. The gargoyle half-buried him in the ground in one crushing blow.

Silence.

Mouths hung agape—even mine.

A thick hand twitched beneath the gargoyle's bum crack. A grinding noise drew everyone's attention upwards.

In a fall that took forever and a moment, the entire section of wall collapsed onto the rest of the blue team, burying their screams beneath brick, shattering gargoyles, and rusty guttering. A cloud of gritty dust swept over the crowd.

I spluttered and buried my face in my cravat, batting fruitlessly at the thick fog of dust. "Fairies..." I managed to splutter. "Use your damn wings."

"We're on strike! We're on strike!"

Bastards. Striking should be made illegal, but someone would probably strike about it. "Fine, *die* then. But your supply of pilfered Halfling Ale will be distributed among what's left of the damn army, *especially the gnomes.*"

There was a barrage of high-pitched swearing and rude noises, and then the sound of beating wings drowned out the groans and occasional plea for help. Slowly, thankfully, with some grudging help from the warlocks who hadn't run screaming from getting their shoes dirty, the dust cleared.

I blinked grit from my eyes. Where the blue team had been now lay a sea of masonry, with the occasional limb, weapon, or piece of guttering sticking out of the stony blight.

Amazingly, the flag still fluttered from its mound, surrounded by carnage. The Assistant to the Pastry Chef stepped over the blocks like they were lily pads, darting smoothly over rubble and plucked the flag from its place before wandering back through the mess and lifting the small copper (plated) trophy from Trudy's fingers.

"And… you are?" Pincher's voice made me jump. For a brief, blissful moment I had forgotten he was there.

The girl's dead eyes lifted to him for a moment. I thought she would perhaps cave his skull in with the ladle. Sadly not.

"The new Head of the Army," grinned Trudy, eyeballing the pathetic battlefield. Pincher looked at me. I looked at the girl, then back at the vague attempts to pull survivors from the rubble.

"Yes… that's correct."

Was it? I didn't know. I was suddenly in a quandary. Did it matter? Did *anything* matter? We'd all likely be dead in a few short weeks anyway. What the fuck. Whatever.

"Yes."

"Pastry," she said.

"Ah… quite." Pincher's eyes swivelled to me. There was no way in all the underworld that I would tell him about any incident involving a weevil. I just hoped that Hammond would escape his notice until it could be realistically disposed of.

Thankfully, or not, at that moment, a piece of falling masonry pulled my attention upward to survey the gaping wound in the side of my castle. From where I stood, I could see into the dilapidated corridors, where dusty suits of armour and portraits leered down at me. Several scamps capered on the edge, tugging their ears and slapping their backsides at their audience. I hated them. I hated everyone. Most of all, I hated the scratching of that infernal pencil.

"You do know that regulations state that you need a permit for a half-derelict castle. And that whole section will require handrails immediately." Pincher tore a sheet off his pad and pressed it against my chest.

I crumpled it up, posted it into his waistcoat pocket, and pushed through the dispersing crowd to the beer tent to drown myself.

9TH JUNN

Scratching everywhere… hard, wooden walls surrounded me, no matter where I turned, and my heart was beating against my rib cage. All around me, the sound tormented me until red ink began to seep through and trail down the walls, pooling at my feet.

"Are you going to lie there all day?"

I burst from sleep to find Francis standing over me, arms folded. This was all I needed.

"Did you know that you smell?"

"You're fired."

"Good luck getting anyone else to help you in this bloody place. Who do you think carried you up here?

"You?" I sat up, my head spinning. I caught the smell of my beer-y clothes and bile hurtled up my throat. A lecture was the last thing I needed. Was she actually a denizen of the underworld, sent to punish me? I don't remember having an especially nasty time as to deserve such a thing.

"Well, no, I got Dagg to do it, but you're lucky I was there."

I struggled out of bed, gave my customary morning finger gesture to Yanna's (now defaced) portrait, and headed into my bathroom to splash water over my face. If only I could slough off the memories of the previous day as they came fully flooding back.

"I thought you were holidaying in the dungeons? What went wrong, not enough to complain about?"

"As bored as you get with red-inked reports from Health and Safety," she sniped, nodding at the heap of official notes that had somehow made their way onto my bedside table. Bastard. I was officially incapacitated; how dare he.

I shoved the door shut and stripped down, hoping she would bugger off and take her stifling cloud of sarcasm with her. There was only room for mine in this castle—no such fortune.

"Anyway," she called through the door, "you should be thanking me… I learned a lot down there."

How to die and decompose? My head was starting to throb and my mouth felt like it had been carpeted in wet dog hair.

"The prisoners in the cell next door—you know, the ones you had fed and then forgot about again…" There was a pause filled with a fug of smug. I wrapped a robe around myself and opened the door.

I would have to ask her, and it pained me.

"Well?"

"They'd been imprisoned by your parents some time ago, after all the others had been killed. Carpenters, ore experts, reporters, and shipbuilders. It was an interesting conversation. About swamps."

"The swamp? With nothing in it? And what shipbuilders?" Through the pounding headache, hope dared flicker.

"No. Swamps. Plural."

"Wait… what?" The other swamp? What the hell was she talking about? Perhaps the aroma of decomposing books and incantations had turned her brain. She wouldn't be the first one.

"There's more than one swamp." Francis let it sink in. I even forgave her for sitting on the edge of my bed. I ran for my wardrobe to throw on the nearest items of clean clothing.

"Brightwood swamp."

"That's a *tourist* destination, I should know, we got dragged there every other summer." The swamp there was purely ornamental – they had even had to import fake trees, or so I heard.

"Well, that's where they're from. Once they'd finished their jobs at the docks, those that weren't killed tried to escape but were hit with a badly constructed memory-loss spell and shipped off here."

I pondered the abilities of our warlocks and how several of them would have appeared to have lied on their application forms when what she had said hit me.

"Dockyard?"

She nodded, looking infuriatingly smug.

"That place is thirty miles inland!"

"Doesn't seem to have stopped them… your parents had a drydock of some sort constructed in the middle of the swamp."

Where they out of their minds? I sighed. I had a nasty feeling that I knew what this meant.

I looked at Francis.

"Nope, no. I'm not traipsing all the way out there to snoop for you. Send one of the misfits."

She saw my rage build. "Anyway, I hurt my leg."

Liar. My whole soul hurt, and you never caught me complaining. Much.

"How the fuck can I leave now? Health and Safety are

breathing down my neck, and everyone is on the verge of a mutiny."

"Hmm... well, there are plenty of accidents that can happen in a swamp... and besides, the minions and army are all sleeping off the fayre and in good moods. It's the talk of the town, apparently."

She had a point. I could imagine Pincher's body sinking beneath the swampy waters like a white horse in a child's book. It would give me something to look forward to, certainly. I hurried away to speak with the prisoners and then would have to organise the misfits, taking as many secret passageways as I could in order to avoid Pincher.

LATER

I sank down onto a stone bench outside the dungeon door, watching Gawain scuttle past with a tray of food (we had a large number of leftovers from the previous day) for what was left of my prisoners. It wasn't my fault. I could never even keep plants alive, let alone people. It didn't bode well, on reflection.

"Why? If the swamp at Needleford didn't ever really have any ore, why focus any activity there? Why hire experts and why pay reporters to spread fake rumours? And what the fuck did they need a shipbuilder and docks for at Brightwood?"

"Diversion. They clearly wanted people to think that there was something there at Needleford that was being hushed up. Makes the rumours seem truer," said Francis.

"But Brightwood swamp, the other place where our prisoners worked, is just a pretentious tourist area. It isn't even a proper swamp. I know, I've visited it when I was a child. My father loved all those places. Anywhere he could bring home a load of junk."

We stared into space.

"And they can't remember everything they did there?"

"No, thanks to that bad memory-wipe spell. Chakk's gone to fetch a warlock to see what they can do, but I wouldn't hold out much hope. Especially not with the head warlock still missing. The vote for the new one has been postponed for the thirty-fifth time, Gawain said."

"My parents went to so much trouble to make it seem like there were riches in one of our swamps... all it's done is rally our enemies. Their campaign of lies will get us invaded. Unless we know what the diversion was for, what's the point?"

I sighed and leant back against the wall. "Who else, besides us, *knows* that it doesn't exist?"

"No one. They're all dead or in here," said Francis.

"Why didn't my father forget the diversion crap and just mine in the Brightwood swamp, keeping it quiet?"

"The ore expert in one of the cells said there was *no* ore in the Brightwood swamp either. It was *all* a lie. There's *nothing* in either swamp. So, who knows what they were doing there? Maybe your parents just wanted to draw out your enemies?"

I stared at her. A trap? Or something else? Perhaps he had been planning something nasty. It made sense.

"Shipbuilders... Yanna found a receipt for an anchor. We don't have any ships, though."

"That you know about."

That made me think.

"Heroes are planning an attack too, the local paper said so."

Well, if my father's goal was to trigger an invasion on multiple fronts, then he had succeeded.

"Maybe he just wanted Sergi out of the way so that he could sneak into their castle and nick his stuff," joked Francis.

A sudden thought hit me like a troll on ice skates. I raced up the dungeon steps, swearing as I slipped, and wound my way through the castle until I found my mother's infernal key cupboard.

They were still on the shelf where I'd left them. A row of jars each containing a shelled crab, increasing in size. I plucked the largest down and shook it. A crab drifted into view in the murky liquid, and I turned the jar until I found the tatty label. "Hermit Crab." It slipped from my fingers, and I slumped against the doorframe.

She was fucking right.

EVEN LATER

"Say that again." Francis cupped her ear and leaned over her desk.

"You were right." I forced the damn words past gritted teeth.

"And how did your parents just expect to march into Sergi's castle once he had left it to invade us? Sergi would have left a watch or guard. They'll see an army coming a mile away, not that you've got much of one anymore. And why was the Brightwood swamp important if the ore isn't real?"

She started stitching a cover back on a tatty volume of plant remedies.

"Docks and ships mean water… there's a huge river in the caverns beneath the castle… maybe that's relevant?" I could feel things starting to form and slide together in my head. "I don't know *why* they were messing around in Brightwood swamp though. And there were goldsmiths in that cell and a number of joiners and builders."

"Goldsmiths? Is there gold in the Brightwood swamp then?" Francis frowned and winced as she pricked her finger.

"Mostly silverscale trees, same as the other one at Needleford. Well, before they were all cut down."

"Silverscale trees…" she frowned again. "Might be worth checking out."

"Fine, I'll wait."

Her eyebrows hiked. She was the damn librarian, after all. I opened my mouth to say as much when Pincher's voice drifted down the corridor. I dived behind Francis' desk.

"Hide me."

"No. Go and look for any books on those trees. Try the botanical section; just watch out for paper mites. And don't disturb Roland, he's sleeping off a trek through the library-dimension."

I stared at up at her as she began colouring in the lettering of a 'Quiet OR ELSE!' sign.

"Don't ask. Librarian thing."

I crawled off among the stacks and straightened up when I could be sure of being out of sight of the main library floor. After many twists and turns among the towering dark bookshelves, and a hair-raising encounter with a swarm of paper mites, I stopped for breath.

"Lost, are we?"

I confess to a small scream.

I looked up. Two small feet swung down from a bookshelf, and a little person dropped to the floor. He reached up to where he had been sleeping and fished down a walking cane with three clawed legs splayed at the bottom and leaned on it. I blinked at him. It had been years since I'd seen Roland. He rubbed a chubby hand over his dark brow, ruffled his curly greying hair, and adjusted his spectacles to scowl up at me.

"You've grown."

"You…" I stopped. My mother would have beaten me for such a remark.

"Say it! Say it then. I *haven't*. Hahahaha, oh, the hilarity. Almost as funny as when your parents tried to bribe me into losing you in the Grand Library at Ferndale."

Bastards.

"Now, if you don't mind doing your oh-so-important

Overlording elsewhere, I'm trying to sleep."

"Had a busy day doing *absolutely nothing*?"

"In fact, I've been hunting shredders in the library dimension. To keep us all safe. You have no idea the horrors that lurk in the average library. I'm the front line!" He slapped his chest and then dissolved into a coughing fit.

Gods help us.

"I'm looking for books on silverscale trees."

He waved me in the right direction and then scrambled back onto the shelf that he'd widened into a cubby-hole bed and pulled a patchwork blanket over him and his terrifying cane. Rumour had it that the claws had been pulled off something in the last library in which he worked, but I like to think otherwise, if just for the sake of my own peaceful sleep at night.

After a long hour, chain-browsing, following a trail from book to book, I let the last tome drop back onto the pile that I had accumulated.

Shipbuilding, carpenters, silverscale trees, and a receipt for an anchor found by Yanna, weeks ago.

I headed out of the stacks, making sure Pincher was absent, and re-joined Francis, who was reading a thick volume and sipping tea from a chipped 'If You Hate Books, You're Shit' mug.

She looked up as I dragged a chair over and sat beside her.

"Well?"

I explained what I had found. "Silverscale and redfern wood are commonly used in shipbuilding, due to their lightweight but hardwearing nature," I finished. "I think that's why Yanna discovered that the trees in Needleford swamp were all cut down. I'm guessing that the logs were shipped to Brightwood to the new docks and used to build a ship."

"Lightweight? Who wants a light warship, though? And what's the point when we're nowhere near the sea? And you can't take over Sergi's castle from Brightwood swamp, either." Her brow crinkled. "I mean, I guess your parents had it built there to keep it away from prying eyes—if it *is* true—but then what did they plan on doing with it and *how?*"

"The lighter your warship, the more you can pack it with people and cannons I suppose? I don't know," I thumbed through a book on small mammals, noting that most of the pictures had been chewed. "And, like I said, there's a river under the castle that flows out of our domain and through Sergi's. My grandfather used to insist that his chamberpot was emptied into it every morning, so that it flowed down there. I suspect that would be the best place to launch a covert invasion by water."

"Well, if they *did* build a ship for an invasion... where is it? Is it still in Brightwood? And how would you transport it *here* in order to sail down the river?"

That I did not know. The river plan would certainly explain why Reginald was faffing around under the castle when he snuffed it, though.

I resolved to make an urgent trip to Brightwood swamp. It was certainly the key to the second part of my father's plan, and it was all starting to solidify in my mind like fat in a kitchen sink. And if it meant either abandoning Pincher or otherwise leading him into a shallow but spongy grave then all the better.

10TH JUNN

I ordered Dave to make fixing our wagon a priority and then went to find Pincher.

LATER

Found Pincher in the largely unused combat training suite. He was just putting on his waistcoat, and his hair was damp.

"Busy?"

"Testing the facilities." He ignored my raised eyebrow and buttoned up his waistcoat.

"I am going on an urgent mission to Brightwood swamp. Do you plan on accompanying us? I need to know whether or not to schedule any assassins for the journey."

He gave a half-smile and shucked on his jacket. "Brightwood swamp… you should be right at home, Mr Evergrim, among the decaying relics of older times, useless swamp creatures, and flashy classless junk that only appeals to tourists. I'll leave you to it. I have work to do here."

He pushed past me with a smirk, and I struggled to process his response. How very dare he? Classless? He wouldn't know class if my cravat slipped around his neck and strangled him.

Fine. I'd be glad of the peace anyway. I would deal with him when I returned. Perhaps I could glue him to the floor of the main vestibule as a gift for Sergi when he invaded. I'd enjoy daydreaming of his torture while I sat on Sergi's throne and sipped frost wine from his famous cellar.

11TH JUNN

Gawain woke me early to let me know that the wagon was ready. I was almost afraid to look.

LATER

After gathering several bags of clothes and essentials and buckling on my sword belt, I made my way downstairs to the yard. I considered dropping into the library to order Francis to accompany me—gods know I would need someone vaguely competent—but she had already told me that under *no* circumstances was she going to 'that fucking swamp'. She also (apparently and conveniently) had a backlog of books to catalogue, an allergy to swamps, an aversion to tourists, two new papercuts, and better things to do in general.

EVEN LATER

Urgh. The wagon was waiting for me in all its tumbledown glory. The axle had been repaired with what looked like part of a flagpole, while half a stable door had been used to replace the door that had fallen off. A barbarian's shield had been used as a wheel. Weariness seeped into my bones, and every step became leaden. It would have to do.

I eyed the misfits who were lined up nearby, rubbing their eyes and yawning. This was my crack team. I was doomed.

"I hope you're all ready because—"

"Will there be toilet stops on the way?" Dave waved his hand in the air.

"No."

"Remember not to drive under an oak tree with three crows in it, it's unlucky," said Chakk, eyeballing a black cat that was lurking under a nearby ladder.

"No."

"Do I have to come?"

"No, I mean, yes. Yes, you do. Why should I bloody suffer alone?" I snapped at Trudy and she scowled at me. "Anyway, shut up all of you. We need to get out of here before—"

"*Nathaniel!*"

I jumped and an icy chill swept through my body.

Arghhhhhhhh.

I *knew* I should not have spent so much time choosing which shirts to pack.

"Why did you not inform me that you were setting off today?" My grandmother swept up with her servants in tow, dressed, once again, in tweed, with a small tweed hat perched atop her tightly coiled bun of silvery hair.

"I did not want to disturb you…"

I watched in dismay as her wagon was fetched and her bags swiftly loaded. Her servants were undoubtedly as keen to get rid of her as I was. The relief on their faces when she had been helped inside the carriage was all too apparent. Lucky bastards.

Just as I was considering where to lose her, her window slid down and she leaned out. "Get a move on, boy, the tea rooms will be out of scones before lunchtime, otherwise. Are you joining me or not? I don't want to be ravaged by bandits."

I'd be happily ravaged by bandits if it meant that I could escape her.

I took one final look at the patched-up wagon and made up my mind. Gone were the last vestiges of any belief that it would be an enjoyable break from the castle, Health and Safety, and responsibility.

I made the misery-laden walk to my grandmother's opulent ride and climbed inside to join her. She had generously made space for me amongst her many bags and was probably looking forward to berating me for the entire journey. I should have worn earplugs.

I ordered the misfits into the shitty wagon and settled back.

The carriages rattled out of the yard, and I rested my head back against the plush, velvet seat, wondering how much of the castle would be left when I returned.

My grandmother sniffed and clicked open a vast canvas bag, from which she extracted a red, diamond-studded lead. On the other end was a handbag-sized orange weevil. I shrieked and plastered myself back against the seat. She just smiled and stroked its wrinkled back. It trilled and wriggled, making me nauseous just to look at it.

"Meet Frank. Isn't he precious?" She placed it on her lap and petted it. My stomach churned, but I was barely aware of it—only a burning loathing for the smug, hateful woman. Frank had been my father's name.

We passed through countless farmsteads and settlements as we left the castle and its surrounds far behind. Only the occasional piece of rotten fruit had been thrown, which was a refreshing change. From the shouts behind us, I suspected that the misfits' carriage did not fare so well. Travelling with a well-known tyrant like my grandmother has its plus points.

Even in the opulent surroundings of my grandmother's carriage, the journey to Brightwood was not pleasant. Every pothole in the road, every corner, every idiotic swerve to miss a peasant led to a mountain of bags crashing down onto me. In the end, I threatened to jettison them, and my grandmother grudgingly had the driver strap them to the roof.

For the most part, she insisted on having her precious new pet on her lap, knowing that it disturbed me. It clicked and hissed at me, constantly. I longed to have the carriage run over it, repeatedly, but she never let it out of her sight, even when we stopped at taverns for meals. Still, thanks to the odious presence of both the weevil and my grandmother, we at least had the places to ourselves.

14TH JUNN

As the wagon bounced over potholes and the occasional furry creature, I couldn't help but wonder if I had done the right thing leaving Pincher unescorted in the castle. What would I come home to? What if Yanna came back? What if the barbarians discovered my hidden wine cellar?

I was disrupted from hateful visions of the castle metamorphosing into a giant silk cushion by my grandmother hawking into a large handkerchief. Feeling my stomach flip, I sought distraction by yanking down the window and scouring the scenery.

"Close that; I'll catch a chill."

"Doubtful, you're wearing more layers than a wedding cake," I muttered. "Besides, your 'pet' smells. It goes, or the window stays open." It didn't smell; I just felt peevish. It was just laying pathetically, occasionally twitching in a wrinkly heap. Perhaps the frilled bonnet and liberally applied scented powder had made it docile. I pressed closer to the side of the carriage. I was taking no chances anyway. I've always liked my legs.

She harrumphed and returned to her newspaper. The headlines screamed out at me:

Enchanted Apple Attacks Queen

Candlemarsh Spa Mud found to be 90% Faeces – Tourist Industry Outraged

Local Dwarf Family to Sue Overlord: Claim That Several Beard Heirlooms Damaged in Recent Skirmish

Wankers. All beards had been retrieved by an emissary of the relatives, as per dwarf code. Well, except for that one that had been eaten by a hellhound. The mutt later choked to death, but that had been little consolation. Even a stuffed presentation of its body did little to pacify the ingrates.

I had just drifted off into a dream about being buried under a stack of books about cushions when something nudged my foot. I started awake to find my grandmother's new pet chewing my boot. She was asleep, snoring. The tassels of the window drapes were jiggling in time to the snuffling pulls of breath as the very oxygen was dragged, screaming to its doom.

I booted the creature in the head and it hit the carriage wall. Its bonnet fell off and it snarled. The carriage screeched to a halt.

"Fuck." I shrivelled back against the wall as it reared up, slitted mouth opening. This was NOT how I wanted to die.

"You're going to die," shouted a voice from outside. I bolted upright and my grandmother snorted awake.

"So... hands UP."

My grandmother tapped her pet on the head with her newspaper and it settled down to a low grumble. Grateful for a diversion, I flung open the door and leapt out. An abnormally tall man was swaying on his feet in front of the carriage with a loaded crossbow aimed at the driver. A black tricorn hat was pulled down over his eyes and the cape was a riot of mud stains and rips. It looked like it had been pulled off a corpse.

"You there, you get back." The bow swung in my direction.

"Certainly *not*. We're on official business, get out of the way."

"Naw."

There was a loud snort from the direction of the misfit carriage, where Trudy and the others were hanging out of the windows.

"Yes."

"Naw."

Fuck SAKE.

"*Do you know who I am?*"

"Naw. You forgotten then, pal? You lost your memory?" The figure started guffawing in the most infuriating way and wobbled slightly. Was he drunk? It was hard to tell beneath the voluminous coat.

"Do you need me to deal with this? Can you do *anything,* Nathaniel?"

My grandmother's dulcet tones boomed through the curtains. A spike of pain lanced through my hands and I realised how hard I was clenching them.

"Move. This highway belongs to me…" I demanded.

"Naw it disnae," cut in the figure in its annoying sing-song voice.

"And—yes it DOES! And that means I can order you to move."

"Naw ye cannae."

"Yes I CAN. I CAN! I fucking *can*! I'm the Overlord. I'm the *bloody Overlord,* and that's my *bloody castle.*" Spit was flying from my mouth and I didn't even care.

"Naw it isnae, that's a pub so it is."

"Well, that's a pub, yes, but back there behind it… somewhere… is my castle—this is all MY domain. I am the Overlord. And you *will* move, or I will *have you moved* at the business end of a sword."

"Naw. We—I've got a Highway License, see." The figure held up a tattered piece of parchment, upon which had been drawn a spiky-haired portrait of a young man. "We can totally legit rob here. That's the law that is."

"I've seen more official-looking things lying at the bottom of ponds," I snorted.

"Name one."

Another snicker from the wagon behind me. Inside my

grandmother's wagon, I could hear her pet gnawing the door. An idea occurred to me. "Anyway, that license has clearly expired."

"The figure peered at the parchment and wobbled again, bending momentarily in a weird disjointed way at the midsection. In one move, I opened the wagon door, grabbed the weevil's collar and swung it. Once, twice, and then let go. It whirled up and hit the figure in the middle, knocking him over. The crossbow discharged, and there was a distant groan from a cow in the adjacent field.

The misfits clattered out of the wagon as I moved closer to the writhing bundle of cloth. The screams, oddly enough, seemed to be coming from the middle. The man ripped open the buttons, his hat tumbling off in the flurry, and wriggled out of the coat before stumbling to his feet.

I blinked.

"Oh, he's half the size," said Chakk.

"There's the rest of 'im."

"The robber took one look at whoever was still wriggling in the confines of the coat, legs flailing out of the bottom, and decided to abandon him to the weevil that was now chewing through the coat. He took off up the road in a cloud of dust.

The coat's legs kicked and gouged the ground as the weevil began to tuck into the half-hidden man. It was entertaining, but we were already running late.

"Shall we?" I picked up the crossbow and mounted the steps beside the driver.

"Errr… is that his guts?" Dave pointed. Chakk was already vomiting at the side of the road.

The driver looked at me and needed no further prompting. He snapped the reins to move the horses, and the misfits ran back to their own wagon. I pulled the traces of the horses to try and drive over the weevil but, sadly, missed. My grandmother scooped it up as we passed and the carriage door banged shut behind it. Better luck next time.

LATER

I had just started to consider that it wasn't so bad after all, being Overlord, if you just forgot about the shit-heap castle for five minutes. The rolling landscape was oddly soul-soothing—the endless greenery. It was mine. It was actually mine, and I had never even seen much of it or even appreciated it before now.

Thrusting hedgerows and dense forests smothered the landscape, peppered with houses and quaint towns (if you didn't look too closely at them, anyway). Only the occasional plume of magical smoke or a burning farmstead disrupted the blue sky. I needed to get out more often. I needed to retain a sharp mind and keen eye if I was to survive, and the calm of these surroundings was regenerating my jaded spirit. After all, what was the point of ruling if you never truly appreciated what you were responsible for.

Nothing ever lasts for long, though, and true to shitty form, the wagon rounded a corner and a man in dusty, torn clothes flagged down the driver, who stupidly stopped (without consulting me).

"All right, pal?" The voice was familiar.

"You?" I struggled to reload the crossbow before I realised I had no bolts. Buggeration.

"Dunno what you mean. Souvenirs?" He held out a chipped tray with a picture of a pretty town painted on it. Scattered over the pockmarked surface were chunks of blue, granite-like stone, some pieces of metal, a handful of spoons, and several folded pieces of paper. Tucked at the back was a broken road sign which read 'Brightwood'. I sighed, the world-weariness creeping back into my bones and driving the blue and green away.

"Did he say souvenirs?" shouted Dave from the other wagon.

"Yes, and stay in the damn wagon," I yelled back.

Too late.

"But I promised my mum I'd get her something."

"You're in luck… I got commemorative spoons, invisible beetles, and lucky stones."

The misfits gathered round.

"Why are they lucky?" said Chakk.

I pinched the bridge of my nose, feeling a headache approaching.

"Cos I found them in the graveyard. No one was using 'em, that's pretty lucky, eh?"

"You mean you nicked the grave chips from some poor bastard's grave?" said Trudy, budging Dave out of the way for a better view.

"Naw. Well… yeah." He shuffled.

"That's unlucky, moron. You'll get cursed," said Trudy.

Chakk looked at her in terror and reared away from the tray.

The man puffed in contemplation and then tipped them off the tray. "Shite."

"What are those bits of paper?" asked the driver, leaning past me.

"Don't you bloody start," I muttered. What was this, a fucking school trip?

"Those are one hundred per cent genuine licenses to rob on this bit of highway."

"Fucking drive on." I elbowed the driver and he clicked at the horses.

"Giz a lift?" called the man as the misfits scattered back to their wagon and leapt in as their driver started to urge the horses forward.

"See this?" Trudy called, sticking two fingers up as they went past. "This is a one hundred per cent guarantee that you can bugger off."

I laughed. Right until a wheel came off the wagon. The frame thunked to the ground, pulling the carriage to one side, and the driver slid into me, almost pushing me off the seat.

"We need to stop," he said.

"I refuse. Keep going."

"But the wheel!"

"Hawhaw! Where's your wheel? Where's your wheel, big man? That's a nice tricycle you've got there." The bastard was walking alongside the wagon, pointing and laughing. We would not stop if the underworld were to open in front of us. I vowed to burn something for this indignity.

The driver, sensing imminent violence inched along the seat away from me and urged the horses onward, the frame gouging a groove out of the road as we went.

LATER, JUST AFTER MIDDAY

We crawled into the town with my grandmother yelling at me from inside the carriage and the driver on the brink of a nervous breakdown. Thankfully, she was, for the most part, drowned out by the cloud of noise from the children and farmhands who had gathered to laugh us into town. Perhaps the only saving grace was that we had lost our gobby escort, who had vanished before the outskirts of the town, no doubt to saw off more signposts.

"It'll take weeks for my bones to stop rattling," Trudy complained, leaping down from the second carriage.

I had a feeling that it would take far longer for my frayed nerves to recover.

I grudgingly held the door open for my grandmother, who

stomped down the steps, swiping away my proffered hand. She snapped her fingers at her driver.

"Bags. Now."

The man moved from the wagon as if he were taking a walk to the gallows. Perhaps that would have been a mercy. He had developed a nervous tic and was red in the face. I could almost have felt sorry for him if I wasn't feeling so sorry for myself.

Turning my back before I could be roped in to help, I surveyed my own fearless team. Dusty, dishevelled, and mutinous. Not good. They were all I had, and I was damned if I was carrying my own luggage.

I took a look around. The sprawling town was just as I remembered, with its large gable-roofed houses and colourful half-timbered frontages lined with bloom-filled window boxes, and sporting ornate porches with iron railings. Upmarket, over the top, and nauseatingly chirpy. Tourist junk shops spilled their tacky wares all over the cobbled streets, while market vendors set out their stupidly expensive fruit besides cheeky chalkboard messages. Many elderly warlocks and pixies were filling up the tea rooms, chewing through plates of cakes as they sloshed tea into paper-thin cups.

"Right. Now we find our own base of operations." I shoved my bag into Chakk's arms.

"Where's she going?" Dave said, barely audible over the crunching of his candied eyeballs. I looked over at my grandmother.

"The underworld if I've any luck left."

Trudy sniggered.

"I'll be in the Bear's Arms Palatial Hotel and Spa," my grandmother called, sweeping her pet into her arms and adjusting its bonnet.

"Ohhh that's dead expensive that place... look at the gold

gargoyles they've got," whispered Chakk, breaking out in a sweat at the sight of the distant glittering gold.

"Probably fake," I said, loathing my grandmother even more. I should be staying there, but since I didn't have a team of crack guards to simply march in and demand a room from the famously terrifying concierge, I thought I would save myself the embarrassment and simmer in my own resentment instead. Gold, hot spas, and room service food that didn't mean hair on your chops. Bliss. Bliss that was not to be mine. Yet.

"Right, we'll find somewhere suitable and come back for the wagons."

"You honestly expecting the wagons to still be here?" Trudy said.

Good point.

I followed her gaze to a nearby cobbled alleyway where several grubby youths were unpacking a tool bag while one scribbled a 'For Sale - One Used Wagon' sign. I decided we'd take everything with us.

LATER AGAIN

Dave located a worn-down manor house on the fringe of town, surrounded by overgrown mature gardens and the remnants of a small orchard.

"This will do."

Dave and the misfits' driver parked the wagons on what was left of the gravel driveway, while Trudy kicked in the front door.

"Uhm… is this the best idea?" said Chakk, peering around Trudy into the dark interior. "It's probably haunted. We're probably all going to die in our sleep."

"We can but hope," I replied.

The boarded-up windows only let in a few cracks of light,

which cut across the wide entrance hall, picking out dusty bannisters and greying shrouds draped over furniture. "But feel free to sleep in the wagon, or wherever my grandmother's driver is being forced to stay."

Chakk visibly paled (more so than usual), and crept through the door after Trudy, who tried to push him away after he stood on her heels.

"Mmm... nice place this. Nice. Fixer-upper." Dave crunched another eyeball and cast an appraising eye over the hallway with its thick, peeling wallpaper and detailed ceiling cornicing.

There was a crunch as Trudy wrenched off several more planks of wood from the windows, sending light spilling over an intricate parquet floor. The once-grand place was sad, but retained a dignified air. I was surprised it had been abandoned. Still, that was someone else's loss. Dust pirouetted in the air, and a pensive musty smell made my nose twitch.

"Well... now that this place is officially ours, we should make ourselves at home. I also require a hot drink."

"Hawhaw."

My blood ran cold.

"Is it a ghost?" Chakk shrank against a velvet curtain that promptly disintegrated in a cloud of dusty fragments, dislodging several large moths. He caught and ate one.

"Sadly," I replied, "it's something far worse."

"H and S?"

"A nasty rash?"

"Same thing," Trudy muttered.

"Hawhaw!"

We moved to the door, Chakk clutching some ancient religious symbol as though the cheap metal would be any use against this hellish creature.

Sure enough, he was standing at the gateway. "A'right big

man? Mr Overlord? How's your new house?" he called.

"Fine. Bugger off."

"That's haunted that. Yous are staying in a haunted house. *Genuine.*"

Of course.

"I've got demons in my basement and vampires in my graveyard—I daresay I can handle this place," I replied, feeling smug about something for the first time in days.

"You wanna buy a ghost repeller? Three gold? That's dead cheap that," he called, waving what looked like a slightly bent metal disc.

"Piss off, we're not tourists," I shouted back. Sadly, murdering him in broad daylight would likely not endear me to the local population.

"Do you have one in another colour?" called Chakk.

"Aye... I got one in green." He rummaged in a belt pouch and fished out a greenish piece of metal.

I felt my will to leave seep out through every pore.

"Would you take two gold?"

"Where did you get two gold?" Dave nudged him.

"My nanna sent me it for my birthday."

"Yeah, but you owe *me* two gold."

"A'right, but you come and get it. I'm not going near the death house, naw. People die in there. Hear screams all the time."

"People are about to die here, too, any minute now," I shouted back.

Chakk scuttled down the path and returned two gold lighter, brandishing the metal disc.

"That's nice that," Dave poked at it. I swear he'd think a gilded orc turd was nice.

"That's mould, you utter moron," I snapped. "And now, we'll never be rid of him. Never encourage people like that. It's like feeding a dog from the table."

EVEN LATER

After tearing boards off most of the windows and de-cloaking the furniture, the place was perfectly habitable. I was actually impressed. The furniture was old but solid. Beneath decades of dust lay cherry wood and dark oak, while the walls were bedecked in regal portraits boxed into heavy, gilded frames. It spoke of a lost opulence. And, to think, the local fools had shut it all away because of a few ghosts. Waste not, want not.

A thought occurred to me.

"Dave. Once you fix our wagon, how much of this stuff can you pile onto it?"

His inrush of breath while his mind whirred was near deafening.

"Anyway," I said after thirty seconds had passed with no crescendo in sight, "I'll leave it with you."

I rounded up the other misfits, who were playing some sort of stick and ball game on a furry green table, and set off to the local guilds to make some enquiries about ships and the activity in the swamp.

MUCH LATER. BACK AT THE MANSION

"You know you'd have got further if you haven't threatened to burn the place down?" muttered Trudy, picking wood-shavings from her hair and smudging blood away from a cut on her cheek.

"I got bored of their damned obfuscation," I said, wincing over my ripped shirt. A hurled set square had very nearly sliced me open. It's amazing how riled up academics can get when challenged. Or called incompetent sponge-fornicators.

"So, they don't know anything about ships or ore," said Gawain, who had escaped from my grandmother and joined us on our afternoon excursion while she took up residence in one of the many local tea rooms.

"There are memorials in the guild chambers for missing members, though," I said. "So, something happened here. Just... what?"

Had my parents kidnapped them, killed them, sworn them to secrecy? Were some of their members the ones currently languishing in my dungeons? I knew I should have made Francis come with us.

"We didn't kill enough of them," said Trudy, cleaning her dagger on the tattered remains of the kitchen curtains. "They were bloody vicious."

"Shiny tools, though," said Chakk, rummaging in the cupboard and buffing up a copper pan with a look of disturbing excitement. I rolled my eyes.

They should be grateful I'd visited their petty guild. It was likely the most exciting thing that had happened in the last decade.

"Now what?" said Gawain.

Dave bustled in, toting a small sack, and whistling. The sound was highly offensive.

"Shopping?" Dave suggested. "I still need to get something for my old mum!"

I groaned into my hands.

"We could just go out to the damn swamp," said Trudy.

"The sign on the road on the way into town said it was closed for refurbishment," said Chakk, licking one of the pots. I hadn't noticed; I had been too busy hanging onto the wagon for dear life and wishing my grandmother would shut up shouting up at me and, perhaps, even die.

"How do you refurbish a swamp?" Gawain said, trying one

of Dave's proffered candies and then instantly regretting it. He ran to the sink to spit it out.

To be honest, I was leaving it until last, as I was dreading finding nothing. I was also dreading finding *something*. I didn't get to be Overlord by throwing caution to the wind and wanted to make sure I knew for *certain* what was out there. The last thing I needed was to get eaten by something. I'm sure H&S would have something to say about that, and I'd likely find half a dozen red-inked notes pinned to the underside of my coffin lid.

"For all we know, we could be walking into an elaborate booby trap laid by my bloody parents."

The pan clattered out of Chakk's hands and startled Trudy, who was busy rummaging through the cupboard under the sink. She banged her head, making the other misfits cackle.

"Wankers." She sat on her heels and rubbed her head. "Anyway, our wagon is buggered, and it will take ages to get out there."

Distressingly, she was right. Patience was not one of my virtues.

"We could use my grandmother's—"

"Erm, sorry, erm, sir, erm... it's gone... She's having the woodwork re-gilded over at the Wagonworks. It won't be available to you, erm, sir." Gawain was wringing his hands again.

Fuck sake. I sighed and then something occurred to me.

"That's a point, why are you here?" I asked Dave. "You're supposed to fixing our wagon. Our fate is in your hands." It was an alarming thought.

"Dinner!" he said, producing a dead chicken and several potatoes from his sack. I realised how hungry I was.

I drummed my fingers on the kitchen table.

"Fine, we'll eat and head to the library tomorrow morning. Francis seems to know bloody everything from her get-together, so we'll see what we can find out there before we make our next move or waste time potentially walking into a trap."

To be honest, I didn't give a damn about traps—that was what the misfits were here for. Truth be told, I was starving, tired, and needed time to recover from the harrowing journey, not to mention nearly being disembowelled by an enraged balding man armed with a set square and some nasty carbuncles.

15ᵀᴴ JUNN

We set off after a breakfast of pilfered eggs and produce from a local garden, and I was feeling quite positive. Dave had 'mostly' finished fixing the wagon and was tagging along, probably in the hope that we would go souvenir shopping at some point.

BRIGHTWOOD LIBRARY

"Yes?"

The small woman looked down her long nose, through a pair of copper-rimmed glasses that were perched on the end. She looked as though she was being devoured by the largest cardigan I have ever seen. The ratio of material to human was massively skewed, and the material appeared to be winning.

"We would like information."

"Come to the right place then, haven't you?"

I explained our quest, and enquired as to what she knew, if anything, about goings-on at the local swamp and any shipbuilding activities.

She sniffed and gave a sigh, indicating what a massive inconvenience it was to even open her mouth to speak.

"I know of no such activities. Ships don't generally get built in swamps."

LORNA REID

She pulled a pencil from her tightly ratcheted hair bun and scribbled a few notes in a ledger in front of her.

"You are still here."

"I'm tenacious. How about work records, expeditions, historical events in that area, magical activity? Massive unmissable deliveries of logs?"

She sniffed and stuffed her pencil into the mouth of a tiny, toad-like creature perched on her desk. It began chewing the wood with a dull grinding sound. She pulled it out, perfectly sharp. "Any relevant records, should they exist, will reside within the Construction Guild."

Damn… somehow, I didn't think they would have had time to clean up the blood from our last visit.

"As for historical events, other than the great drowning of the entire town choir at Winter Festival, and the Big Crush of '77 after the giant cheese wheel rolled over fifty spectators during the Great Cheese Chase, nothing much of note. Brightwood is a beautiful, peaceful town. Not… *grubby*." Her eyes flicked to my shirt, Trudy's cut face, and Dave in general. "It is polite, cultured, and respected. Your mother was a great patron of ours in the past. Rest her soul."

I didn't want to disappoint the woman by telling her that my mother didn't have a bloody soul. And anyway, even if she had, I certainly didn't want it resting after the inconvenience she had caused me.

"So, she can't give us any sodding answers?" muttered Trudy, drawing stern glares from a pair of dwarves reading newspapers in comfy chairs by the fire. "Let's just help ourselves to a decent wagon from somewhere and go and check the swamp for a ship."

"You'd notice traffic coming to the town, surely? Anyone bringing logs or other resources would have shopped or eaten

185

locally. Erm… miss." Gawain quivered under the librarian's well-practised steely gaze.

I wish I'd thought of those points. I had been busy thinking of all the points of all the railings I'd like to impale the woman on.

"Mrs," the woman snapped.

"How did *that* happen?" muttered Trudy. I couldn't help but let out an involuntary snort of amusement. I was starting to like her.

"Perhaps if you asked the right questions in the first place," the woman snapped. Her eyes swivelled to Chakk, who was licking the silver 'Quiet OR ELSE' sign screwed to a nearby column. I've never seen a letter opener flung with such anger, or a magpie demon move with such speed.

"In the interests of getting rid of all of you…" her eyes moved to Dave, who had begun to pick mud from the treads of his boots with a tourist information leaflet. "Yes, your parents began the restoration of the local swamp some time ago. Resources were brought in, and some locals were hired to help, although… there were several *accidents*, I am given to understand. After a particularly devastating event, in which many people died, including the head of the Construction Guild, the project was suspended."

Hah! I knew it.

"It was most distressing. Had word got out, we could have lost half a star AT LEAST in the Kingdom Guidebook."

"What—"

"If you have any further queries, direct them to the former head of the Construction Guild." She slammed shut her ledger, puffing dust into my face and stood up.

"We didn't pack a fucking spirit board." I planted my fists on the desk, but was forced to retreat when she slammed down her mug, slopping boiling tea over my left hand. "Perhaps I should have one sent to your husband—he'll soon be needing one when you sadly pass on," I snarled.

"Oak Park Cemetery, Overlord Evergrim. On Wheatfield Lane. Don't upset her; it's been a distressing enough time. I can't *imagine* what a visit from you and your cohorts will do for her state of mind."

I stared at her in confusion before it clicked. "She chose to return?"

"After your visit, she may well change her mind and choose to vacate. And on that subject, I *politely* request that you do the same." Her grinding teeth and the dangerous way she was fingering a heavy, metal stamp suggested that it was indeed time to leave.

I made sure to empty the Librarian's Benevolent Fund box on the way out.

LATER

After sending Dave back to move the wagon's status from 'mostly fixed' to 'actually fucking fixed', we stopped for food from a street vendor before wandering in search of the cemetery. At one point, we passed a newsstand, and I glanced at the headlines in the afternoon edition of the local rag:

Overlord in Debauched Palace of Lust: Brightwood Residents in Shock

Bastards. Chance would be a fine thing. I haven't been debauched for ages.

After getting lost twice, an elderly dwarf took pity on us and pointed us in the right direction. It wasn't that my orienteering skills were lax, merely that anyone would have become disoriented among the countless tea rooms and craft shops.

"This looks like the place."

"Cursed!" muttered Chakk.

"Shut up, or you'll be a bloody inhabitant, and we can cram more nice furniture onto the wagon."

"I hate graveyards; they're bad luck," he complained as we climbed the steps to the imposing stone entrance. The squat building skulked in front of the sprawling grounds beyond, poised. Waiting for fresh meat to feed its maw. I decided I hated it. What emerged was, perhaps, more offensive.

"Ahhh... visitors... welcome, *welcome*." A smarmy, oiled man in a pinstriped suit scurried out, rubbing his hands together. His beady eyes roved expertly over the group before landing back on me. Creatures like him could sense money and status. The moustachioed little weasel was sizing up how much gold I had. He was about to be disappointed.

"We are looking for information."

"But of course, of *course*. We have a great many plans for *post-death* here." A colourful sheaf of leaflets was pulled from his inside pocket in a split second and fanned in front of me.

"No."

"Insurance then, after all, we mustn't neglect the living." He chuckled to himself.

I saw Trudy's eye-roll and raised it a thousand.

"Look, Mr..."

"Vito."

"I have fuck-all gold and an angry disposition, the former mainly contributing to the latter. I do not want insurance or a grave. I want to talk to someone about the former head of the Construction Guild. I believe she is interred here?"

The man visibly stiffened and gave another sniff. Bitterness twitched over his ruddy face. I was happy to have disappointed him.

"Miss Dartmouth, I believe. You will want Franklin, our keeper. He's tending to our guests."

"The live ones?"

"Sadly not." He swept a pudgy hand, bearing more rings than anyone should be able to realistically lift, towards the doors and we passed inside.

"Erm… you okay, Chakk?" Gawain looked at the magpie demon, who was mopping his brow with a red and white spotted handkerchief.

"Those rings… so *shiny*."

"Wonder if he pulled them off or cut them off," said Trudy.

"Eh?"

"One of them was an elven wedding band—does he look elven to you?"

"That's bad luck!" squeaked the idiot magpie demon. "If you wear someone else's wedding band you're doomed to suffer bad luck."

"In his case, we can only pray," I said. "Now shut up."

We clacked across the marbled foyer and followed the gilded signs for the Gardens of Eternal Rest. I started to picture what my eternal rest would look like. At this rate, it would be a sack on the compost heap if I didn't shake loose some cash. Maybe I should have asked Vito about special offers.

"This is a posh place, innit?" said an unexpected Dave.

Trudy actually yelped in shock while I struggled to keep my surprise in. Little bastard.

"What are you doing here? I gave you a job to do," I snapped, willing my heart to stop racing. Maybe just to stop altogether.

"Mostly nearly sorted. Can start loading her up this evening, or once we get back from the swamp. Will be a bit of a squeeze, mind, but it's all good," said Dave, offering round his paper bag. "Anyway, I thought we'd be popping to one of the shops."

I rolled my eyes. They'd be the death of me. At least I was in the right place.

No one accepted Dave's offer, and he stuffed an eyeball into his mouth, shifting and clacking it against his teeth in a way that made me want to commit physical harm.

I dreaded to think what he had done to 'mostly nearly' fix the wagon, but at least there was someone vaguely competent around. I didn't feel quite as lonely. I also suspected that we wouldn't get much further with it until we'd debased ourselves by visiting one of those wretched shops.

After the cold marble building, the graveyard seemed inappropriately bright and warm. Surely there was some tedious regulation that said it had to be run-down, perpetually cold, and full of foreboding. The place was almost welcoming. I felt somewhat affronted.

"This is fancy too. Look at all the white stone," cooed Dave. "All my old nan got was a stick and a few daisies."

"Cos the town's posh," said Trudy, wrinkling her nose despite obviously being impressed.

"My nan was posh-ish," Dave said, rustling in his bag. "She had one of them clocks where the demon's eyes and tail move to and fro, and she had nice crockery. No cracks."

"Then her passing was a loss to us all," I said, feeling a headache sidle over the horizon. "Now, where's this Franklin?"

I cast around the pleasant rows of white, and occasionally blue, polished marble headstones and spotted a figure hunched over in the distance. The figure stood up from working on a grave and spotted us.

"A'right there, big man?" came a horribly familiar shout.

"Oh, fuck. Someone hide me."

Trudy and Dave shuffled in front of me but, given that I was a head taller than them (two heads taller than Dave), it had little effect.

"Fancy some lucky stones?" He brandished a handful of blue stone chips.

"Changed your mind about them being cursed then," shouted Trudy.

"Aye."

"Oi!" A voice bellowed from behind us, giving me my second near-heart-attack of the morning. "I've warned you, you little bastard."

"What you gonnae do, grandpa? Eh, hawhaw! What you gonnae do?" He cackled and mimed a doddery old man walking along before stooping down and shovelling as many chips as he could into a leather satchel.

"Bastard." The old man with spiky white hair gave a shrill whistle. Two hellhounds burst from a large white kennel beside the rear door and streaked across the graves, their clawed feet kicking up small divots.

He stopped beside me and leaned on his knobbly cane.

"Every week, that little bastard. Well, they listened to me, finally, and upped my budget. I have *two* hellhounds now. *Bastard.*" He shifted his false teeth backwards and forwards, and I felt my stomach roll.

"Ahhhh! You bastard!" came a distant screech. The yob took off with the hounds on his heels and scrabbled up and over the wall with the aid of a small garden bin, stone chips raining down behind him.

"Bastard," came the yell from over the wall. The rest was drowned out by the screeching yap of the hounds as they leapt and clawed at the stonework.

"I'll bury you alive, you little bastard, I ever get hold of you."
The old man waved his stick in the way that only enraged elderly
gentlemen do.

I wondered if he would come and work for me for free scamp
meat? He was a damn sight more ferocious than most of my
flaccid army. *Never* underestimate a rancorous old man with a
stick. My back could testify to that after scrumping in numerous
orchards as a child.

"As much as I hate to interrupt your entertainment…"

"He'll be back. Bastard. Someone's been prising the metal
row markers off the fence posts, too."

Out of the corner of my eye, I saw Chakk re-examine his
'ghost repeller' before wisely tucking it away out of sight.

"Well, I'm setting broken glass in mortar on top of the walls
tonight. He'll get a shock. Bastard."

"Miss Dartmouth—we wanted to know more about her."

"Hmm. Dead. That's about it." He flicked his teeth in and
out with a revolting sucking noise. Everyone around me cringed.
"You relatives?"

"Yes." I stuck an elbow in Dave's ribs when he opened his
mouth.

"Hmmm. This way. She's in the 'other part'. Maybe you
should have turned up sooner with a bit of gold, eh? Guild refused
to pay out of their budget—they voted to spend their excess on
new chairs instead. Bastards."

"What other part?" Trudy said.

We followed Franklin along the edge of the graves and
through a white gate in the wall. The 'DO NOT ENTER' sign
was all too prominent. Chakk started fumbling beneath his shirt
for one of his many lucky charms.

The door swung open.

"I thought stuff in graveyards was supposed to be all creaky and atmospheric?" said Gawain.

"This is a garden of eternal rest. *That's* a graveyard." The old man pointed through the doorway with his polished, twisting cane.

I believe the sun actually went down. You can't buy drama like that.

Sprawled over a low hillside of patchy, yellowing grass were graves as far as the eye could see. Sad, chipped slabs were leaning drunkenly or lying broken in the grass, while other, slightly more ambitious, tombs sulked on the hillside, with chained gates and the occasional splash of graffiti the only respite from the depressing grey stone. The sun never lingered here.

No one spoke. It was as soulless as my grandmother.

"How's yer atmosphere now, eh?" Franklin gave a mirthless laugh that had clearly been well-honed over many years and led us down a winding path and through a rusted gate. It creaked in the way one would expect, and I found myself nodding in approval. Overlords have been known to pay good money for graveyards like this.

We skirted past several open graves, and I regretted that my grandmother was not along for the walk. There was so much she could trip on.

A bundle of what I had believed to be clothes shifted as we passed and a weathered face, besieged by wrinkles, looked up at us. Knitting needles clicked in her hands. "Don't mind old Betty, she knits scarves for the dead," said Franklin.

"'Scuse me?" said Chakk, looking horrified.

The man nodded. Several tombs had scarves tied around the stones.

"Don't they get nicked?" said Dave.

"Someone tried once. They were found hanging from the lightning tree in the morning; scarf had nearly severed his head."

As one, everyone looked across the hillside's broken teeth to a bare, split tree near the distant iron gate.

This place was clearly not bucking the trend of graveyards in the realm being bloody weird places.

"Mmm... here she is. Your basic plot."

As graves go, it was unassuming, with a plain headstone and tasteful black lettering. I could feel the man's eyes boring into me—since I wanted to know more, I grudging feigned some semblance of sadness.

"Do you know who killed her?"

"Weren't me."

The misfits stared at me, and I could feel the weight of their expectation hanging over me like a pus-filled tarantula. I suddenly realised that I had no real idea of what was supposed to happen now. Did I expect everything I wanted to know to be chiselled on her headstone?

The wind that somehow had not been present in the garden of remembrance whirled around my ankles, stirring dead leaves into semi-apathetic eddies among the graves.

The keeper hawked into a handkerchief and shuffled his feet. "You gonna stand there all day then?"

"I'm overcome with grief," I snapped.

"You didn't honestly expect a conversation, did you?" said Trudy, eyeing a man in the distance who was stooping over a grave.

"Don't mean to rush your 'grief'," the man said, "but the lunch buffet starts in five minutes..."

He rolled his eyes and huffed past me. He reached out a gnarled hand and rapped on the top of the gravestone. "Hello?"

Trudy rolled her eyes.

"Oi... I know you're in there."

"Bugger off," came a miserable voice from nowhere. Chakk screamed, and even Trudy looked startled.

"There's folk here to see you, and I'm going to miss lunch," he grumbled. "You know the bastarding rules." He rapped on the headstone again, this time with the top of his stick.

Of course, there were rules. There are always rules—about everything.

I tried to remain composed as a woman apparated in front of us. She had tanned skin, straight black hair, and was dressed in a pale blue dress and hobnail boots. She wore a scowl from her almond eyes to her small mouth that made my entire body sigh in weary despondency. I resolved to pass a law in which no one was allowed to be more unhappy than I. Miserable staff were the bane of my life. I spoke too soon.

Just as the phantom opened its mouth to speak, the grave keeper yelled, scaring the living daylights out of everyone, including the ghost, who ran through Dave to hide behind Trudy.

"You! Oi, you thieving bastard!" He waved his cane at the distant figure who was scooping something into a satchel.

"Hawhaw!"

I suspected that I would be hearing that laugh in my nightmares.

"See you tomorrow ya old bastard."

"Bastard." The man rushed as fast as he could manage across the graveyard in pursuit of the fleeing figure. If I were him, I'd be setting traps. I'd be digging a pit with traps at the bottom with traps inside the traps. I suddenly sympathised with the old man. It was a rare feeling. I was glad when it dissipated.

"Don't lick my grave," snapped the ghost, taking her place back in front of her headstone.

Chakk backed away looking guilty. I can't take these idiots anywhere.

"You'll get germs. The last person that licked something here died."

"They were in the right place then," said Trudy, earning a glare.

"And did you know your dagger is rusty," she eyed Trudy's waist. "You could get a disease from that. A woman two rows over had a husband die from that."

"Just the one?"

The sound of someone clearing their throat came from behind her, and she looked even more miserable. A woman appeared, wearing the most ruthlessly sensible clothes that I had ever seen—even her leather elbow patches had patches. The clipboard, neat shoes, and tight curls told me that trouble was coming.

"Now dear… remember your induction. Let's try again, shall we?"

Perky question intonation should mean instant extermination.

"Sake," the ghost muttered. She cleared her throat and started speaking with a wailing, undulating tone. "A woman two rooows overrrrr haaaaad a husbaaaand—" She stopped suddenly and shook her head. "Look, this is fucking embarrassing; I can't do this. I won't."

The older woman clucked and peeled something off a waxed sheet on her clipboard. She stuck a sticker of a glowing ghostly caterpillar to the front of the younger woman's dress. It read 'Good Effort!' The caterpillar's annoying grin was making me angry just to look at it.

"I used to be a bloody academic. Head of a guild. I refuse to do this."

The older woman cocked her round head to one side. "You'll get there, dear. But you won't get to level two apparition status unless you meet all the requirements."

"I want to go home."

"You can't leave your place of interment until you are at *least* a level five entity. And then only on probation."

"I wish I were dead," she muttered.

A strange noise made the woman's head swivel in the way that only an elderly woman's could, such as when a cat was about to be sick on some prized piece of furniture. "Stefan, put *down* that bioluminescent ectoplasm, it isn't yours."

"And it's unhygienic—they drink it all the time."

"Ah, shaddit." There was a hideous burp.

"And look!" The woman's chest puffed up beneath her pearl-buttoned cream shirt. "*What* is that phantom doing with that planchet?" She marched off, purple tweed jacket flapping.

One glance told me that it was something far more unhygienic than drinking ectoplasm going on. You wouldn't get this sort of behaviour in the Garden of Remembrance. Dave and the other misfits were staring, open-mouthed.

"You have to get me *out* of here," the ghost pleaded.

"We came in to find out who killed you and why. And to find out what the fuck was going on at the swamp."

"Oh, *did* you… I'm amazed anyone cares. Do you know what it's like here, do you know how filthy everything is? Do you know how late the catacomb ghosts stay up, getting smashed on the weird supernatural secretions down there? This whole place is an abomination."

"It's supposed to be."

She seemed to be under the impression that I was someone who cared. While the graveyard keeper vanished over the horizon waving his stick, and the tweed ghost lectured a transparent young man wearing a planchet on his nethers like an absurd, oversized erotic wedding ring, I could feel my irritation rising.

"I don't care. I want to find out what you know."

She glared at me, and then I saw a half-smile that I knew meant trouble.

"It'll cost you."

"What? What the hell can you spend money on, even if I had any, which I don't."

"Get me out of here."

"I thought you couldn't leave."

"I read the whole stupid book that I got on my induction day…" she wiggled her fingers into quotes. "I haunt this grave. The stones here are part of that. Take one with you, and I can probably go with it. Loophole."

I had to admit it was genius, but I was reluctant to pick up another party member with issues. There was only really room for my issues. However, I sensed I would have little choice.

Also, the castle didn't have any proper ghosts, so it would perhaps raise our standing, and at least she wouldn't need feeding. On that note, perhaps I should just kill everyone in the castle?

I considered what it would be like to watch the whole thing crumble down on top of every last miserable minion and staff member… a hot flush of pleasure passed through me but, of course, was not permitted to last long. Something told me that Francis would only end up surviving and filing a whining complaint about damaged books or something.

"Sounds good. I wanna get out of here," said Trudy, scooping up a smooth green stone from the grave.

I pinched the bridge of my nose, just wanting an easy life. "Fine. Fine, fucking fine. Shall we leave?"

MUCH LATER

The wagon was apparently fixed enough to get out to the swamp, so we parked up as close as possible, given that the road had been blocked by two huge boulders. I prayed that it was still there when we returned. That said, given that one of the wheels hadn't been properly secured, any would-be thief would likely not get far.

"Where's this swamp then?" Dave said, after approximately ten seconds of walking, craning around as we headed into the trees along a rough path.

"In that direction, I should think." Trudy pointed at an ornate sign with swirly writing, which read 'Swamp – It's Deadly!'. Under it was pinned a notice with stern warnings about dumping rubbish and lighting barbeques. At this point, I could happily have upended the whole castle into it.

So much for a distressing trek through deadly swampland. The neat, stone-lined path wound its way through uniform trees, many of which had warnings about swamp beasts, which used far too many exclamations marks for my liking. The thickening mist was a blessing, really. Until I tripped over Dave, who had tripped over Chakk.

"Get a room," sniggered Trudy, hauling Dave up as I dusted myself down.

"Urgh…!" came Chakk's strangled cry. If he couldn't take someone of Dave's stature falling on him, then he was pretty bloody flimsy. "Monster! It's the curse!"

We all stared past his quivering finger. It was a painted wooden monster. Lizard-like, it appeared to be breathing fire that had been half snapped off—presumably by the same vandal who had daubed spectacles and a monstrous phallus on it. Gods, I fucking hate tourist resorts.

"The sign says to check it off our scavenger list, did anyone get one?" said Gawain.

Everyone looked around; Dave even checked his pockets. Urghhhh. I pushed past, wishing I didn't need any of them.

"I don't remember this place being so misty," I said, after a time. It didn't seem like a real mist… the faint blue tinge told me that it was magical. So, someone had conjured it for a reason.

LATER STILL

The reason became clear as we passed the dick-daubed monster for the fifth time.

"Someone find *something*," I demanded. "NOW!"

"There's an old cake packet on the floor," Dave offered.

I rubbed my temples.

"And something's pissed up the fence over there..." said Chakk.

Rubbed harder. Wished for death.

"And there's a bloke over there buried under a bag of firewood," said Trudy, pointing.

Rubbing suspended.

There was indeed a lanky man, whose limbs and head were protruding from beneath a huge sack of charred wood. I did what any curious person would do in such circumstances and sent someone more expendable to investigate. Trudy swore as she stumbled over a tree root and poked at the man.

"Oi," he muttered. "Bloody help me up, eh?"

"Is he dead?" called Dave.

"He wouldn't be bloody speaking, would he?" snapped the ghost. "Anyway, I'm the only dead one around here."

Not for long, at this rate.

Trudy rolled the bag off and hauled the man up. He was dressed in an alarmingly garish orange tunic and black trousers, with an upside-down name badge on his chest.

"Hiroki." Gawain read the badge.

"That's me. I work at Fingal's Fingers Art Supplies. Oh, I saw your face on a mug the other day," he said, peering at me.

"Lucky you," I said.

"Don't s'pose you seen a dock around here?" Dave said, offering him an eyeball. He took it and rolled it around his mouth.

"Yeah, what's left of it. That's where I got this stuff." He motioned towards the bag of charred wood. "We sell it to the tourists as premium charcoal art supplies 'from the heart of the Brightwood Swamp'. They can't get enough of it."

"Nor can you, clearly. Show us where it is," I ordered.

Dave offered another eyeball and the man, perhaps realising that we weren't a threat to his art operation, conceded and led us through the undulating landscape, eventually emerging from a break in the trees.

I could understand why he had a never-ending supply of charcoal. In the middle of a vast clearing was a dockyard. Correction… were the blackened remains of a dockyard—more of my inheritance up in smoke.

LATER AGAIN

I sat on a blackened stump by what was once some sort of outbuilding and tried to stop the nervous twitch that was developing in one eye. Somewhere behind me the misfits were playing some sort of bat and ball game with charred pieces of wood and a large skull.

What in the underworld were my parents playing at? Not for the first time, I wished them back to life so that I could slay them. I tried to think back over the things I may have done in my past to deserve such a fate and had to stop, as the list was rather overwhelming.

Why build a fucking dock and burn it? Was it because some idiot built it in a swamp, inland? It would explain why everyone connected with it was dead or imprisoned— that level of incompetence beats anything I have yet had to deal with, which is saying a lot.

Something in my nasty guts told me that it was something more.

A skull whistled past my left ear and thwapped into the muddy fringe of the swamp. Gawain ran to pull it out, battling a small green tentacle that had reached out and coiled around it. A tug of war commenced.

I decided to leave them to it and wander along the ruined shore, kicking over pieces of timber and squashing any tiny wood fairies that scuttled out. It made me feel a little better in a way that only casual cruelty could.

The ones who avoided my heeled boots swarmed up and, by the time I'd reached a blackened fence around the remains of a building, there was a cloud of them trying to spit in my ears and nip my face.

I swatted them away, and my foot hit against something. I plucked it from the ash and realised that it was some sort of glass dome. What it was for, I had no idea, but what it *was* useful for was trapping several of the more tenacious fairies. They batted against the glass, chittering obscenities, while I flipped open a few trunks that I'd had Dave haul from under a heap of timber.

"Nasty little buggers them, ain't they?" said Dave, tapping the glass. One of them kicked at his knuckle, and another pressed a tiny pair of buttocks against the inside of the glass. "You should pour some water in there, like, and make a snow globe. Be unique that. Nice and fancy. My aunt had one like that. Only her fairies were dead. Her dog knocked it off the shelf and broke it… you wouldn't believe the smell."

His droning faded into the background as I stared at the glass dome. I felt something move in the back of my mind again. Before I could catch hold of what it was, it slithered back to the depths.

"Place has rather gone downhill since I was last here."

I looked up to see the phantom woman glide through several pieces of burned furniture.

"Where are the ships?" I said.

"No idea," she replied. "And I have other things to worry about. You know… like being dead."

"Maybe they burned the ships too," said Trudy.

Why would my parents waste our resources? Were they stupider than I thought? Something told me that it had been the opposite. I had always thought myself smarter than them. After all, I always avoided their traps, and they fell right into mine. Now, however, I was having to reassess. It was like having teeth pulled. And not in a nice way.

I decided that I'd had enough. I snatched the miserable ghost's stone from Trudy and strode out of the hut, batting away several more fairies as I marched to the edge of the swamp.

"What are you doing?" demanded the ghost.

I held the stone out over the swamp mud. It was time for answers. My boots were ruined, and I had a headache and several fairy bites. I was no longer in a gaming mood. And my parents' grinning faces were haunting me. Taunting me. "Tell me everything, or you'll spend eternity here."

The ghost looked furious. "How *dare* you threaten me?"

"I'm the Overlord, remember. It's my job."

"I want to lodge a complaint."

"Tell it to the swamp mud."

I could feel the misfits' eyes pinging back and forth between us. Silence. A silence broken only by rustling paper and cracking eyeball sounds.

"There were two ships here. All fancy. Lots of gold."

Everyone's attention snapped to her, and I felt my heart jolt. I had to stop myself from screaming in joy! All rustling, sucking, and cracking stopped. Even Chakk stopped licking a charred signpost.

"Gold? How much gold?"

"I don't bloody know. It was everywhere. I've never seen

anything so *tacky* in all my life," she snapped.

"Or death," Trudy remarked, earning a foul look.

"Yeah, rub it in. You'll be dead too, one day."

"We can but hope," I snapped. "Anyway… the gold?"

"I told you; it was everywhere. Gold busts, gold mastheads, gold cannons, gold fixtures and fittings, lamps… you name it. Someone claimed they even saw a gold chamber pot in the master cabin. Disgusting display of wealth." She folded her arms.

Son of a demon. That's where they hid it. All this time. They hid it in plain sight. They didn't store the damn stuff, they *made* things with it, *coated* things with it. Gold.

"The shipbuilders were always arguing with your father's advisors, about how low the ships were riding and how much water they'd draw because they were so heavy," the ghost added.

I looked over at the ruined docks, half-expecting the ships to materialise in front of me, to the sounds of glorious and uplifting orchestral music. Only the plopping sound of a tentacle retreating into the swamp with a fairy in its embrace broke the stillness.

So, where were they? Did they get so heavy that they sank in the swamp? I looked over the filthy water, with its tiny clusters of muddy land and tenacious trees, stooping to sweep the surface. The thought of having to drag something out of this mess was more than depressing. Before I could run through the possibilities of who I could force to do the work, Dave cut in.

"So, did they sink or what?"

"No idea," said the ghost. "Last I saw, everyone who worked here was rounded up. Some were killed, others escaped and were later caught and shipped off somewhere. Probably to some dungeon."

I thought about what remained of those in the castle.

"I hid under a wagon and watched their big fancy warlocks swish through here and start messing about on the docks. Didn't see what happened after that. I made a run for it with a couple of carpenters."

"So… I have some of those escapees in my custody just now?"

"What's left of them," muttered Trudy.

"They were hit with a bad memory spell, I heard. One of the low-level warlocks botched it. It's why some retained their memories."

Warlocks. Hmmm. Arrogant pains in the neck, but very useful. I'm amazed my parents got them out here. Anything that even suggests that their robes and cloaks might get dirty usually leads to instant revolt, sulking, and protest voting.

If they got the high-level snobs out of the castle and out here, then it *must* have been serious. Big magic. Perhaps it explained the absence of the ships.

"They make em lighter or something?" Dave said.

"No idea. You'd have to ask the big head warlock that was strutting around here. He was in charge of the magic when he wasn't complaining about his purple suede shoes getting ruined." The ghost rolled her eyes. I knew how she felt.

"Maybe they're invisible?" said Gawain.

We stared over at the ruined docks.

"Invisible stuff still burns. No, they've moved them, somehow. They had to have done, before they destroyed any evidence as to their existence." I pondered for a time. "You've been incredibly helpful." I told the ghost. I had to say I was surprised. People actually being useful and proving their worth was something of a rarity.

I considered hurling the ghost's stone into the middle of the swamp anyway, but I know one of the misfits would tell Francis and I would never hear the end of it. Besides, she may still have useful information. And the castle really did need a ghost. It would, perhaps, get us an extra star in the Kingdom Guidebook next year. It would bring us to a grand total of one star.

Just as I was handing the stone back to Trudy, a tentacle whipped out of the lake and snatched it away, vanishing under the mud with a foul sucking sound. The ghost screeched in horror.

Bugger. Bye-bye, guidebook star.

Trudy stared at me and then everyone else. They clearly blamed her. Good.

"Ah well; you win some, you lose some."

"You not trying to get it back so she isn't stuck here?" Trudy said, glaring.

"Why would I do that?" I marched away, determined to interrogate the head warlock about the ships. Now I had purpose, and confidence was surging through my veins. Now our enemies would look out. Even if ~~my parents' ships~~ my ships would take an age to actually get anywhere. We now had a solid plan. Secret, gold-laden ships, designed to sail up-river and invade Sergi once he had been lured away from his domain by the lies about valuable ore. Now I just had to *find* the ships.

Howls of rage from the ghost fell at our heels as we made a hasty retreat, passing several chancers with sack loads of 'art supplies', busy shaping charcoal into sticks and slipping them into colourful packaging.

TOURIST TAT SHOP

Given the good news, I had to give in. I wanted to make sure that morale stayed high, since the plan was within a gnat's hair of being put into action. I hated myself.

It was what I imagined the underworld to look like. Nauseatingly jaunty—bright walls with flimsy, over-saturated wall hangings depicting famous landmarks. Rows of identical resin figures from history stood stoic on shelves, decked in hand-lettered signs 'ONLY 1 GOLD!!!!!'. 'LIMITED EDISHUN'. 'BUY NOW!!!!' Below them were pewter trinkets in wicker trays, sword letter openers, miniature treasure chests, collectable dwarves ('each one has a different scowl – collect 'em ALL'). It was depressingly endless. Junk as far as the eye could see. How any customer was supposed to move among the racks of saucy-elf postcards and baskets of crystal fortune-telling orbs (glass) was beyond me.

I had sudden visions of being trapped under a cascade of badly embroidered parasols and cock-eyed stuffed toy orcs and turned to make an exit.

"Cor... it's nice in here, ain't it?" Dave was barring my way, eyes wide as they soaked in all the tourist 'treasure'. "My old mum would love this place."

I watched them fan out, cooing over flimsy wooden shields and clay towers ('NOW WITH FREE WRAITH!!!'). Trudy skulked near the postcard rack, pretending not to eye up the nudes.

I pondered, momentarily, what life would be like with a crack team of bodyguards and trusted assistants. Assassins, engineers, wizards, and strategists. Instead... I had *them*. It was no wonder I was doomed to fail.

"Look, this orc's nadgers are poseable!" Chakk shouted across the shop. Two elderly halflings with curling white toe hair fanned their faces and looked shocked. Trudy sniggered.

"You break them nadgers, you buy 'em, you hear?" snapped the towering shopkeeper, planting his fists on the cluttered counter. His blue apron was bristling with daggers, and I wondered just what level of violence he expected in a tourist tat shop. But then, after just a few minutes of being there, I was feeling inclined to severe violence myself. On myself, mostly.

"Sven, don't be rude—that's our new Overlord." A curly

white head popped around the doorframe and a wrinkly face split into a beaming smile. Recognition. Finally. The man grunted and gave a curt nod.

"Ma'am," I smiled. I could use all the support I could get.

"I'm just unpacking the last of the new Overlord steins now!" The woman bustled out of the back room, wiping her hands on a floral apron.

"They mostly got your nose right."

I felt everyone study my face. The two elderly halflings leaned around a rack of grotesque door knockers and stared at me. It made my skin start to itch.

"Hopefully you won't be assassinated before the ink dries on the posters." She pumped my hand and scuttled back into the bowels of the shop. "We're very honoured anyway, dearie," she called back.

I blinked. I never pictured my face on crockery before. It felt... odd. My father's face had appeared on a privy seat cover that my grandmother had specially made, however. I also once had a school bully threaten to quaff ale from my skull. But this was bizarre. Still, in an odd way, Snipper, the barbarian scourge of year five, would get his wish. Not that he could drink now. He mysteriously had his mouth stitched shut on a school trip to the Firewalls of Blight. Tragic. On a completely unrelated note, hiding a spool of thread internally was not an experience I'd like to repeat.

I decided to move away before I was asked to sign any tawdry relics and found myself confronted by a window display of snow globes. I couldn't help but lift one. Inside a glass bubble was the famous upside-down shrine of Kalen-Vale, built by ancient druids during the Mushroom Renaissance. It had been crudely hacked out of red clay, had paint thrown at it, and been glued to a baseboard. Dandruff-y flakes lay in repose over the miserable scene, and I was moved to give it a shake.

The lazy swirl eclipsed the building and, for a moment, I was thrown back to my childhood. I collected a snow globe from every location my family visited or conquered. Every quashed township, every tedious holiday destination. They lay somewhere in a cupboard in my old childhood bedroom. For a brief moment, I wanted nothing more than to be back there, when the world was someone else's problem.

Something at the back of my mind nagged me but refused to be coaxed out, and I set the globe back with an odd moment of sadness.

A calloused hand reached past and snatched it back. "Ohhh, this is nice," Dave cooed, peering into the flakey swirl with a moronic grin of delight. "My mum'll love this."

"How are you paying for it?" I enquired, as he pushed past Chakk, who was browsing through a large basket of lucky charms, and slapped it on the counter.

"I got gold saved. My old mum ain't getting any younger. Gotta save for a nice headstone."

"Well, we all have to have goals."

Why did everyone have more money than me? Still, I'd rather burn it than spend it in this place.

Unable to take any more, I left the misfits to their wandering and headed back to our makeshift domicile. There was a queue at the gate. Apparently, no one was prepared to venture closer. Expecting trouble, I sighed. I had on a clean shirt, and rotten fruit plays havoc with silk.

"Yes?"

"You're the Overlord... erm... sir?"

"Last I checked, yes." I eyed the barbarian at the front of the line. His hulking frame in battered armour was becoming a less common sight in my castle. The ones who hadn't drunk themselves to death had mostly departed for better-paying jobs. Some had returned, however, having got lost on the way, or else sobered up and forgotten what they had left for. And that was just the ones who hadn't had been too stupid to find their way out of the wine cellar in the first place; having a pull door that is marked 'push' has likely been the culprit.

"Well, I'm looking for a placement."

Perfect. Then a sinking thought sidled into my brain.

"Sadly, we have gold issues at this moment in time." I held my hands up as a groan passed along the queue. The barbarian, an elven archer, and two orcs left, heading for the nearest pub, dragging clubs and shields behind them.

I surveyed what was left. Two mucus demons, three little people, a drunk blacksmith, a water terror, and a nervous-looking pixie who was being eyed-up by the mucus demons, one of whom appeared to be measuring her with a long, stale bread roll.

"And we have no food either," I said. The bread roll snapped shut, and the two corpulent mucus demons slithered away, muttering in wet baritone snorts. As vile as they were, like bags of wrinkled yellow-green flesh dropped from a height, it was a shame. They were excellent fighters, with black horns and powerful arms (not to mention their vile flatulence) and my now-depleted army could do with a boost. If only they could be relied upon to eat weevils. It took a rich Overlord with a large food supply to sustain the damn creatures.

The pixie waved her hand. "Ah, do you possibly have gardens?"

"Of a sort... they've become... somewhat out of control." It was a gross understatement. Images of the sprawling mass surrounding most of the castle flashed into my head. She looked pleased and smoothed down her patched green-and-blue tunic and straightened her pointy green hat.

"I'd like to apply for Head Gardener. No gold needed." She waved off my protest.

"*Everyone* wants something."

"Just a garden. Maybe some good fertiliser." She gave a beaming smile. It was unnerving. No one I knew was that happy.

"We have a well-stocked compost heap. Plenty of corpses."

She mulled over the possibilities and nodded.

"Fine. You're hired. Fall in." I jerked my thumb back at the house, and she walked tentatively down the path, eyes darting everywhere.

"And you?" I addressed the three little people dressed in cream trousers and red and white striped jackets with wide lapels.

"We require a stage," said one of them.

"A what? Who are you?"

"We're 'When the Going Gets Gruff'—the Brightwood Barber Quartet."

"There are three of you."

"Yes, Jeff spontaneously combusted last week. That's the third Tenor in two years."

"Reeeessttt…"

"Hiiiiissss,"

"SOUUUULLLLLLL!" The three joined together in chorus, sweeping their straw hats off and clutching them to their chests as they looked skywards. Yanna would have loathed them. She had once told me that she was allergic to musicians.

"Hired. Fall in. Don't expect gold."

"We work for tips. And maybe fried rat tails."

I didn't like to tell them that the last travelling players to visit the castle were tipped with the shrunken heads of another group. They headed towards the mansion, pulling their jaunty-coloured wheeled luggage behind them.

The drunk blacksmith (who appeared to have a hammer

tangled in his wild beard) and the water terror (dressed in thigh-length leather boots and a dark tunic, with a nasty curved sword on her back) enquired as to the availability of a warm forge and a dark river respectively and wandered down the path, once I had confirmed the presence of such things.

The blacksmith took several attempts to climb up the two steps to the front door. He eventually had to be rolled through by the terror, her pale aqua skin flashing orange with the effort. In the end, she flicked her blue hair back over her pointed ears and stepped over him, making sure to squash his nose as she did so—more fine additions to the forces.

Half an hour later, after the misfits had returned, loaded with tourist tat, I was regretting everything.

The quartet of three was performing a series of disgusting-sounding vocal exercises in the hall, the drunk blacksmith was arguing with the bannisters, the water terror was sitting on the kitchen counter with her feet in the sink, and the gardening pixie was passing around some suspicious-looking herbal cigarettes to the misfits who seemed delighted to have more company. They hadn't yet realised that it meant less room on the wagon, especially if Dave had managed to get anything on there. Why do I do this to myself?

After putting up with the chatter for as long as I could bear, I decided to vacate the best seat by the fire and hunt for any hidden vaults or safes. The basement was the most likely place to yield riches.

The door opened with a suitably impressive creak and I descended into the musty gloom—the cold driving into my skin, even with a flaming torch in my hand.

Aside from an impressive wine collection I didn't have time to notice much due to the fact that I nearly walked into a fucking HUGE giant tarantula nest. I was still slumped in an alcove, having palpitations, when whispers reached my ears and the sound of scraping. I started to think that perhaps I was hearing things—that's stress for you—but crept to investigate, nonetheless.

It was ghastly. Vile. Just… hideous.

In a large chain of storerooms at the far reaches of the basement was a small stage, lit by magical lanterns. Mismatched chairs and tables were crowded with an array of chattering creatures wearing the gaudy trappings of tourists. Tat-shop bags lay under tables and hung on chairs, and pixie wait staff whirled around tables, serving colourful drinks with olives and fairy skulls poking out on little sticks. Two trolls in suits guarded a staircase, presumably leading to an illicit entrance.

Was it some sort of secret gambling den? Had I lucked out?

No.

No, I hadn't.

Sadly not, because life is just not that *fucking* generous. As soon as a sleazy-looking young man, with a gap in his teeth you could drive a medium-sized wagon through, sauntered on stage and swung a speaking cone on a stick in front of him, I had a sinking feeling.

By the time he was two minutes into his comedy routine about singing vegetables and halfling pubic hair, I wanted to commit serious harm, not only to everyone in the room who was guffawing at him, but to myself for not immediately setting the whole place (and myself) on fire to erase the audial assault.

Of all the illicit dens of iniquity that an Overlord could be blessed with on holiday—gambling clubs, risqué sex dens, advanced torture classes, kinky pottery sessions, pyromaniacs anonymous—what did I get? A fucking ghastly alternative comedy club.

By the third act (best joke being when he accidentally fell off stage and broke his back), I had to leave. I barely made the stairs before vomiting onto a lurking tarantula. It scarpered. So did I.

Trudy dragged me from the stairwell, dagger drawn.

"I heard screams."

"That was me. It was terrible."

I explained the terror that lurked beneath our feet and she paled, her purple hair seeming to deepen in colour. She immediately offered to set fire to the basement, or "drive that fucking scum out", but I did not want to risk our temporary home. Her desire for extreme violence, however, was something of a turn-on.

We settled with cutting the tarantula nest loose and using a tarpaulin to help roll it down to the end of the cellar before giving it a few kicks and running like buggery.

When the final nail was hammered into the boards that covered the basement door, I breathed a sigh of relief. I have had some unpleasant experiences in my time, but an underground stand-up comedy club was one of the worst.

In a moment of weakness, I was tempted to invite Trudy to join me upstairs to test the new bed but, sadly, she had already headed for the kitchen to explain where the rumours about ghastly noises and cackling had come from.

I decided to get some fresh air. I stepped over the now-sleeping blacksmith who had a smouldering cigarette in one hand, and a hammer clutched possessively to his chest with the other, and found my way through the house to the backyard. I nearly had a heart attack at the beastly sight lying in wait.

Once I had recovered myself enough to swing a lantern up, I realised that it was our wagon. Or what remained beneath the contents of the house that had been secured on top of it.

Dave had clearly taken my orders to heart. Now fully fixed, the whole wagon looked like a deformed, kleptomaniac snail. I had no idea how I was supposed to get inside, but I was impressed.

There was even a velvet upholstered fainting couch strapped to the rear windowsill. Several dusty curtains were wrapped around a large wardrobe which was acting as a surface for all the other furniture piled on top of it. In one half-open desk drawer, I could see a collection of gilded door handles and hinges.

He had certainly been thorough, and I was actually impressed. I tried not to let the fact that the wagon was now sinking into the mud, due to the weight, fragment my mood and headed inside to crawl into bed.

16TH JUNN

It was the second-best night's sleep that I have enjoyed in a long time, despite not actually having a bed (or anyone with whom to share it). The four-poster from the master bedroom had been somehow disassembled by Dave and loaded onto the wagon, so I spent the night in a nest of plush blankets in an armchair and awoke just after dawn to the sound of banging on the front door.

LATER

My arm is killing me from signing so many limited-edition Overlord mugs for one of the more enterprising tat shops. Once the old lady had gone merrily on her way to accost some early rising tourists, I was able to get to the kitchen where Dave was frying a brace of rats. Chakk was crunching on a couple of deep-fried tails and flicking through the morning paper, which I relieved him of.

Local Man Moves Into Giant Clam

Overlord Seen Mourning Dead Parsnip

Jam Fight at Local Tea Room – 7 Dead

I shook my head at what passed for journalism and scoured the pages for anything relating to the swamp and our visit. Nothing. Good—if word got back to my enemies, it might prompt them to attack sooner than they clearly planned to. I had to get back and speak with the warlocks. I wanted that gold.

It was time.

Sadly, our departure was delayed by the fact that no one could leave the kitchen. The door handle had been removed by Dave during breakfast and added to our haul. Trudy and the water terror ("call me Millie") scrambled out of the window, while Chakk tried the back door. It collapsed inwards and fell on top of the sleeping blacksmith. He snuffled and turned over, never even removing his thumb from his mouth.

LATER AGAIN

Outrageous. Having to hang around, waiting, while my grandmother poured herself out of her third tea room of the day and finished terrorising the local traders over prices of cocoa beans and gaudy statues was not something I wanted to be doing. It was beneath me to wait for anyone.

I considered abandoning her. While I was contemplating her likely reaction, I was accosted by a group of townsfolk. At first, I thought they were adoring peons; however, their complaints soon put paid to that.

I was bombarded by all manner of whinges—when was the

swamp going to be properly restored, what was I going to do about unclogging the main sewer, why has no one dealt with the problem of tourists taking home pieces of the cobblestones as souvenirs… and so it went on. Taxes, state of the roads, lewd behaviour from tourists using the local hot springs for inappropriate purposes, mucus demon faeces exploding in the summer heat…

I was displeased at having my good mood fragmented. This was *not* how I wanted my trip to Brightwood to end. So, I invited them back to the castle for a discussion and locked them in my grandmother's carriage with her pet weevil. I gave it a good ten minutes after the screams had stopped to take a peek and concluded that I would be taking my own carriage home, furniture laden or not. Several onlookers rushed away, so I decided that it would be best to make myself scarce. I don't want to demoralise any townships who may then be motivated to offer assistance to either Heroes or rival Overlords.

MUCH LATER

I closed my ears off to my grandmother's ranting and watched, smirking, as her driver and an unlucky passer-by were press-ganged into cleaning up her carriage and disposing of the body parts. My own team of misfits and new recruits (they caught on quickly) were hiding under our carriage or in pieces of the furniture piled on top of it to avoid being drafted into the clean-up crew.

It wasn't the only thing angering her to the point of foaming incoherence.

Having accepted defeat as far as space went on our wagon, Dave, under express orders, had utilised all available space on my grandmother's. Several carved cabinets were strapped to the roof beneath a pyramid of fine chairs, while other bits and bobs hung off the side so that it now resembled an overladen packhorse.

It was most satisfying. If I had known it would annoy her this much, I'd have had him load up twice as much. I was also pleased to note that he had thought to remove the fine porcelain sink from the master bathroom and strap it to the back. The kitchen one had been too heavy to move, apparently.

As her helpers finished sluicing out the wagon, several enterprising locals swooped on the pile of severed limbs and gobs of flesh and carted them off to the small alleyways that backed onto some of the higher-end restaurants.

I leant on the carriage window sill and took one last look around the town. It was far nicer than I remembered, but sadly, I had an evil domain to run, so I couldn't linger as much as some pathetic part of me wanted to. Overall, it had been a good trip— my grandmother's inconvenience was merely the delicious icing.

I grudgingly allowed Gawain and Trudy to slither into the wagon through the other window, past an overhanging sofa and some fireside tools, while the others rode in pieces of the strapped-on furniture or squeezed in beside the driver.

"Are you going to move that eyesore or not?"

I looked over at my grandmother's wagon and smirked.

"Drive on." I banged on the roof of the carriage.

I plonked my feet up on a small sewing machine and closed my eyes and ears to her shouted abuse. Trudy and Gawain started playing with a pack of dog-eared cards and the misfits outside were singing along with the not-quartet as we trundled slowly out of town.

Could this be contentment? Not *yet*. I suspect that it's more gold-coloured, but this was perilously close.

EVEN LATER

As the wagon pulled into a siding for the driver to take a short break and for some of our new recruits to sneak into a nearby field and steal a few more horses to help pull the wagons, I decided to stretch my legs.

"Hawhaw!"

Shit. I considered making a run for it, but it was too late. I rounded the end of the wagon, narrowly missing losing an eye on a table leg, and saw the bane of my life surrounded by the misfits, with the exception of the blacksmith (snoring in a wardrobe on the wagon), and Trudy, who was lurking nearby, arms folded, but interested, nonetheless. The pixie was sitting on Chakk's shoulders for a better view, while the not-quartet was perched on a rock, craning to see.

This time, the annoying chancer had a more ornate tray with a tea-room name emblazoned on it. Scattered over the surface were a number of squashed cakes, stones, and what looked like street cobbles.

"Them's genuine!" he said, nodding at the cobbles. "Take a part of the town with you. That's dead lucky, that is."

Eyebrows were raised among the misfits, and they began scrabbling in pockets and purses. Why they didn't just help themselves when we were actually *in* the fucking town is a mystery. There is something about a tat seller with a tray that turns people's heads.

"I forbid anyone to throw gold away on cobbles," I said. There were several despondent looks, and Trudy rolled her eyes.

"How about some lucky stones then, Mister Overlord?"

Everything was lucky, it would seem. I was amazed he wasn't selling lucky bottles of horse urine.

"What's that one?" Trudy asked, succumbing to her own interest and wandering over to examine the stones.

"That's *really* lucky that one."

Colour me fucking surprised.

"Genuine haunted stone."

Everyone but Trudy backed away. She narrowed her eyes. "It looks familiar. Where did it come from?"

"I'll sodding well *tell* you where it came from." The ghost apparated next to her, and Trudy actually screamed. My laughter earned a withering glare. The pixie toppled off Chakk's shoulders in shock, while the thud from inside the wardrobe told me that the blacksmith had woken up with a start and then regretted it.

"It took me *ages* to figure out how to get back to the bloody graveyard. And then I got a written warning for absconding. I'm supposed to report to the management next Friday now."

"You buying or what?" The chancer leaned past the ghost to look at Trudy.

"I'm not for sale," snapped the ghost.

"Hawhaw, but your stone is."

"Not now, it isn't." Trudy snatched the stone off the tray, gave the thief the finger and walked back to the wagon, now-smug ghost in tow.

I took great pleasure in letting the dust cloud from the wagons envelop the annoying bastard, and we headed back down the road, with another passenger on board. At least it wouldn't cost anything to feed this one.

19TH JUNN

Thankfully, no one had been eaten or killed in my absence, and only Francis griping about mould and a shortage of tea was there to greet me. According to her, Pincher was out inspecting the grounds. With any luck, he'd fall into or onto something deadly. I had sent most of the misfits off to help the new additions settle in and to show the new pixie to the gardens and the mammoth task that awaited her. I seriously doubted whether we'd see her again. If nothing ate her on the way there, then she'd likely become lost in moments. Trudy, however, I trusted to go and spy on Pincher, to check he wasn't stirring trouble.

In the meantime, I poured out our findings to Francis over a cup of tea and a thick biscuit from a tin that I had decided to requisition for her at the last moment (from my grandmother's shopping)—she is one of the few competent staff members I have, and the only one who will at least pretend to listen to my woes.

Never underestimate the effect of a pretty tin of biscuits and a large mug of tea on a crabby book-person. It had a near-instant calming effect, and I was able to glean much gossip.

"So, are my quarters currently papered in notes from dear Mr Pincher?" I blew steam off my tea and shifted in my overstuffed chair.

She puffed. "No idea. He has been in a few times."

I bet he has. Any woman who can kill a book thief with a well-flung library stamp is instantly alluring, in spite of her incessant complaints.

"He spends part of his days down in the combat training place. I heard he's quite muscular, works up quite a sweat."

"Heard or spied?"

Her face went bright red, and she busied herself by rummaging in the biscuit tin.

Hah!

Well, she needn't get too attached to the image of the man working out... he'd be on the compost heap with the rest of them as soon as I had resolved my other issues. She could watch his alleged muscles slowly decompose.

After telling me that the warlocks could be found in their grand chamber, holding a round of votes, this time on who was Head of Tea Selection, she headed off to lecture Gawain, who was opening a book too much that it risked bruising the spine.

Looking at half the books on her to-be-repaired pile, a slightly damaged spine was the least of her worries. Blood is not an easy stain to shift, and as for repairing teeth marks... I dropped the last book back onto the pile and scrubbed my hands on my waistcoat. Urgh.

I leant back a while, enjoying the peace—something I'd not enjoyed for days. So, of course, it had to be ruined.

Trudy strode into the library and her gaze lit on me. She motioned me back, and I frowned. I realised her warning too late and, with a roll of her eyes, she stepped aside to let Pincher past.

"Mr Evergrim. Nice holiday?"

"Passable. Nice snoop? Killed any joy, lately?"

"There appears to be an issue with your... ah... thing."

I felt heat rise to my cheeks, and my fingers dug into the arms of my chair. How fucking *dare* he!

Trudy sniggered.

How in all that's unholy do these people find these things out? I hadn't bedded anyone since Yanna, sadly.

"I absolutely do NOT, Mr Pincher. It is likely a vicious rumour spread by my former and hopefully-soon-to-be-dead mistress."

Confusion cycled across his bright eyes before morphing smoothly into realisation and then amusement.

"No no no no no..." he said through a poorly masked grin. "I was referring to a creature known..." he riffled through a thick wad of notes attached to his clipboard. "...as Hammond."

Buggeryfuckanation.

I cleared my throat. "Uhm... yes... yes... no... erm, do we?" My face was refusing to de-redden. Trudy's open smirk was not helping.

Pincher's smirking stare was also doing nothing to mitigate it. A fact of which he was well aware. In a panic, I looked again at Trudy and Dave. One sighed, and the other shook his head and drew in a familiar, rattling breath.

"Well… if you want it to stay in the pit… then, nah. But if you want it out…" Dave's words hung and twisted slowly in the air like a condemned pirate.

"It's eaten itself into a coma at present, anyway," said Trudy, folding her arms. "Not a problem."

"Not *quite* true," Pincher said, paging through some notes. "It needs to be properly domiciled, as should all minions."

"Ain't a minion, is it? Warlocks wouldn't like that." Dave popped an eyeball in his mouth and clacked it around. Pincher wrinkled his nose.

Those fussy, snobby bastards don't like anything.

"You will need to do something with it."

"Well, why don't we make the pit 'is home… chuck a few cushions in or summat?"

"Sadly, given its apparent growth rate, it needs a larger domicile with better facilities," Pincher said.

"Yes, let's wallpaper a fucking suite for it while we're at it," I raged. "I'll pay for a sodding mosaic floor and diamond fixtures."

"What if it ain't a minion, then…" Dave wondered.

"Then it needs to be promptly disposed of," replied Pincher, smirking.

"How many victims did it claim?" I asked.

Trudy shrugged.

"Thirty-one and a half. I knows because I won half a magazine an' a goat hoof ashtray from someone on a bet," said Dave. Pincher's eyebrows twitched upwards. He had made several enquiries as to the whereabouts of his goat but, sadly, no one knew. A tragedy. A tasty tragedy.

"Bollocks. I refuse to spend any lives on its destruction. We'll attempt to move it," I growled. "*Someone* will get to work on it right away."

Without turning, I snapped out a hand and grabbed Trudy's collar mid-escape. I dragged her back and shoved her towards Dave, who'd also been about to make his escape, but wasn't as quick off the mark as Trudy.

"You're on the Hammond removal squad."

Trudy scraped a strand of purple hair from her eyes. For the first time, I noticed that they were a fetching shade of lilac. "Are you serious? HOW? Where are we even going to put it?"

"Decorum prohibits me from making any suggestions."

I rubbed my hands together, feeling good about myself. A problem offloaded is a problem vanished. "Oh, if you intend to supervise the proceedings, Mr Pincher, then you should be careful. It would indeed be *tragic* if something were to happen to you."

I shot him a smirk and sat down at the desk to pour myself another cup of tea, listening to them leave.

LATER

Read papers. Wished I hadn't.

Wear-Your-Neighbour's-Skin-to-Work Day a Moderate Success

Overlord to Holiday in Swamp

Several Tourists Missing After Spider Rampage at Brightwood Comedy Venue

I binned them and began browsing in the stacks, trying to ignore

Francis' complaints to Roland about the secretions emanating from some of the older, demonic volumes, when Pincher arrived back.

Sadly, there was no time to hide. Still, the spectacle turned out to be worth it. He was covered in mud, and one arm had been torn off his jacket. There was a thin cut on his cheek, and his usually tidy hair was dishevelled in a way that, as much as I hated to admit it, oddly suited him.

"You're looking well, Mr Pincher. Busy day?" I moved to greet them and made sure to display my amusement in the most irritating way I could.

"I took a tumble into Hammond's pit."

And he survived? Why do the gods hate me so?

"Oh *dear*." I clucked my tongue in mock-sympathy. "How did *that* happen. More to the point, how did you get out, and how can we stop that from happening again?"

"A flagpole fell down and just sort of knocked him in," said Trudy, flicking her hair back and shrugging.

"Must 'ave been the wind," Dave volunteered.

Pincher turned to fix her with a fiery stare. "Yes," he said slowly. "A flagpole which seemed to have five fingers and a palm."

He got nothing but a look of bored disdain as she fiddled with her black fingerless leather gloves.

Perhaps I had underestimated her. While Pincher brushed mud from his clipboard, muttering under his breath, I glanced at Trudy. I have never seen her smile, but it was so fleeting, perhaps I imagined it, and the wink that followed in my direction. I was impressed. Not something that happened often—at least not around here. I would also have to watch my back. I did not need any assassination attempts to add to my woes. Although the thought of wrestling with her was... appealing.

"And yet, alas, you survived, Mr Pincher."

A glare. "Fortunately, I was shielded by the corpse of an orc, and the thing's previous meals had also made it sluggish."

"Well, I hope that you haven't damaged our newest addition to the roster, Mr Pincher, or we will have to file a claim with your superiors."

Trudy's snicker gave me a dart of pleasure, as did the look of utter loathing in his eyes. He was about to retort when Francis stormed over, a book from the high-magic section dangling from one hand.

"*What* is that?" she jabbed a finger at the mud on the floor. I don't know how she noticed it among the general dust and debris of the library floor, but there we are.

"A gift from Mr Pincher."

She eyeballed him. "Are you going to clean that up?"

It seemed that Pincher had had about as much as he could tolerate for the day, what with being covered in mud, losing half his jacket... oh, and nearly being eaten.

"Would it honestly make a difference in here?" he snapped in a rare moment of lost composure.

She puffed up, and Trudy and I shared a look and stepped back.

"Well excuse the *fuck* out of me, but we aren't quite up to H and S' palatial standards here," she snapped back. "Perhaps if you pull that stick out of your arse for five minutes, you could attach it to a mop head and do something useful for once in your officious little life."

Whooooa.

Trudy gave a silent fist-bump to the air.

Pincher squared up to her, fists balled, chest starting to heave. This promised to be glorious.

Sadly, before a full-scale row could erupt, there was a scream from somewhere up in the stacks on the upper level, followed by a roar. Heads spun. No one was stupid enough to move.

"Kill it! Kill it!" screamed someone.

"Run!" came another distant screech. A volley of magic erupted, sending light spilling from the upper level. A large bolt of magic suddenly exploded from between the stacks and whistled down, heading directly for Trudy.

Francis reflexively whipped up the book she was holding and, in a flash, the bolt ricocheted away and knocked an elderly warlock off a distant ladder.

Everyone stared at her. She lowered the book and examined the scorch mark on the linen cover. "Well. Bugger."

LATER

I dragged Gawain with me up to the warlock's chambers. He could help deal with the awkward bastards. He was the only magical person that I vaguely trusted at this point and, even then, it was a stretch.

I hadn't been up to the warlock's chambers in years, and nothing had changed much, there was just slightly more dust. Plush furnishings, expensive wood panelling, and chairs so vast and soft that you could lose an army down the back of one. Rich colours and the smell of old magic abounded.

Many of the magical blowhards were lolling in chairs, mouths gaping in sleep, while others sat around a large table, squabbling over tea, cake, and crockery. Arseholes. Elitist bastards.

"Greetings, Overlord Evergrim." They stood as one to welcome me, and I considered that I had, perhaps, been too harsh.

A few minutes later, after finding out that they could not help me, however, I decided that I had not been harsh enough. In a rage, I upended several chairs and their inhabitants. Even Gawain flinched when I lit a taper and held it to an opulent velvet couch.

"*Please*, Overlord, we can't help you! None of us were there that day. Only those hand-picked by the head warlock were taken on the special mission," pleaded the snivelling warlock who appeared to be in charge, trying to move between me and the couch.

"What mission?"

The man wrung his long white beard and looked at his fellow spell-slingers for aid. None was forthcoming.

"We don't know... *we* weren't chosen."

Bitterness laced his tone. I respected that. I knew that feeling all too well. I lowered the taper a little. There was a collective sigh of relief.

"And those who were?"

"Were never seen again. We were told that their wagon veered off a cliff and there were, sadly, no survivors."

"How tragically inconvenient," I snapped, waving the taper.

"Am I interrupting, Overlord Evergrim?"

"Always, Mr Pincher."

"Good."

He moved to join me, hair wet, presumably from bathing. The ruined jacket was gone, leaving just his waistcoat and shirt. He folded his arms and scowled around, eyeing the warlocks who were clustered together, muttering under their breath and glaring at me. Many were still asleep, despite having had furniture upended on them.

"If you wish to discuss our newest addition to the minion ranks, however, now is NOT a good time."

He looked at the taper and then at the trepidatious faces and nodded.

"Fire safety checks," I said, glancing his way, daring him to interfere.

He nodded again. "Quite right. Although... if you wanted

better results, I would say that you should start with those volumes there." He pointed behind the warlocks to a shelf of dark leather books with silver embossed spines.

The barely-concealed horror on many of their faces told me that they would be appalling card players.

"Thank you, Mr Pincher." I smiled and moved towards the shelves. It seemed that his bad mood over his near-death experience made him more amenable to boorish behaviour.

"G-go ahead and burn them!" trilled the stand-in head warlock, voice cracking as he forced restraint. He wrung his hands and bounced on the balls of his feet.

"They're old volumes, third editions, worthless anyway, sir." I read the panic in his eyes. *Feasted* on it.

"Hmm…" Pincher moved through the crowd and pulled a book from the shelf. "First edition, I think you will find. *Demonix Heartland Volume II*. Each first edition said to be hand-made from the skin of a crawler dragon. Rare. Exquisite. *Dangerous*." He turned to stare at them. Many flinched, several shuffled away from him.

"They're extinct!" squeaked Gawain, wide-eyed.

"They are indeed." Pincher slid the book back and stared at the pale, shocked faces of the assembled warlocks once again.

"How… how would a simple Health and Safety man know about… *that* book?" breathed the not-head warlock.

"I'm starting to think that there is nothing simple about Mr Pincher," I said, studying him. What may have been a smile flashed over his face and was gone. I stowed the thought for another time.

I pushed past the warlocks, and they screeched, uncertain of whether to challenge me to save their books or to stay away.

"Wait, sir. I have remembered something."

Of course.

"Indeed?"

"Ah… the head warlock was the only survivor to return. He received a handsome wage thereafter and moved into a large suite."

"Yeah, he's a right snob," muttered Gawain. "He rejected my application eleven times." Several warlocks sneered over at him, and he shrunk back, stroking his hair down and tugging up the hood of his frayed cloak.

"Anything about ships? Anything brought home with him?"

"He had a small box. Would not let anyone touch it. Something glassy was inside I think because he nearly dropped it when he slipped on some scamp mess downstairs," said the not-head warlock. "Which reminds me, Overlord… about the issue with scamp mess—"

"Nope." I pushed past him.

A quick search of the missing oaf's luxurious chambers turned up a box at the bottom of a wooden chest. Inside were an empty glass dome and several small discs of marble.

"Looks like the one Dave brought a couple of fairies home in, sir." Gawain tapped on one. "He was gonna pour whiskey in there with some troll dandruff to see if the fairies lasted longer."

The image flashed through my mind. Dave, the dome, the trapped fairies and the improvised snow globe. Then the tourist tat shop. And suddenly I was five again, travelling home from Brightwood after a long summer break, clutching another snow globe for my collection. A collection that lay in my old chambers gathering dust. Long forgotten.

No.

No. Surely not.

Bastard geniuses.

In a daze, I wandered back out of the bedchamber. The warlocks were busy hiding the rare books behind several other books. Pincher watched with a vaguely disgusted look, shaking his head. I liberated a brace of fine vintage wines from the warlock's extensive rack, and then, since they were too busy to notice me, I dropped the taper on the sofa. I tossed a bottle to Pincher, who caught it with surprise, and left the warlocks to their panicked screams while I made my exit.

With a look at me that seemed to be a blend of amusement, faint respect, and physical exhaustion, Mr Pincher left us to continue his inspection of the grounds (or the bottle, no doubt) while I hurried inside. Gawain vanished at some point, probably to go and tattle-tale to whoever would listen.

MY CHILDHOOD QUARTERS

Dust whirled drunkenly as I flung open the moth-eaten curtains and let in the afternoon light. It was as I remembered it. A quilted duvet decorated with embroidered swords and torture devices, atop which lay Mr Boo, my faithful toy ghost. Shelves trailed around the room, laden with books and ornaments, and the occasional trophy from school.

But I had no time to reminisce.

I yanked open the large, ornate cupboard that lined half of one wall and there they were. Shelves of tat from tourist destinations across the lands, from family holidays long since faded into the lost halls of memory. In pride of place were my snow globes. Except two. Those… looked different. New.

I took one down and shook it gently. Blue-tinted snow whirled up around a fine, warship with gold fixtures. At once, a magical aurora of blues, greens, and gold shimmered over the backdrop, picking out the glittering parts of the ship and dazzling me. I could sense the magic; it made my hands ache.

Here. Finally. This was how I was going to win. All along, it had been here. Correction: *they* had been here. I lifted down the other one and bound them both up in several old cloaks from my chest.

Now what?

Of course, *I had to show them off.* And then it suddenly occurred to me that I had no one with whom to share my treasures. An odd feeling of sadness stirred inside me, but I trampled on it until it died and then headed off to find someone to show off to. For some reason, my feet led me to the library.

LIBRARY

"You again?"

"Lovely to see you too, Francis."

She looked momentarily taken aback by the use of her name.

"You look like the cat who got the cream."

"Gold-top cream." I smiled, laying my precious bundle on her messy desk.

She finished stamping a return date into several books on pest management for the new pixie and then flopped into her chair.

After waiting for the pixie to drag the books onto a long board on wheels and push them away, I took one more look around to make sure we were not observed and then gently unfolded the cloth. I took a breath and waited. Francis looked at me, and then back at the snow globes. And then back at me.

"And?"

"Don't you know what this is?"

Why couldn't she just be happy for me and like my things?

"Cheap tourist tat. Please don't tell me that you paid for those."

"This is it!"

She looked at me as if I had grown a second head.

"The ships. From the swamp… my parents hid them here. It's how they could transport them all the way from Brightwood."

Realisation.

"Bloody hell, that's smart."

Yes, it was. I had to give them that. Albeit grudgingly.

"So… I'm guessing they used the warlocks. So now you have to just get them to unshrink them."

Ah. I had not thought as far ahead as that. If I had known, then I would not have set anything alight in the warlocks' quarters.

Francis must have seen my expression because she stopped examining the globes and sat back.

"What have you done?"

I told her.

She shook her head and then covered her face.

"Urghhhh." Her voice was muffled by her fingers and the chunky skull rings.

I explained that the warlocks who had been present at the time had been conveniently disposed of anyway, bar the head warlock.

"Erm… Mr Overlord, erm, sir…"

Gawain. Harbinger of doom. I watched him sidle closer, paper in hand. I felt a tidal wave of despair move towards me.

"What now?"

He cleared his throat, gave Francis a terrified look, and then handed me the paper.

"Nathaniel," I read aloud, "why did you not inform me of Sergi Grimhaven's impending invasion? You know that I need time to pack. I have been told by my knitting circle that his army set off yesterday. Deal with this *immediately*. Also, I am missing a tin of biscuits. Have you seen it? Your ever-patient grandmother."

"She also said to give you this, sir." The worm handed me the evening papers. On the front page was a picture of the morons at the local Heroes' Guild, decked out in their armour, posing in front of the local tavern and signing autographs. Utter, *utter* bastards.

Francis appeared beside me and read the headlines. "Guild poses with adoring locals before setting off for historic invasion. 'We aim to be hanging our washing out on the castle battlements in three days, including lunch breaks,' says guild leader Clementine Sandbank."

She rolled her eyes. "What a tosser. And that cape is far too long to be practical in battle."

I couldn't really speak. My body appeared to have seized up. Although my testicles had no trouble vanishing inside my body in terror. Invasion? From two sides? Wasn't there some sort of rule? I mean, this was my first time as Overlord. "This isn't fair!"

"Erm… Sergi's forces will also reach our domain in around three days," said Gawain, trembling.

I looked up, barely registering Trudy and the rest of the misfits arriving. The looks on their faces told me that they already knew.

"We running or fighting?" said Trudy.

I looked down at the snow globes.

"I have found a way out. A way for us to launch a counter-invasion."

Looks were exchanged, and the little surge of power that it gave me woke me a little. This was my time. This was my chance to prove myself as Overlord and lead my people, however ragtag, to victory.

"Really?" Dave said, a crooked smile spreading over his stubbly face.

I showed them the snow globes and explained the situation, including the unlikely idea that the warlocks would help. "We need the head warlock—he likely masterminded the magic that did this, and the others are all dead. However, he's not been seen for days."

Trudy suggested that we start investigating. I concurred and sent Dave to help round up, fix, or steal enough carts to pack up what things of value that we could find and ferry them down into the caverns beneath the castle. Francis had a fit about not leaving the books and would not be pacified until I promised at *least* one transport made available for her to load up with books.

As Trudy, Gawain, and I set off for the warlock's chambers, she vanished into the stacks with a small hand-pulled child's wagon, yelling for Roland to move his backside and help her. It was a 'Code One', apparently.

WARLOCKS' QUARTERS

Every window was open, but the smell of smoke lingered, along with the acrid smell of singed robes. It appeared that, although the books were important enough to save, several slumbering warlocks were not. I received several sulky glares from those not on ladders, scrubbing the sooty ceiling with wet brooms.

I explained the predicament.

I received bemused looks.

I explained again, louder, and more violently. Several pieces of furniture moved from survived, to deceased.

When Trudy suggested that we ban suede from the castle, they were more forthcoming. The head warlock had still not appeared, and he was likely the only one who could help.

"We have no idea as to his whereabouts, Overlord. It is as inconvenient for us, we can assure you. He was supposed to take charge of ordering in this season's wines from Mothweald, and choosing the location for the annual warlock ball."

"Riveting. Where was he last seen?"

"Uhm, he went out weeks ago for his usual morning stroll, taking his book. He liked to find a spot in the gardens to sit and read."

A nasty, needling feeling spread up my chest.

THE HERB GARDEN

"Shit."

We stared down at the decomposing remains of the head warlock, pinned by an ornate chair to a bed of herbs.

"Why the fuck did he have to have been sitting here?" I raged. Did everyone die just to spite me? Worse, there was no one else that I could blame.

"Now what?" said Trudy, picking up a soggy book and examining it.

"Now we have two ships full of gold and a way out of this place but no way of accessing any of it." I kicked at the chair and instantly regretted it, as my toes bent back. I uttered a small scream.

"Can't the other warlocks sort it out?" she asked.

"Not if they don't know how it was done. Anyone else who was there died," said Gawain.

"Can't they just figure it out, for fuck's sake?" said Trudy. "I mean, their bloody lives depend on it too."

We both looked at Gawain. He shuffled and fiddled with his colourful hair. "Uhm… they are a bit distracted at the moment, and it would probably take them ages to nominate someone to take charge, then they'd hold a few votes and then probably argue over who gets to do the good bits of magic…" He looked thoughtful as he ran through the whole likely scenario while I lost the will to live. Then something occurred to me.

"You."

"Wh-what?"

"You. Magic. *You* bloody do it."

Trudy looked at me as if I'd gone mad and Gawain started trembling. "B-but I'm not a warlock."

"And? I don't give a rat's knackers what title you have. Your so-called label does not bloody define you. You managed to infect the whole bloody castle with giant weevils…"

"That was an accident," he muttered. "I was practising a transformation spell."

"Perfect."

"Yes, but…" he sighed, giving up trying to argue.

Trudy edged closer. "This wise, Overlord? He could turn those ships into weevils or something weird."

That was a fair point. But not one that I wanted to hear.

"We'll get the globes down to the river and then work out the next step. Anything you need, we can take from the warlock's quarters."

I had to practically drag him through the castle, made harder by the throngs of panicking minions and clusters of whispering staff. The news of invasion had clearly spread.

The dank passageways ran past the cellars and abandoned storage rooms, and opened up into a large cavern cut down the middle by the vast river. Luminous spindly vegetation grew by the black waters, while flickering magical lanterns hung from mouldy wooden posts marking a wide path along the riverbank.

It was satisfyingly dramatic.

"Someone's been busy," I noted, as we approached two long wooden spits thrusting out over the water. These certainly were not as mouldy and rotten as the rest of the castle. It occurred to me that the banging and hammering from the reconstruction work on the west wing, which wasn't far from this place, was not all it seemed—the perfect cover. Again, perhaps I had underestimated my parents' planning skills.

The bones lying around the docks suggested the reason as to why it had remained a secret.

"Smells funny down 'ere, don't it?"

Trudy screamed.

Gawain screamed.

I screamed.

"What the buttery-fuck are you doing here?" I demanded, clutching my chest. Dave shrugged and offered round his paper bag. There were no takers.

"Rustled up a few carts."

Good. Something was going to plan, at least.

"Miss Francis took 'em, though. Said it was 'Urgent Library Business'."

Fuck's *sake*.

"Still, I banged together a few somethings out of a couple of wardrobe doors and some dwarf shields. It'll do."

"Fine," I pinched the bridge of my nose, feeling my old friend headache on the way. "It isn't as if we have much worth bloody taking with us anyway."

I placed the cloak down on a barrel and removed a globe before we walked along the nearest dock, the boards creaking as black water lapped at the posts. The boards were strewn with coils of rope and some odds and ends of metal. It was about as tidy as the rest of the place.

"I don't think I can do this." Gawain looked as though he wanted to either puke or run. Probably both, actually.

"Yes, you can."

"I can't... I can't do it with everyone watching, anyway."

"Can you be killed or tortured with everyone watching? Because that's what will happen."

Dave and Trudy nodded, and he grew even more pale. He lifted the globe from my hands and gave it a shake. The magical aura swirled around the ship trapped inside, and everyone shuffled closer.

"Corrr…" Dave was so mesmerised he didn't blink when a drunk fairy crash-landed nearby and vomited onto his boot. The glowing green mess spattered the boards—nasty little things.

I booted it off the dock and opened my mouth to issue orders to Trudy to fetch whatever Gawain decided that he needed from the warlocks' quarters. I never had the chance, because the next thing I knew, an enraged fairy divebombed me.

Everyone batted and swiped at it. Gawain swore and ducked and, in one heart-stopping moment, slipped on the fairy vomit. The globe flew out of his hands and smashed against some metal scrap.

Noooooooooooo. No. Nonononono.

Trudy punched the fairy out of the air, and we clustered in horror around the smashed globe. The magical glow was growing in intensity, the liquid from the broken globe seeping across the wooden boards, reflecting the strata of magical colours.

Gawain drew a sudden breath and grabbed the ship. He threw it into the water. I screamed again, clutching my head. "What have you DONE?"

"You might want to back away, sir."

There was a burst of rainbow magic, and a ship erupted from the water, no longer tiny, no longer imprisoned. It lunged and rolled drunkenly, water cascading from the decks. A large wave hit us full-on, sweeping us into the water.

The shock of the freezing water was instant, and I barely struggled to the shore. The others hauled themselves dripping from the river, Gawain hauling Dave, who was still clutching his candies.

I looked back and watched the ship lurching and settling, water running off the masts, the furled sails, the decks. In the lamplight, the gold masthead of a mermaid shone. The more I looked, the more details I could see picked out in gold.

Yes.

I laughed. An odd feeling came over me. Happiness.

"We going to check 'er out?" Dave said.

I wished we had time. But we didn't. I wanted more than anything to roll around in a gold bed, with gold curtains, and pick my clothes from a wardrobe with gold doors.

I directed Gawain to take care of the other snow globe, and he vanished along the river to the second dock. There was a large flare of magic and a second ship burst from the water—a matching pair.

But of course, I was afforded little time to gloat. There was an odd screeching sound that was all too familiar, and several weevils slithered through a large crack in the wall.

"It was the magic that drew them here... run!" Gawain bolted, and we squelched after him, no one daring to look back.

Somehow, in the confusion, we took a wrong turn and ended up in a series of storage chambers. Light filtering in from a grate high up, coupled with a smell of flowers told me that we were beneath the front of the castle, near my grandmother's flowerbeds.

"Here." I ran for a screen of broken crates and heaps of spoiled flour. The rumbling grew closer. I'd rather go out on the point of a sword than be torn apart by some vile weevil. "If we die here, I'm holding you personally responsible." I jabbed a finger at Gawain.

He stared down at his hands, and, for a moment, I thought he was about to cry. My lip barely curled in disgust when he stood up and, with all his might (not much), flung a large ball of magic. It surprised even him, and he stumbled back and fell on top of

Dave. The magic whistled across the dank room and through a doorway into the next chamber.

A sickening mass of wrinkled, screeching weevils tumbled into the room and chased the magic. Everyone huddled up and prayed until the sounds receded.

"Help me." Gawain pinched Dave's arm and ran to the door.

A suicide?

Between them they pulled the heavy door shut and I sat on a crate and watched Trudy help them pull sacks and boxes across the door, giving me occasional foul looks. The last thing I needed was splinters.

"This probably won't hold them," she said, leaning down to heave a final sack onto the heap blocking the door.

"Long enough for us to get out of this place," I said.

"They've got stuff to eat with these old sacks and whatnot," said Dave. "Make 'em happy for a while."

We made a hasty exit, blocking the outer door which was, fortunately, metal braced.

Now we could get out of here, and there would be a lovely bonus waiting for Sergi in the cellars once he got here. The thought warmed my freezing wet body all the way back up into the castle to direct the evacuation.

21ST JUNN

Panicked minions, arguments over luggage, a (failed) attempt to board my grandmother up in her quarters, and other stressful things all filled my time. Pincher hovered around, watching everything, and I had to get the army to help the warlocks ferry their magical books downstairs. There were several clashes with Francis, who was also press-ganging people into service moving books from the library. More than one fistfight broke out between her helpers and those of the warlocks. Francis was terrifying when books were in danger, and I stayed clear.

After using some tacky slime to seal the doors to my grandmother's chambers shut while she was packing, I made my way through the oddly quiet castle to the lower passages where the minions and troops were gathering, bundles of property (some was even their own) slung over their shoulders. I was joined on the way by Pincher. I should have sealed him up, too. Still, decks were slippery, and anything could be made to happen before we reached Sergi's castle.

For some reason, Francis was flapping around near the entrance to the river cavern, screeching at two hastily departing soldiers as others flowed or staggered past. One pair of enterprising barbarians were carrying a liquor cabinet between them, while a drunk fairy rode on top.

"Why, in buggeration, are you not on board yet?" Looking at the riverside, it appeared that no one was. The misfits were idling nearby. All they had to do was board a damn ship. Walking up a piece of wood is apparently too much for them, and I'm not even surprised. Not in the least, and I haven't even the heart to be disgusted.

"The bloody wheel's broken off the cart," she stormed. From somewhere atop the wagon of books came the sound of Roland's snoring. His feet were just visible poking over the edge.

"And? Their army will be on our doorstep within the hour. Get on the damn ship, or we'll sail without you."

"I *won't* go without my books."

Pincher stepped in to try and reason with her, and I stepped back. He grabbed her arm to pull her towards the river, and she doubled him over with one punch, clearly beyond reason. My heart skipped in one weak moment of attraction.

"MY books, and fine. Sodding well stay then," I shouted.

I pushed past her and clattered along the dock, shoving aside several older or injured minions. "Why is no one on board?"

"The guards said we wasn't allowed yet!" said Chakk, staggering under a ragged knapsack with bits of shiny metal and odds and ends poking out.

What guards, what was he babbling about? I looked towards the end of the dock. For some reason, the ship was already pulling away. Was I mistaken? For a moment, I thought that Dave or some other incompetent had failed to moor it properly. And then I realised that it was far, far worse.

My heart plummeted. Across the increasing gulf of water, a familiar figure appeared, looking over the rail. Thin, terrifying, and expensively dressed. For a moment, I thought I smelled cushions.

"Thank you for this parting gift, my darling." Yanna's voice cracked across the black water, each word cutting into my soul.

"You're *actually* stealing my ship? My gold... my everything?"

"What's yours is mine." The chiding mockery made me want to scream.

The former Head of the Army sidled up beside her and slid a proprietary arm around her shoulder, earning himself a slap. He snivelled and cowered away.

How?

"How the—"

"You really should have sealed up the Hero tunnels under the west wing, darling. And I'm offended that you didn't bring my painting with you..."

It hit me—that *cursed* painting. She'd used it to spy on me. I *knew* I should have taken a knife rather than a black pen to it. A moustache and demon horns are nothing compared to gouged eyes and a slashed neck.

"You..." words briefly departed in fear, like tides sucking away before a tsunami.

DIARY OF AN EVIL OVERLORD

"Fired, divorced, dead, dismissed, over, out, fired, fucking GONE!"

Her smirk gradually faded into the enveloping darkness along with my inheritance and the second last hope of actioning my parents' well-laid plan.

"Oh, *well put*, Mr Evergrim." Pincher's sarcasm snaked around my twitching body, punctuated by Trudy's snigger. "Very erudite. I'd wager she was cut to the quick."

"Chance would be a fine thing," muttered Trudy.

"I'll burn every one of your wretched cushions!" foam bubbled at the corners of my mouth.

"Yeah, but we sold most of 'em, remember?" Dave's dulcet tones emanated from behind me. "Anyway, cheer up. There's still that other ship, ain't there?"

"But... I don't WANT one; I want TWO!" The toddler in me was stamping his feet.

I wanted two, deserved two. I deserved MORE than two. This was *not* supposed to be how it ended. I despised sharing anything.

I could feel all their wretched eyes boring into me, burning into my back until I felt it would ignite. No, this wasn't *my* fault. How could it be? I needed someone else to blame. Anyone else.

I spun around, seeking a victim. Soldiers, minions, and misfits peeled away. It was the first time that I had ever had such an effect, but I was not even in the mood to savour or appreciate it.

At the end of the tunnel of idiot-flesh was Francis, planted in front of her overflowing wagon of books, arms folded.

Aha! My mouth had barely twitched...

"How are you going to blame this on me? Hmm? Or any of us, for that matter?"

I would die trying to find a way. Sadly, I could not do it swiftly enough. Not with everyone watching, anyway.

"She had half the army with her," said Gawain, his voice wobbling.

"Yes, my army."

"Not anymore." He cringed as I turned to eyeball him.

"It was the better half, too," muttered Trudy.

"Oi!" came a feeble protest from somewhere in the assembled ranks.

"Why the hell are you all hanging around here when you should be on the other ship?" I demanded. For a pathetic moment, I was grateful that they hadn't been on the first ship, or they would have gone, too. From the look on some of their faces, they clearly wished that they had been.

"Yeah, especially if Miss Yanna comes back for it." Gawain's words drew looks of horror, especially from me.

Bugger.

I pushed through them, leaving Francis to enlist help with her wagon of tomes. I was struck with a sudden urge to get aboard before Yanna and the better, more sober half of my army returned for the other ship.

I found myself running… I could see the gold… taste the gold… the opportunity, the freedom from this mouldy, higgledy heap of stone. I barely heard the footfalls behind me—carried away by thoughts of stretching out in Sergi's bed, plundering his legendary wine cellar, and enjoying his face via scrying spells when he saw what he had 'won' from me.

"Who parked it all the way along here?" Dave wheezed, somewhere behind.

"You don't park a ship," replied Trudy.

"Ohhh, it looks right fancy this one, don't it?"

"It's just a ship."

"Nah, I mean the ornaments. All them tentacles."

I stopped, and Trudy and Dave cannoned into the back of

me, jerking me forward. I jolted again as the scurrying minions and soldiers piled into the back of them.

Trying not to shudder at the odour and the thought of fleas, I stared at the ship. He was right. Why had I not noticed the distinctive and oddly intrusive marine motif before? And then something moved.

"Corr, it's alive!"

"Cursed, we're all cursed!"

"Told you," sniffed the ghost.

The tentacles draped over the stern moved, and, with a creaking noise wrapped around, tightening. Water boiled around the ship, and a pointed head arose from the dark water, purple mottled skin glistening in the flickering magical light. A powerful odour rose with it, and even the least hygienically motivated creatures began to complain.

I had a dreadful feeling.

Baleful yellow eyes swivelled to me and, suddenly, I was a teenager again, emptying a large bucket and its thrashing contents down the privy as recompense for some misdeed of my father's.

Bugger.

Timbers creaked, and the behemoth tightened its grasp around my golden vessel. I could only watch in abject horror as, masts toppling and sails rent, the ship was slowly dragged beneath the dark waters. Somewhere in the background, over the sound of splintering timbers, the infernal not-quartet was reaching the crescendo of their backing song.

LATER

A hand passed in front of my face a few times, blocking out the bobbing debris field that remained of our last hope.

"Well... now what?" said Francis. Why was she always here

to demand answers of me?

"Was that an *actual* Kraken?" said Pincher.

"If you tell me it isn't on our list of permissible registered creatures, I'm going to kill myself."

"As enjoyable as that would be, Mr Evergrim… it is." He sounded disappointed. It was a minuscule saving grace.

"So, our way out is now decorating the riverbed," said Trudy. "My gold…"

"OUR gold more like," came an angry voice.

"Yeah! Gold!" Other jeering voices rose up and jabbed into the sludge of my pounding headache. I rubbed my temples, wishing that they had all sunk with the damn ship.

A loud and completely unnecessary clearing of the throat emanated from behind me.

The newly-elected-for-now head warlock pushed his way through the crowd while trying not to touch anyone, his oversized robes held gingerly away from the ground. Nob.

"I regret to inform you, master, but the enemy are, in fact, but a few miles away." He slapped away several hands that reached from the crowd to feel the material swaddling his over-privileged form. "They also appear to have brought a siege weapon with them."

"Why bother? The front door's rotten anyway," said Trudy.

Before I could issue any orders or put forward a call to arms, there was a mutiny.

"Well, we ain't going nowhere," came a bold voice hidden within the crowd. It was joined by others.

"Yeah, we ain't fightin'. Why should we."

"Yeah, if we stay here, they might not find us."

There was a murmur of assent as the idiocy rippled through the crowd. Did they actually believe that they could hide down here? Urgh.

Treacherous worms, all of them.

LATER

After a brief but decisive vote, the wretched minions and soldiers decided to stage a strike—as if they ever worked at the best of times. They refused to leave the waterside to be slaughtered by Sergi's army. What they *actually* planned on doing was beyond me. At this point, I was just hoping they all committed mass suicide. The warlocks had already retreated back to their quarters to barricade themselves in.

Indeed, I was reluctant to spend time in my newly-renovated torture chamber—new wash-hand basin or not.

I strode purposefully away until I was out of sight along one of the dank passageways back to the castle and then ran. I may have growled out a manly sob.

The damp stone chilled my spine as I leant back against one of the least mouldy walls and sucked in several ragged breaths. Through the mould spores and taste of decaying brick, I could smell something else.

It was a familiar combination of candied eyeballs, dagger polish, stale magic, and old books.

"Now what?" demanded Francis. The woman must stroll around with folded arms unless someone has glued them together.

"Bit late to put a boat together now," Dave said, mouth thick with candy.

"Ship. And fuck *sake*. Can't H and S put a stop to the attack on some stupid technicality?" Trudy said, glaring at Pincher. I had never heard him arrive. I hoped he would not die as quietly when I eventually got around to dealing with him.

Hope flickered within my carcass.

Pincher pushed his glasses further up his sharp but crooked nose and sighed.

Hope faded.

"It is not Health and Safety policy to interfere with or become involved in disputes, wars, lawsuits, arm wrestling, general name-calling, or other machinations of rival Overlords. We must *and will* remain… impartial."

Hope: DOA.

"What a load of bureaucratic bollocks," muttered Trudy, earning smirks from Gawain and Francis. Pincher cleared his throat and pretended not to have heard her.

"So…" Dave was clearly still catching up. "So… that's like if you're writin' one of them nature magazines and you see a lion eatin' a mushroom or summat, and you don't interfere 'cause it's nature…"

Silence. Brief, golden silence.

"What kind of lion?" asked Gawain.

"Mushrooms are poisonous," muttered the ghost.

"Why would a lion eat a bloody mushroom?" said Francis and Trudy, almost as one.

"Depends whether it's tasty looking," said Gawain.

I intervened before a heated debate could get into full swing about mushrooms and their attraction for lions, but couldn't help noticing Pincher rubbing his temples. *Welcome to my world.*

"You got a plan B or C?" said Trudy, shuffling in her patchy cloak and looking at me with a weary expression.

I shook my head, suddenly feeling the weight of their expectation. It was heavier than I had thought possible, and suddenly I could barely meet their gaze.

I felt… ashamed? How was this possible? For someone who got consistent top grades in dark combat, I should have had many plans. I had been too consumed with my parents' plan. I had… *failed.*

I finally looked around at them, thinking over the past weeks, and my eyes lit on a tatty fire-safety notice on the wall behind

Gawain. I frowned. A scraping noise drew my attention. It was Chakk, scraping some substance off his boot with half a brick.

"Eugh… looks like fairy puke," said Dave, wrinkling his nose. "Little bastards. Course, the cellars are nearby, an' that's where they stash their booze."

"That is disgusting. Don't you have standards in this castle?" The ghost appeared next to Chakk, terrifying him into a near heart attack.

"Sadly, it appears not," said Pincher.

"How are you here, anyway?" I snapped at the ghost, finally deigning to acknowledge the miserable creature. Trudy reached into her bodice and yanked out a familiar-looking stone set into a clasp on the end of a thick cord necklace. It appeared that the ghost was now officially part of the misfit's crew.

I rolled my eyes.

"You need to watch out, if one of those weevils sees that, they'll go for you. Anything that glows, not just magic," said Gawain, eyeing Chakk's boot.

The warning faded slightly… everything faded into the background as things moved and click, click, clicked in my head. It was terrible, ridiculous even. I looked at the poster behind Gawain, and then at the glowing fairy sick.

"The weevils are still trapped in the storage rooms below the front lobby?" I asked.

"Yeah," said Trudy.

"And the fairies?"

She looked confused. Everyone was now staring at me.

"Probably drunk in their cellar."

I nodded.

"You can't even fail upwards…" I breathed, my grandmother's harangue pinballing around my head.

Gawain's wonky handwriting was partially obscured as he

leant back, orange and red striped hair spreading over the poster.

Yes… just maybe we *could* fail upwards. Something crackled to life within me. I had a *plan*.

Everyone stared.

"We'll need several large sacks—thick ones." I paced, feeling an odd buzz of energy tempered by a sudden calm.

"Dave, how long would it take you to engineer a small but powerful catapult?"

"Few days."

"You've got about two hours."

"Wouldn't hold up to much." He shook his head and delivered a truncated version of his air-suck.

"I'll only need one shot. Hopefully. And the basin thing needs to be wide."

"Why?"

"To fit in all the drunk, pukey fairies," I replied, cracking my knuckles.

Trudy laughed.

"We gettin' rid of them?" Dave looked more confused than he normally did.

"Temporarily… above the enemy, once they've had a good shake." I grinned at their faces. "And then, we release the weevils."

"But… hang on, sir… how do we get them?" said Gawain.

"That's where *you* come in."

He cringed back as I turned to give him my best evil smile. "You'll be finding a way of getting them up from the cellar to the battlefield, which is likely to be at the front of the castle. Sergi isn't smart enough to attack from the sides."

"What, like use a tube or summat for 'em?" said Dave. "I've seen some old pipes knocking about."

"Then you can help."

I detailed exactly what I needed them to do, and where. No

one questioned the absurdity of it; we were beyond the point of reason.

"Anything else?" said Trudy when I'd finished with Dave, Gawain, and Chakk.

"Yes… when I give the signal, Chakk will set off the fucking fire alarm—the rally point is in front of the castle, which is, conveniently, where we want everyone to be."

They laughed. It made me feel good.

"That'll bloody move them," said Chakk.

"Could be a stampede, and that's dangerous," said the ghost.

"If it gets them outside to meet that tosser Sergi, then I can live with a few squashed gnomes. They won't have a damn choice but to fight once they're out there."

I was feeling exceedingly smug with myself until I remembered the other problem—the Heroes. I looked around and caught sight of Pincher, glasses now off, rubbing his temples again. He looked quite different without them and, for the first time, I noticed his ring. Thick gold, with the H&S crest carved into a garnet. It flashed in the light. In a split-second that lasted an oddly long time, the recognition flashed into my head and popped, oozing and seeping into the cracks of memory.

The ring. *That ring.*

That man.

That picture.

Perfect.

A VERY HURRIED TREK TO MY PARENTS' ROOM LATER

After gaining a brace of papercuts from rummaging through my mother's paperwork, I finally had the picture in all it putrescent glory. It was even better than I remembered. A naked man wearing a lime-green witchy party hat, getting *extremely* intimate with a tentacled water demon (also wearing a hat). It was a moment of pure bliss. For him as much as me.

BACK IN THE DEPTHS

Bar decapitation, seldom have I seen colour drain from someone's face so quickly as it did Pincher's.

"I… where?"

"My mother did not believe in conventional insurance policies."

"She destroyed it… she said…"

"She most certainly did *not*." Whispers surrounded us as the misfits drew closer, curiosity like catnip.

"Put that away," hissed Pincher, glancing at them. I savoured the desperation in his voice and the attempts to mask it. This level of nastiness was where I excelled.

I have *missed* this feeling.

"I'll consider it."

"Is that… a tentacle… or something else?" said Gawain, whispering loudly. Pincher tried to step in front of the picture, gritting his teeth as I whipped it away from a sudden snatch of his hand.

Trudy sniggered.

Green eyes bored into my own. Anger, frustration, fear, desperation, hatred… *humanity*. Finally. *So, there you are,* Mr Pincher. *There* you are. *Now I see you.*

"I can destroy you, Mr Evergrim."

"Ditto. But then, I have less far to fall. Look around you. How much worse do you think this could get for me? Compared to, say… you?"

He glanced around, clearly weighing the reality of my words against his instinct and obvious desire to crush me.

"What do you want?"

"You to lend a helping hand... you're good at that."

Trudy snickered. His face had moved from porcelain to flame red.

"I can't intervene, I'll—"

"No no no no," I chuckled, tucking the picture into my waistcoat pocket. "But you can 'inspect' the tunnels at the west wing, where the Heroes will soon be turning up."

Confusion crinkled across his brow. "The supports are... slipshod, weak, and even a cursory inspection could see the whole wing come down. It would be a tragedy if it were to happen during an invasion."

"Surely the morons at the local Heroes' Guild would not be stupid enough to attack via the same place as last time?" His eyes strayed to my pocket. I had already wormed the picture through the secret slit at the back and into a hidden secondary compartment.

"Yes, they would." There was a murmur of assent and 'yeah's.

"They're lazy, stupid, and have under-invested in excavation tools," said Francis. "Besides, they have an invasion quota to meet, and we're the easiest option, so I heard."

Pincher looked at her, searching her face, perhaps for understanding or support, but she refused to look at him. Her eyes flicked to the pocket where the picture had been secured and slid away.

Interesting. I saved this moment for a rainy-day piece of needling.

"Fine."

"Can you afford to lose the entire west wing. Again?" Francis said.

I shrugged. What did she care as long as the library was safe? I said as much, and it shut her up—another victory.

"Anyway, we can if Mr Pincher has an accident. I presume that H and S will compensate us more than adequately? Rules work both ways, after all."

Something approaching a smile flickered briefly in his eyes, and he nodded, more to himself than anyone else. There was contemplation. Conclusion. He drew a sharp breath.

"I appear to have underestimated you, Mr Evergrim. I won't do so again. And we *will* have a… *discussion* another time about this."

We locked eyes for a long moment, and then he handed Gawain his clipboard, rolled up his sleeves, and removed and pocketed his glasses. "Shall we?" he sighed.

"Tunnels are that way. Wait until you can smell the beer and cheap armour polish."

"And then?"

"You're a darkly creative soul, Mr Pincher, I've no doubt."

"You have *no* idea."

I wasn't ever going to give him the chance to demonstrate it. And he would try, of that, I had no doubt now.

I made a sweeping gesture towards the tunnels, which was reciprocated by a very un-H&S one before he departed.

For some reason, something seemed to have finally clicked, and I felt, for the first time, at home in my desired role. Well… almost.

A debate about mushrooms had sprung up between several of the misfits, and the other half were discussing the photograph. I saw several expansive gestures and allowed myself a smirk.

If, by some miracle, we survived, I imagine the gossip would spread faster than a contagious skin disease at a Randy Minion Retreat.

Now… let's see if we should have taken our chances with my father's Kraken after all.

GRAND LOBBY

I peered through a cracked glass pane beside the main doors. Sergi's army was amassed across the fields and gardens at the front.

It was time. I sighed.

"Trudy."

"I'm not here."

"Go out there and ask him if he can come back tomorrow."

"What?"

"That's 'what, *sir*?'," I said, turning to motion her towards the door. A few whispered bets were placed among the watching minions—mostly misfits, new/Brightwood misfits, and some minions whose curiosity had got the better of them.

Shooting me a look of incredulity, Trudy stepped over the drunk blacksmith who was passed out on the doormat, cracked open the door, and slipped outside. Dave and the other misfits pressed to every available window and crack in the wall, watching her stalk down the steps, one middle finger raised back at us. Her other hand twitched over the hilt of her sheathed sword.

"Are you crazy?" hissed Francis from the far side of the doors.

"You said we needed to buy some time."

"With the corpse of a good fighter?"

"How would you know?" I said. Her questions and truth were starting to needle me, and it came out in my tone.

"I've watched her train in the combat arena, actually."

"When? *Actually*."

"When I was down there confiscating some books that were being used to prop up an attack dummy, *actually*."

"Do you mind, some of us are trying to listen!" trilled the gardening pixie.

I pulled a face at Francis and gazed outside. Trust her to spoil it.

Trudy rolled her shoulders, rested her hand on her sword hilt and called out: "The Overlord says, can you all please fuck right off and come back tomorrow?"

Whatever they had been expecting, this clearly wasn't it. The rows of amassed soldiers and creatures turned in confusion to someone—guess who—in polished silver armour and a ridiculously spiked battle helm. It took him three attempts to flick the visor up, and nearly snipped off a finger when it accidentally slid back down.

"Tell Na—Overlord Evergrim to get his cravenly arse out here now."

"Sooo, that's a 'no' then? How about next week? Would you consider making an appointment for when we give a shit?" she shrugged and spread her hands wide.

Everyone in the lobby snickered.

Sergi's visor slipped down again before being rammed back up.

"NO! Tell him to get out here NOW and surrender to me, or I'll take this castle and all the lands and treasures contained therein, by *force*."

"By what, sorry?" she called.

"Force."

She cupped a hand to her ear. "What, sorry?"

Everyone snickered again.

"I'll take it all by force!"

"Four what?" She cupped the other ear.

"By force, force, I'll bloody kill you all and take your stuff," Sergi screamed, startling his own horse so much that it danced to one side and trampled over two soldiers.

One of the goblin quartet wet himself laughing.

"Why didn't you just *say* that? Nob." Trudy turned and began a very slow walk back up the steps.

Where the fuck was Dave? And Gawain? I looked around. We couldn't do this without them.

"Well," muttered Chakk, "at least they're two soldiers down."

No one said anything. When you are hopelessly outnumbered, two didn't make much of a difference. Especially when one minion had just wet himself, one was blind drunk, and one was now puffing on a herbal cigarette and at risk of wobbling off the window sill into a bin.

A door bust open at the back of the hall and Gawain stumbled out. I swear he'd fall over a pin. He scuttled across the floor, alone.

He was alone.

I couldn't help but notice how *fucking alone* he was.

"Oh, perfect." Francis rolled her eyes.

"Ah, they are coming, sir, but…"

"What?"

"Well… they're stuck."

"They what?"

"Uhm… well, sir, two trolls pushed to the front of the scrum and tried to get through the door, erm… at the same time… sir." He trailed off.

I was about to explode when someone else got there first, and a hideous voice boomed from somewhere above.

"Nathaniel!"

Shit shit *shit*. She'd obviously freed herself. Too late, I remembered the secret passage from her quarters that my mother had mentioned.

"Why are those people on our front lawn?"

"Collecting for the poor," I yelled back.

"They're crushing my rhododendrons. Where's my battle armour?" she yelled down.

I'd heard enough and made my escape outside. I'd rather face Sergi's army.

He was waiting on the fringe of his troops and creatures on a large black horse that he could barely control. He called out in his annoying, smug tone.

"Well, well, well... finally you've crawled out of your hole."

"Walked. Through the doors, actually. They're right there." I pointed over my shoulder.

"I know that," he snapped. "You always have to be so difficult."

Ah, he wounds me.

"Well, if you would just bugger off and bother someone else, I'd be perfectly pleasant."

"I have come to claim this castle and your domain by force."

Did this dickhead have any other words?

"How inconvenient. Do you have an appointment? Because our crochet club starts at four and there are Brightwood scones on offer."

Buoyed up by snickering and giggles from the misfits and new recruits, I smirked. "You are more than welcome to join us."

"Silence! And no, I WILL NOT."

"Not a scone fan then? Cupcake?"

"ENOUGH!"

"*Can* one have enough cupcakes?"

He was as fidgety as his warhorse. I just hoped that Dave had done his job; given the way Sergi was foaming at the mouth, battle was imminent.

Just as Sergi opened his mouth to speak, there was a distant rumble, and the ground shook under our feet. Everyone turned, just in time to see the west wing of the castle sink slightly. Just when everything appeared to have settled, one of the towers wobbled and toppled off. There was a crashing sound from whatever it crushed.

I looked at Sergi. He looked at me. I shrugged. He cleared his throat and composed himself before speaking. "You WILL surrender and... oh WHAT NOW!"

A tumultuous cascade of shrieks, shouts, and clanking was boiling from within the castle behind us and, finally, our rag-tag army and multitude of assorted minions spilled out of the doors behind us.

"Fire! Fire!"

"It was terrible."

"Where's the rally point?"

"How's Annie?"

"I've spilled my fucking beer!"

"The fire has pulled the castle down!"

Voices and shrieks spilled over us as the masses surged around us.

I folded my arms and waited. One by one, they noticed the army in front of them and silence swept over them like poisonous little dominoes.

"Ahhh, shite," came one lone voice.

"Kind of you to join us. Glad to see that you remembered your weapons. You'll be needing them." I turned and faced Sergi's forces, relief barely soothing my knotting stomach. By now, Francis should be locking the door from the inside before finding another exit. Most of our army was too stupid to think of going around the back.

Sergi laughed, looked around, and was dutifully joined by his soldiers and minions.

Trudy made the wanker sign and rolled her eyes. Chakk snorted and giggled.

"Is this all you have?" Sergi called, mocking.

"The rest of our army got lost in the mail," I snapped. "Besides, it'll be enough to beat you." Fuck me, I hoped so. I didn't want him leering over me in my torture chamber. He always spits when he talks.

"You think so, do you?" He beckoned to something or someone behind him. The low rumbling sound did not bode well.

"It's a bloody siege weapon," someone shouted.

It was indeed—a great, hulking metal catapult on a wooden chassis, pulled by a team of black horses. The wheels groaned through the churned-up grass. Perfect.

"Ohh, nice. A Belcher Mark Three," came a voice from the ranks.

"I think you'll find it's a Mark Four," argued his companion.

"Are you takin' the piss? The Mark Three has green flames on the wheels."

"The model A, yes, but later that year—"

A look from me sent the argument into furious whispers instead.

"That siege weapon looks a bit iffy," I called. "Couldn't you afford a good one?"

"It's fine, as you'll soon bloody find out and it's worth more than your castle, anyway," Sergi yelled back.

Bastard. He was probably right.

"Wheels look a little loose. When was it last inspected... maybe Health and Safety should check it out?" This could stop everything in its tracks if...

I looked over to Pincher, who was perched on top of an old crate lying beside the front doors. He unfurled his arms and scrawled something on his clipboard. He held it up. In big red pen, across the page was the word 'IMPARTIAL'. He gave a wide grin and settled back against the wall, arms folded again.

Bastard.

There was a faint creaking from behind me, and the crowd parted. A small makeshift catapult jerked its way over the uneven ground, the wooden arm (looked like it had been removed from a fence) swaying. Dave raised his head and mopped his brow.

"Not late, am I?"

"Just in time," I said. He pushed it forward until it sat beside us. Compared to Sergi's, it was tiny.

"What is *that*?" Sergi pointed and laughed.

"This is our own siege weapon." I patted the side, and a piece fell off. Most of it looked as though it had been cobbled together from various pieces of exercise and sparring equipment from the training halls, with a few shields for wheels. I recognised a vast fruit-bowl from the warlocks' quarters that had been utilised as the basin. It was the fanciest piece of the whole thing.

It looked... Gods awful, if I'm honest.

"That thing's ridiculous." Sergi laughed and looked around. His army obediently cackled along with him. Dave puffed his chest out and folded his arms.

"Oi, yer shiny tosser, it's rustic," he shouted.

"Rusty, more like," shouted back one of Sergi's people.

"Couldn't put a dent in an apple with that little thing!"

More laughter.

I'd heard enough. No one insulted my staff except me. "Chakk?" I shouted.

The magpie demon staggered through the crowd, dragging a large sack. Francis followed, hauling an even larger one.

"They've been biting through the bloody sack." She scowled and dumped it on the floor before giving it a kick.

"Let's get this over with," shouted Sergi. "Fire when ready."

There was a heavy wooden thunk, and then a whine as a large rock whistled over our heads and smashed into one of the towers. Stone and slate tumbled down, and part of the wall collapsed to cheers from Sergi's forces.

"Load the little fuckers up," I ordered, wincing as another

projectile whistled overhead and took out the rest of the tower. Francis and Chakk heaved the sacks up with the help of a few soldiers and emptied the contents into the large bowl. A writhing heap of limbs, wings, and glowing vomit spread out, swearing and shrieking.

"Attack!" I turned to yell at the army, who were watching with interest as the enemy siege weapon was reloaded by a team of armoured trolls. Several bottles of beer were being passed among them, along with a few bets. "ATTACK! Bloody attack!"

None of them moved.

"Bloody move! Do you all want to die?"

"Hurr hurrr…" An enemy swamp rambler guffawed and pointed, and a halfling in armour two sizes too big for her cackled along. "Scared, are yers?"

"Of your hygiene, you bloody cheese wreckage," shouted the ghost, eliciting cheers from those of our minions who knew what hygiene was.

And then the dripping green swamp rambler, betraying the few dabs of intellect that it had, threw a rock. It shattered a bottle of beer being downed by a barbarian, spraying him and his companions (one of whom was the Brightwood blacksmith) with glass and froth.

Nobody moved.

Narrowed eyes turned to the culprit who was now not so cocky. Everyone around sucked in their breath. The sun slithered behind a cloud, and the field darkened.

With a bloodcurdling scream, the barbarians and blacksmith charged. With a glance at one another and, unable to think for themselves, everyone else charged with them, the surge of adrenaline and anger seeming to ensnare them all. The sides clashed, and battle was finally joined. Thank goodness for stupidity.

"Dave, will this thing work?" Francis ducked as a spiked

metal projectile zipped past us and shattered against the wall not far from Pincher, who looked more amused than concerned.

"Yeah, 'course! The Fairy Flinger Two Thousand is solid."

"Why two Thousand?" Francis said, raising her voice over the clash of weapons, name-calling, and the screech of projectiles.

"If you put two thousand on the end of any name, it sounds dead fancy."

He had a point, and I saw them all silently consider it.

"Chakk, where are the weevils?"

Another shot from the siege weapon took out the top of another tower. That would be a prick to fix.

"Are you sure about this?" Francis grabbed my arm, and we both ducked as an arrow thunked into the catapult.

"It's the best shot we've got. CHAKK!"

"Ready!" came a distant voice.

"Dave, bloody fire!" I yelled, grabbing a soldier and using him as a shield against several rocks and an axe. Dave leaned heavily on the lever and, with a thunk, the arm jerked forward, hurling the bowl's drunken contents skyward.

Fairy shrieks filled the air, and they were buffeted and bowled by the momentum, tumbling and spreading out over the battlefield below as they tried to right themselves.

The turbulence and alcohol took its revenge. Gobs of glowing vomit rained down as they hurtled over Sergi's troops, shrieking and gagging. Minions and soldiers screamed in horror as it spattered everywhere.

"Chakk, now!" I yelled, running back towards the castle. He was dragging a large fabric tube, the other end of which jammed into a grate at the base of one of the castle's casements.

"They're eating through it, sir!"

I pushed him aside and used my sword to cut the metal cap off the end (bin lid). There was a rumbling sound, and then one of the grotesque creatures burst from the end.

I ran. We all ran.

"If you can move, bloody move!" yelled our new Head of the Army, finding her voice and dragging several soldiers behind a stunned minotaur for cover. Our minions already knew better and shifted as best they could as the weevils flooded from the tube and reoriented themselves. The glowing patches spattering the enemy caught their attention and they slithered into the fray, screams welcoming them. Our troops took the chance to disengage themselves and staggered back to the castle front as the weevils slowly wreaked havoc on the field.

Drunk fairies who had survived the rocky flight slowly fluttered back, crash landing beside the front doors, chittering abuse. Nearby soldiers wisely vacated the area not wanting to be puked on and marked for death. I was tempted to see if I could grab one and hurl it at Sergi, but he had surrounded himself with large minions in a cowardly bid to keep away from the weevils. Anyway, I've had enough of fairy bites.

"Booze, booze!" they chanted.

"Shaddup," yelled Chakk, grabbing a discarded cloak and throwing it over a group of them who had vomited on themselves. Quick thinking. I did not want to lose any more troops or creatures to weevils… a couple of our own had already been unlucky enough to have been spattered in vomit and then torn apart by the bastards.

There was a yell from Sergi somewhere, and another projectile crunched into the castle, this time, ripping away a chunk of the battlements and sending debris raining down on some of the soldiers who were sheltering near the walls.

Fuck sake. Even if we did get rid of him, by some miracle, we'd not have anywhere left to bloody shelter. "Sir, we need rid of that siege weapon," yelled the Head of the Army/Assistant to the

Pastry Chef (now formally known as Atty).

"I'm open to sodding suggestions," I yelled, running and ducking behind an ornamental wall with Trudy and Francis as a stray rock zipped past and knocked out a slime wraith. Anyone venturing out there was just as likely to get mauled by a weevil as to be killed by one of Sergi's creatures.

"Where are our warlocks, for fuck sake?" said Francis, picking up a spiked projectile and hurling it back, taking out a halfling who was hacking frantically at a blue weevil.

"Same place as theirs, probably—avoiding getting their shoes dirty while they vote on something," I replied. I wasn't the only one who glanced up at the castle. Several warlocks ducked out of sight of the windows.

I'd be setting more than a sofa alight when this was over.

"Bastards," yelled up Trudy.

"Right, I'm not having this." Francis clenched her fists and then stood up and ran for the doors before remembering that she had locked them from the inside.

"Shit, shit, shit." She ducked a rain of debris from a hit to the battlements and then ran, heading for the side of the castle, and vanishing out of sight.

Trudy eyed the troops loading up the siege weapon for another hit. This looked to be the biggest one yet, and they were straining to load it.

"We'll never get close enough to take it out," she said. Her eyes narrowed. "Where's the ghost?" she suddenly said, touching a familiar-looking stone on a pendant around her neck.

"Right here, and I do have a name, you know," said the ghost.

"You actually carry that thing around?" said the pixie, eyeballing the stone.

Trudy shrugged. "Can you get over there and spook those horses?"

Brilliant.

"No, it's too far, they've moved it back to get out of the way of those disgusting things," she said, crouching (as if anything could actually damage her).

"What if I get you there?" Trudy said.

"Don't be stupid…" But I was too late. Trudy leapt the wall and took off at a run.

"Fuck sake," I yelled, following suit before I realised what I was doing. I was aware of others scrambling to follow, and plunged into the considerably thinned enemy ranks. Trudy was hacking and stabbing her way through mangled soldiers and angry minions, ducking wide, meaty swings from trolls and stabs from goblins. She barely stopped to fight, doing the bare minimum as to not lose momentum.

I cut down two soldiers with one sweep of my blade and stabbed another in the eye with a dagger before being doubled over by a green stench cloud from an enemy mucus demon. As I vomited over a dead weevil and the remains of the person it had been eating, I thanked my lucky stars we had not brought any home from Brightwood after all—the smell alone would have been enough to drive everyone away.

Two orange weevils charged it, and it groaned and tried to make an escape, smashing at them with its thick arms and biting one's head off. In the moment of respite it gave me, I caught sight of Trudy.

She was closer, but still not close enough. She'd just jump-kicked a dark assassin in the face and cut down a hellhound when a huge mass rose up in front of her. It looked like a heap of slimy rock dressed in pieces of ill-fitting leather armour.

"Cor, that's a warven! Bet that was expensive, you have to import 'em." Dave tiptoed to see, bloody hammer dangling from one hand, the other looped through the handle of a large

DIARY OF AN EVIL OVERLORD

reinforced bin lid which had been painted with the words 'Big Shield 2000'.

"Our fire demon would have incinerated that thing," I said in a tone dripping with bitterness.

"Yeah... 'cept now you'd have to use the bits to start a fire," said Dave. I wondered if I could feed him to the weevils.

For a moment, chest heaving, Trudy regarded the huge beast. I thought I was about to lose one of my best fighters and an odd feeling of... regret? ... washed over me.

What was wrong with me? I wiped my brow. I was clearly unwell.

She had clearly had enough because I could see her swearing at it before snatching up a weevil that had been severed in two and flinging it low. It hit the creature in the groin, and it let out a pitiful howl as it doubled over.

Trudy ripped off her necklace and ran, leaping up onto the creature's back and using it as a springboard. She flung the ghost's stone with all her might towards the siege weapon before she crashed down into the mud.

A dark assassin started towards her, blade flashing, and then suddenly fell backwards, an arrow embedded in his eye socket.

Trudy turned. I turned. Only Mr Pincher stood in the direction it had flown, leaning against the wall, arms folded. Then *who*?

There was no time to wonder as our attention jerked back to the stone as it landed in front of the scrum protecting the siege weapon. The ghost appeared from nowhere in front of the horses and screeched at them, waving her arms. They reared up, eyes rolling in terror, and thrashed around, trying to escape.

As they wrenched around, the wagon was dragged sideways through the mud before it started to tip over. The wooden crossbars splintered, allowing the horses to bolt, dragging their traces.

Sergi's scream of rage was sweet music to my ears.

Enemy troops scrambled as the siege weapon toppled off the wagon bed, discharging its last projectile as it hit the ground. The huge boulder, intended for the front of the castle, was fired sideways into Sergi's army, obliterating a huge swathe of what was left after the weevil wave.

I allowed myself a maniacal laugh and then vowed never to do it again—my throat felt shredded. I don't know how some of the legendary Overlords did it.

While I spluttered, cheers went up from our remaining army and, given a second wind, they waded back into the thinned crowd. Most did, anyway. Some pointed and laughed at the mangled remains of humans and minions and the beleaguered siege weapon. I couldn't blame them; it was pretty amusing. Especially as the bolting horses had trampled over the few remaining archers Sergi had left.

I had no idea that my wretched army could actually fight when needed and took a brief moment to be half impressed. Of course, they were more than likely defending whatever wine supply remained in the castle, but still, it was a gesture that I appreciated.

After expertly cutting down a barbarian and two waxbeasts, I enjoyed a brief respite to survey the carnage. The garden pixie was scuttling between minions, firing at troops with a spiky wooden V-catapult. Her projectiles exploded over chests and in faces with a puff of green magic, spawning nests of stinging nettles that enveloped their heads. I winced at the screams.

Chakk had dropped his weapon and was busy tying several pieces of shiny armour up in a bundle fashioned from a muddy cloak. Before I could yell across the fray at him, a bolt of magic whistled from the rear of Sergi's troops and exploded nearby, knocking over two bonewraiths and a hellhound. It seemed that

Sergi's warlocks had finally been coaxed into battle.

Magic roared over my head, and with relief churning in my belly, I turned to see our warlocks leaning out of the windows— reluctant to risk themselves but as least making a fucking effort. Finally. Gods know what Francis said to them, but they appeared motivated.

Feeling re-energised, I was too busy stamping on an enemy fairy who had stabbed me in the ankle to notice what was going on, but a yell made me look up. Too late, I saw a nasty sliver of blue magic slicing through the air towards me.

"Look out!" Something slammed in front of me, and the magic ricocheted away, slicing through the armour of an enemy fire titan and felling him like a tree. Well, felling the top half. Blood spurted out of what remained standing.

I looked at Francis as she lowered her shield.

"Are those… book covers?" I said.

She nodded and wiped her brow with her free hand. The other was looped through two leather straps that had been attached to a circle of tattered magical book covers in a rainbow of colours, now partially obliterated by a scorch mark.

I stared at her, and then over at the half of the fire titan, which fell slowly backwards, spraying blood over two wrestling soldiers who shrieked and ran. "Erm… thank you." I didn't know what else to say. She nodded and then pulled a metal library stamp from the cluster tucked into her belt.

"You're welcome, Overlord."

I wanted to tell her to call me Nathaniel, but she had gone, jumping over a pair of hissing, biting gnomes and charging at a warlock who had strayed too close to the fight. The library stamp made a nasty dent in his forehead. Discarded, indeed.

After surviving a brief duel with a drunk soldier, I staggered back, exhaustion starting to weigh down my arms. And I still hadn't dealt with the coward Sergi, who was now prancing around inside a cluster of protective minions, occasionally swinging a battle mace at anyone who strayed close.

"Warlocks, summon my champion," he screeched, holding up his visor.

His warlocks, clustered together behind a row of shields and soldiers to keep them safe, held up their hands and I felt magic crackle in the air. So did everyone else, and most creatures stopped mid-fight, teeth locked around limbs, swords half-buried in foes, and looked around... waiting.

A swirling pukey green puddle of magic opened up in a clearing amid the wreckage of battle and a hideous green-grey creature emerged. Long, swinging arms and a large head with a gaping black mouth and slitted green eyes elicited shrieks from those close to it.

A moss beast? Perfect. This was *all* I needed. For a brief, stupid moment, I had allowed myself to think that we may actually be victorious.

"Where did 'e get that?" yelled Dave. "They're dead limited edition, them!"

I didn't care where the bastard had got it; the fact was that it was here and it was screeching in rage. Its mossy limbs swinging as it tested its freedom. Sensing the magic, a couple of the remaining weevils made a beeline for it. I sighed in relief. Relief that choked in my throat as the thing swung its arms down, swept them up, and hurled them across the field.

They smashed into the castle wall, spraying guts and green blood everywhere. It would stink to blazes once the sun had worked on it.

"I hope you're going to pay to get that cleaned," I screamed at Sergi. I got a finger gesture and a laugh in response. He returned to batting away my fairies who were hurling shards of beer-bottle glass at him. "Flash git, flash git!" they trilled.

I had other things on my mind, however. Francis was beside me, along with Dave, Gawain, and Trudy. Each was injured in some way, and Trudy was nursing a bloody wound on her side.

"You may want to reconsider your positions because we're about to be pulped," I said. Should I apologise? No, absolutely not.

"Nah, it's all right here," said Dave, examining his hammer.

"Nothing we can't handle." Trudy rolled her eyes and headed back into the fray, one hand to her injured side, the other swinging a blade at a harpy, who dropped down to be repeatedly kicked in the head by a swarm of brick gnomes. Other, more foolhardy, battle-crazed minions and soldiers were darting in to slash at the moss creature, having little effect.

A bolt of magic arced through the air and took out two of our soldiers and we scrambled for cover behind an unconscious rock troll.

"Bastards. If you can come up with a way of distracting that moss thing… I think I've got an idea to deal with his warlocks." Francis grabbed Gawain and ran back towards the castle. What the fuck was she doing? For one horrible moment, I thought she might be abandoning me.

I stood up and watched her go. It was worse than the punch to the back and the dagger slashing my ribs. That's what I get for not looking. I spun and slashed at the grey harpy, and its wild death swing caught me in the chest, flooring me.

For a moment, I saw stars.

It wasn't just the indignity of laying half-conscious on my back amid the battle, but that I was wearing an expensive waistcoat that was now covered in mud, blood, and some odd green secretion from the now-dead harpy beside me.

A burning ache in my head sent ripples of pain through me

but, beyond that, I could feel something else.

Someone crouched beside me and, for a moment, I expected a blade to end me. Instead, I felt something slip inside my waistcoat pocket. I cracked open an eye.

Pincher was beside me, dagger in one hand, the other in my pocket. He swore to himself and glared at me. Had he honestly thought I would have left it there? I half-opened my eyes, and suddenly his blade was at my throat, green fire burning into me, glasses long gone.

"Looking for something, Mr Pincher?" the point of his blade twisted in the hollow of my throat and I couldn't help laughing at the absurdity and the wonderful pleasure of his frustrated anger.

I could see the ache in him to finish me. We both knew he could and that no one would be any the wiser in all this mess. The contemplation crawled across his mind, reflected in his eyes. It was a side of H&S that I had not yet encountered—it was rather invigorating.

He withdrew the blade and stood to leave.

Without warning, a soldier lurched over. I groped for my sword, but his was already raised to strike down at me. And then he paused, confusion cycling over his face.

Pincher's fist, dagger and all, was buried in his stomach. He pulled it free, and, with a swift stab to the neck, shoved the already-dead man backwards into the mud.

I sat up and gaped. He glanced around, looking suddenly uncomfortable and reached down a hand to me. I took it and was surprised by his strength as he hauled me up. Before I could really register any of it, the dagger had vanished somewhere beneath his waistcoat. With a quick mutter of "Get this fucking mess over with, I've got work to be getting on with," he vanished back to the castle.

With aches competing for dominance in my weary body, I

found my sword and sucked in a breath. The air smelled of horse. And lavender. A snort behind me had me scuttling aside, and my grandmother's steed clopped past me, unconcerned about where or upon whom it trod—rather like her.

She flipped her visor up with a dull clank and hung her bloodied mace on her saddle. "Look at the state of your shirt."

What?!

"What?" My voice cracked with incredulity.

Before she could answer, there was a yell from somewhere among Sergi's ranks.

"Myrtle? Is that you?"

My grandmother pulled off her helmet and sat taller, staring over the scrum of fighters. "Gwendoline?"

"Hello, dear!"

"Fancy seeing you here!"

Slowly, the bizarre sight of two elderly women in battle armour, hailing one another across the field of battle sank in, and the fighting and slaughter ground to a halt. Even the moss beast thing looked confused and ceased pulling one of my soldiers in half for a moment. Trust my grandmother and one of her cronies to desecrate a sacred event like a traditional battle.

Sergi removed his stupidly large battle helmet and looked as pissed off as I felt.

"Ohh, I haven't seen you in *ages*, dear," shouted Sergi's grandmother, waving.

"Grandmother!" Sergi hissed. He was ignored.

"Oh, I know! Not since that siege at the Little Toadstool Tea Rooms," my grandmother called back.

"Oh, I know! They never did find everyone's limbs."

"Grandmother!"

"Oh, I know!" said my grandmother.

Sergi rolled his eyes and shot me a look. I shrugged in reply.

I had no intention of wasting my breath.

"What's that you've got there, dear?" Heads swivelled from one woman to the other. Even the orcs on both sides had now stopped pummelling people into the ground.

"My magical weevil." My grandmother held up her repulsive pet, which was decked out in a miniature riding hat and tweed coat. Many minions close to her recoiled in horror.

"Oh, isn't he *precious*!" her crony cooed. Attention ricocheted back to her. "Sergi!" her head snapped around, and her voice took on that nasty, sharp edge reserved only for nuisance grandchildren. I saw him brace himself.

"Why don't *we* have a magical weevil?"

He cringed. I knew that feeling only too well and was grateful that, for once, it wasn't me.

"I don't know."

"How much are they?"

"I don't *know*." His voice was testy and defensive.

"Well, where do you get them?"

"*I don't know!*" he snapped.

"You don't know *much*, do you?"

He slammed his helmet down in temper, crushing a small goblin.

"DON'T take that tone with ME!" she shouted.

"I didn't HAVE a tone; I didn't even SAY anything," he snapped back, fists clenching, face bright red. Several knowing members of his army backed away.

I was enjoying the scene until my own grandmother's attention turned to me. Because of course.

"Nathaniel! What are you smirking at?"

"Nothing," I said, sullenly.

"What was that?"

"I SAID, 'NOTHING'." My face was scarlet, and my

headache was hammering around the inside of my head like a doped-up fairy.

"Don't you *dare* speak to me like that in public."

"Perhaps you'd like to come inside then."

"You'll be bloody sorry if I do, young man."

It was Sergi's turn to smirk. Give me five minutes alone with him and a cheese grater, and he'd not have a face to smirk with.

"Honestly, dear, I don't know why you bother," called Sergi's grandmother.

"Quite right. Bloody leave them to it. They couldn't organise a piss-up in a privy factory, the pair of them," my grandmother snapped. She clopped away, and the pair of them rode off in the direction of Waterford, their complaints vanishing over the horizon.

Good bloody riddance. I saw Sergi's chest heave in similar relief.

"Incoming, incoming!" came a collective trill from some nearby fairies, and a bolt of fire hit the moss beast in the chest. While there was too much slime to do much damage, bar singeing it and making it angrier, it certainly ignited the fighting once more.

I hid behind the remains of a wall and surveyed the battlefield. Amazingly, we had more troops and minions left than Sergi. However, his vile moss beast could easily turn the tide, and his warlocks were now holed up behind their shield wall, deflecting much of the fire from our own warlocks—useless cretins. They would need to be dealt with.

Where the bloody hell was Francis? Still, the moss thing would flatten us all before she likely showed up anyway.

A screech drew my attention. Chakk was busy yanking a shiny breastplate away from a similar creature to him, with blue-black hair and blue eyes. They pulled it back and forth in a tug of war, hissing at one another and snarling abuse. I recognised it as a jackdaw demon and, like Chakk (magpie demon through and through), it had already requisitioned a number of shiny items from the battlefield, which could be seen poking out of various pockets.

"Mine!"

"No, MINE!"

More hissing and then, frustrated, Chakk pulled the breastplate down and let it go. The released tension flipped it up, and it smacked his rival in the face, knocking him cold. The idiot picked up his spoils, booted his opponent in the ribs, and then and held up his shiny treasure.

"Look what I got!" the sun caught it and bounced the light into the eyes of the moss beast. It howled and held up a hand to shield itself. It was the chance that we needed. Well, that someone more expendable needed.

Atty broke cover, ignoring shouted warnings, and ran. With two leaps, she sprang off a stepladder of two unconscious ascending-sized soldiers and slashed her whisk weapon across the moss beast's face, taking out one eye. To cheers, she landed on its back and clung on to the thick clumps of moss on the back of its neck, repeatedly stabbing it in the head. It was grim but, nonetheless, effective.

I approved.

To a howl of rage from Sergi and a rousing cheer from our own troops, the thing gave one last groan and toppled over. Atty dropped away, rolling as she hit the ground. It splatted into the mud inches from her. She stood up, mud and blood spattered over her face, and stared. Silence.

Another cheer went up among my army and minions, and several of the cockier ones ran and clambered onto the moss creature and danced a quick jig.

Before I could shout something smug to Sergi, a bolt of magic sliced across the battlefield and cut a dancing troll in half. It looked very surprised as its two halves tumbled to the ground. Bugger.

Another bolt of magic flew high and then shattered, raining fire down. Everyone ran, taking what little cover there was. One shard of flaming magic barely missed me, while several minions were not as lucky and danced around, screaming while their compatriots cackled. One or two of the more compassionate ones ran to roll them in the mud to extinguish the flames and drag them back to safety.

Bastard warlocks. Sergi's troops may have been thin on the ground, but if his warlocks kept ours pinned down, there was little we could do as we were slowly picked off. Our own warlocks were doing little damage, especially given how many of the enemy there were compared to ours—of course, it didn't help that many of ours were so ancient they had practically morphed into the furniture where they spent their lives dozing. In fact, many were likely still there, trying to achieve enough escape velocity to free themselves of the squishy cushions.

By the time they arrived, we'd likely all be dead.

I ducked another bolt of magic, and there was a yell from Dave. I looked in the direction he was pointing and nearly keeled over. *What was she thinking?* She could get us all killed. I'd rather take my chances against the sodding warlocks...

I could only stare in horror as Francis hurtled towards the battlefield, throwing a glance behind her. One hand was holding up her muddy dress above her chunky boots, while the other trailed a torch with a magical light pulsing at the end, leaving mesmerising trails in the air behind her.

Screeching behind, in slithering pursuit, was Hammond. Somehow, she and Gawain had got it out of the pit and had deliberately set the thing loose on the battlefield. I froze.

"Clear the way," yelled Atty, waving people back. No one needed telling twice, and fighters disengaged and scrambled madly to get out of the way. Those who were already hiding curled up and prayed.

Francis leapt over a few bodies, including one bright soldier who had played dead for the majority of the battle and who, I suspected, was now asleep. She took one last glance back as Hammond closed the gap between them and then flung the torch with her perfect librarian's aim.

It bounced off the head of a wood elf and rolled to a halt in front of the shield wall protecting the enemy warlocks. Cloaked heads peeped over the top to look at it.

Francis veered off, slithering behind the shields of several of our minions and soldiers, including Dave and his Big Shield 2000, and gave Trudy a high five.

Hammond made a beeline for the torch before scenting the stronger traces of magic from the warlocks. With a triumphant screech, he reared up and crashed through their defences, crushing several warlocks beneath shields before attacking another and ripping off his foot.

Those that could were already running, much to Sergi's frothing chagrin.

"Get back here now, you bloody cowards!" he raged after them to no avail.

More screams from his warlocks half-drowned him out, and more and more of his few remaining troops were vanishing into the distance.

I stood up and laughed.

"I hate you, Evergrim, I—" Something zipped past me and bounced off his chest plate before plopping into the mud. He looked down, then looked around, confused.

I laughed myself into a coughing fit as the ghost popped up inside the circle and shrieked at his horse. It reared up, depositing him in the mud and bolted, trampling a pair of soldiers as it went.

Trudy stood cackling nearby, leaning on Dave for support, blood seeping through a wad of cloth clutched to her side. One of the dark assassins made towards her, but a whirling straw-coloured disc sliced his head off. I blinked. It appeared to be a straw boater with a jaunty chequered band around it. I spun turned as the other two of the not-quartet hurled their hats. They whistled through the air, one decapitating a halfling and the other embedding itself in the chest of the largest assassin still guarding Sergi. At that point, the others decided to retreat, leaving only a handful of hangers on to prise Sergi out of the mud.

Bloody, muddy, and scarlet-faced to the point of passing out, he screamed abuse at everyone (but mostly me) as his lackeys helped him stagger away. It took them seventeen attempts to get him back on his horse, given the weight of his ridiculous armour. By the time he made it up there, he'd drawn a crowd, who were whistling, shouting abuse, and making bets. I felt my headache vanish to the depths, and the fading sun warmed me. Happiness.

Slowly, Sergi and the remains of his army retreated from the field.

"Expect a bill for this bloody mess," I called. No response. He always was a sore loser.

"Why'd you let him live?" said Trudy.

"More fun this way… he has to live with this." I grinned. Besides… always better an enemy you know, than a replacement you don't.

I looked around the field at the dead, wounded, unconscious, and those playing dead. Among the debris of battle, lay a plethora of coloured weevils. Some were dead, and others had merely eaten themselves into a comatose state. So, it seemed, had Hammond.

Little remained of a large number of warlocks, save for some suede shoes. They were too pretentious for even a mutant weevil to eat.

"Did… did we win, sir?" said Gawain, looking around.

"We did."

A cheer rolled around the field, and I felt a smile rise from the dark depths of my body and spread across my face.

"What now?"

"Now we either kill that thing or somehow wrestle it back where it came from." I pointed at Hammond.

"Shame to kill 'im," said Dave. "Could widen up his pit a bit again until we can put together somethin' nicer."

"And you intend to move it how?"

"That shiny tosser's cart that pulled the see-gee thing, that'll do it."

"That's your job, then."

He faltered, not clearly having through it through. "Bugger."

LATER AGAIN

I spent the next hour—before the light fully faded and the local vultures moved in—directing people to cart off and tend to the injured, gather everything that could be used or sold, and sent Gawain to the town to bring back several weapons merchants who made a quick deal for Sergi's siege weapon.

I had never known the troops and minions so motivated, and there was little argument. There is nothing like a good battle and significant bloodshed to put people in a good mood.

The cells were filled with prisoners, and the remaining non-Hammond weevils were wheeled off in barrows to a network of sealed drainage ditches that the pixie had discovered at the rear of the gardens, where they could rumble around safely without mutilating anyone. It also meant that we had our kitchen back.

Weary but elated, with a cartload of gold from the local merchants who had been sold much of the battle spoils, what remained of my army retreated to the slightly worse for wear castle to celebrate. Not a word I ever expected to be using, but I surprised even myself.

OLD BALLROOM

My parents loved to throw opulent parties back in the day, but in recent years, the grand old ballroom had fallen into disrepair, with fairy graffiti marring many of the elaborate panels, and much of the gilt work licked off by persons unknown but strongly fucking suspected.

It was the ideal place to dump the remaining spoils of battle and divvy up the gold to the exhausted, injured but happy minions and soldiers. My grandmother had still not returned from whichever tea room she was frequenting, which was a bonus.

The not-quartet (hats retrieved and cleaned) was singing on the stage, and people and creatures were milling about, comparing wounds, getting patched up by busy first-aiders. Others were rummaging in the pile of spoils. It was a pleasant hubbub. Until someone tapped me on the shoulder.

"Mr Evergrim."

I turned and sighed.

"Mr Pincher."

"I believe we need to have... a discussion." Something in his eyes told me exactly what this would be. I nodded, wanting this over with, and followed him down the hall to an abandoned guard room.

The door clicked shut, and Pincher turned and locked it. I watched the key vanish into his waistcoat pocket—a mirror of the one that I had used to secrete his photograph. Even though I knew what I had been heading into, my eyes roamed, instinctively searching for an exit. It would be better for me, in the long run, however, if I did not run.

He leaned against the door, arms folded, watching me. Studying. His usually neat dark hair was now messy, trailing over his forehead and startlingly green eyes in a manner that made him look suddenly appealing, (were it not for what was about to happen). This was no time for my treacherous libido, however.

"I thought it best we get our... *discussion* out of the way now, so that you can celebrate your victory. I know how rare they are."

Sarcasm aside, it was a courtesy I had not expected. I said as much, and he nodded an acknowledgement. He re-rolled one of his sleeves that had started to creep down his arms. Only then did I notice the lean muscles and trailing tattoos. He was certainly H&S with a dark side, and I wondered who he *really* was and how I could use it to my advantage. Right now, I chose to let him have the upper hand.

He was almost conversational as he slipped on a rather fetching set of brass knuckles.

"No use healing twice, or spoiling your afterparty."

"No. Quite right." I exhaled deeply. This was not unexpected, and given the havoc he could bring down on me and everyone here, I was getting off lightly... besides, this was personal and that I *did* understand.

Sometimes, most of the time, I hate this damn job.

"Before we begin, I should mention that the picture..."

"Oh, I know I won't be getting it back any time soon. That will be a work in progress—a personal one. I also know..." he moved closer.

I didn't bother to back up. This was nothing that I hadn't faced before, usually for far less.

"...that I don't appreciate this misstep of yours. I have

worked hard and faced… many challenges to reach the position I'm in today."

"That day too, but I expect the alcohol and tentacles helped." I couldn't help myself. Sarcastic in the face of physical harm, I have always been a fool unto myself.

His smile was as terrifying as my mother's when I accidentally-on-purpose knocked over her collection of hideous dwarven collectable plates. Some of them had had to be knocked over two or three times before they eventually broke. So did I, as it happened.

SOME PAINFUL TIME LATER

I didn't remember the point at which I eventually hit the ground and stayed there, but I remember someone turning me over. Cool hands touched my face, checked my eyes, breathing, and I gradually focussed on Pincher with far more respect than I previously had.

He held out a hand. Astonished, I looked into his eyes for a long moment, waiting for the trick. There was none. I grasped his hand, and my ribs, kidneys, stomach and face screamed in protest as I sat up.

"Are we done?" I managed, determined to salvage some semblance of dignity. I had not felt so oddly exhilarated for a long time. Here was an H&S person worthy of my attention, grudging respect, and vengeful machinations. My apathy and boredom lifted a little, and I felt… perversely alive.

"We are. For now."

Like a half-paralysed beetle, I struggled to get up until he pulled me up.

"I must say, I'm impressed, Mr Evergrim. Your resilience is to be commended."

Was that... respect? Perhaps just a flicker.

"Thank you. I must compliment you on your choice of 'discussion aids'. Birthday gift from your grandmother?" I winced as I straightened up.

He smiled. "No, they give them out in the crackers at the H and S New Year parties."

I couldn't tell whether or not he was joking. Could H&S joke? Was it allowed?

For a long moment, we stared one another down. This wasn't over, but some scales had been balanced somehow, if only for now. With the picture still in my possession, I was protected from some of the worst he could bring to bear on us, and our 'discussion' had been a worthwhile price to pay for damage control. Pride had been satisfied, however minimally, for now.

To my surprise, he reached out and wiped a streak of blood from my cheek. I was too tired to flinch much.

"You have a celebration to attend, I believe."

I sighed. "Yes. An Overlord's work is never done."

"You are suggesting that it ever begins?"

A smirk. I banked it for future reprisals.

"I don't suppose there are any low-work, high-paid positions at H and S headquarters?"

He unlocked the door and pushed it open. "Alas, no. Besides, I don't quite hate you or them enough to inflict you upon one another."

He slid his glasses back on, along with his usual smirking mask. Suddenly he was less human and more H&S. I liked him less this way. Or hated him more, I wasn't sure.

I drew myself up as best I could with ribs that felt as though they'd been stir-fried in lava and cleared my throat.

"Well, if you can tear yourself away from your clipboard at some point, I expect I will see you at the celebrations, sucking the joy from the room... *Jimmy*."

I limped past him into the hallway. Faint noise filtered through the corridors.

"Yes... I'm sure you'll see me there, while you puff up like a putrefying pit viper and take credit for everyone else's hard work... *Nate*."

For some reason a grin sprang to my face and, with a nod of acknowledgement, I shuffled away in as dignified manner as I possibly could (which was not very, especially when I was overtaken by an asthmatic goblin).

LATE

Drunk on victory, some of the barbarians had mounted a traditional raid on a local tavern, and there was plenty of alcohol to go around, for once. Those who weren't drunk and dancing on furniture were passed out beneath it, or otherwise engaged in ever-more dramatic retellings of their brief battle.

There is certainly nothing like a victory to raise spirits. Of course, in addition to the sale of the siege weapon, the swift sale of discarded armour and weapons from Sergi's army had already fetched a pretty penny from a local vendor (who would likely go on to sell them back to Sergi for a profit next week).

Wages were paid—finally. The army was kitted out with mostly-new gear (again, thanks to Sergi) and resettling into their old quarters once more, which had been decorated with the remaining cushions that lingered in the castle, along with Yanna's more putrid fabrics. I have developed an allergic reaction to cushions, so I was glad to see them go.

I sat in a suitably high-backed chair and tried not to look too injured as the merriment wove around me, the not-quartet now performing a jaunty variety of victory songs.

I closed my eyes a moment, and I could feel the odd, arcane magic that ran through an Overlord's veins begin to slowly heal me. It was one of the few perks of the job.

In the far corner, Dave was hammering the dents out of a stack of breastplates and shields, a souvenir moss beast claw hanging proudly around his neck on a waxed cord. The ghost looked on, issuing dire warnings about moss-related germs.

Trudy was showing off her newly acquired scars to a seven-foot barbarian who had only managed to acquire a nasty papercut, while Gawain was trying to hide his multi-coloured hair under a fancy hooded warlock cloak pilfered from the battlefield, twisting and admiring himself in front of a mirror.

Chakk was pawing through the pile of spoils and battle junk that had yet to be sorted, sold, or stolen, pausing to lick anything shiny. Atty polished her ladle weapon with what looked like a piece of moss, while several young soldiers lingered nearby, trying to earn her attention with their loud stories of imagined valour.

Francis drifted around the pile, kicking at things and wrinkling her nose at the odd severed head still in its helmet. Nothing appeared to be to her liking, typically.

Pincher joined her, falling into step with her as she walked and surveyed the heap. He suddenly reached past her and pulled a stained book from the pocket of a scorched robe with some charred necromancer feet protruding from it. He wiped the cover on his waistcoat and handed it to her without a word, but a small, hopeful smile.

I was disappointed that she didn't smack him in the face with it. Instead, she took it with a shy smile that stirred something strange in me. I hoped the pile would collapse down and smother the pair of them.

Their faces were thankfully lost in the ebb and flow of soldiers and minions and the drinking, singing, vomiting, and stabbings before they had the chance to ruin my mood.

I closed my eyes and sank back into the velvet embrace of the chair, feeling the imperceptible gears of history grinding and clicking and settling. A sense of some invisible hurdle overcome—or at least stumbled over. The first of many, I suspected but, in the end, despite wishing myself dead many times, I had prevailed. I am the Overlord, and I acquitted myself well.

I wondered if my parents were watching benevolently over the celebrations, perhaps with knowing smiles and sober, glowing robes. I cracked open a bruised eye. They weren't, thankfully. I'd had enough misery and smirkiness for one day, and anyway, my ghost was too sulky to be set upon them.

Overlord… perhaps, just *perhaps* I could do this. I looked again at the misfits. At my engineer, hammering; my assassin boasting; the head of my army polishing; my magician de-cloaking. In the corner, my librarian—the second most intelligent person in the castle and the closest thing I had to a friend—was perched on top of a sleeping troll, nose deep in her new/old book. I hadn't got what I wanted, or expected, or deserved. But… I had done the best with what I had and, together, somehow, we had failed upwards. It was a start.

The End

READERS' CLUB

If you liked what you just read, then consider signing up to my mailing list. As part of my exclusive Readers' Club you'll receive newsletters featuring updates on my books, promos, bonus content, sneak peeks, and more.

I value your privacy, and will never sell or pass on your details and you will not be spammed. Once you fill in your details and sign up, don't forget to check your inbox for the confirmation email - you'll need to confirm that you definitely want into the club and consent to being added to the mailing list.

And remember, you can unsubscribe at any time without issue!

Visit here to join:
https://landing.mailerlite.com/webforms/landing/n9f2r0

THANKS FOR READING

If you enjoyed the book, then please consider leaving a **review**. As an indie author, without the backing and might of one of the 'Big Five' publishers, reviews are crucial in gaining a foothold in online retailers, and in helping market my work so that I can continue writing.

Each one makes a difference and just five minutes of your time to write a quick review (it doesn't have to be anything elaborate) would be much appreciated.

ACKNOWLEDGEMENTS

This is the part of the book in which I am supposed to wax lyrical about those kindly souls who have helped or inspired me, blah blah, etc. No. Not this time.

Thank you to... **me**, for not giving up too often and throwing this whole thing into the sea. Thank you to me for opening my eyes, venturing back into the world from this dark prison of depression, and finding the hope and joy there. Thank you to me for lifting my old acting dreams among the ashes of my past, dusting them off, and realising that I might be able to light that spark. Thank you to me for starting to believe in that talent uncoiling again inside after all this time... it wants to stretch...

Thank you to me for finally, after many years of faffing and putting it off, finishing this book. I am rather in love with it.

And... thanks to Nate. You are a grumpy, stubborn bastard. It took you long enough to get your story together in my head, and you fought me most of the way. I hope you're happy, you prick, this took ages. Anyway, I'll expect you back for the sequel sometime soon.

ABOUT THE AUTHOR

Lorna Reid is a writer and aspiring actor, who currently lives in the gloomy climes of Scotland, surrounded by books, an excess of stationery, and far too many mugs of half-finished tea. She studied performing arts at Canterbury College, and currently enjoys the lively environment of CityLit's online courses, as well as rediscovering her love of Shakespeare.

Words, movies, and an incurable Columbo and Poirot habit (not to mention true crime) tend to dominate much of her time, and she has been taking advantage of lockdown to build up her acting toolbox and confidence in order to try and catch hold of the dreams that she let slip, too long ago. She writes a bit, too.

Made of shadows and tea.

Printed in Great Britain
by Amazon